UNSEEN

A SHAYE ARCHER NOVEL

JANA DELEON

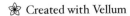

1

Friday, December 18, 2015
The French Quarter, New Orleans

Madison Avery looked out the glass wall of her unlit penthouse apartment and across the city. It was an impressive view and an expensive one, but it had been worth every penny as far as Madison was concerned. The view from the floor below her was also excellent, and the unit had been listed for 20 percent less than what she'd paid for her penthouse, but being on the top floor meant no one was above her banging and knocking around. She could disappear in her retreat in the sky and be alone with her work and her thoughts.

Just the way she liked it.

The sun had set hours ago, and the night lights of the French Quarter created a glow of color over the city.

Below, people bustled back and forth across streets and down sidewalks. Some were visiting and taking in all the culture and fun the city had to offer. Others lived in the city or one of the nearby suburbs and were shopping for gifts for the upcoming Christmas holiday. Many came into the city for the food alone. The incredible dining offerings were the one thing that consistently drew Madison out of her apartment.

Sure, she appreciated art as much as anyone, but she could see and order it online and look at it in her own apartment. Same with music. But not every restaurant delivered and even if they did, some things simply weren't good unless experienced in person. Great food was one of them. Styrofoam containers and the time it took to deliver minimized the chefs' efforts with loss of heat and flavor. Sauces didn't pack the same punch. Meat wasn't as tender.

So she forced herself out at least one night a week to a different restaurant and kept a list with ratings of them all. Seventy-eight weeks she'd lived in New Orleans. Tonight, she'd eaten at her seventy-eighth restaurant without a single repeat. And she was still nowhere near repeating herself. From tiny cafes to five-star restaurants, New Orleans was a mecca of eating pleasure.

A light flickered on in the building across the street and she looked down at the open windows of the empty apartment. Realtors had been showing it with regularity, and Madison figured that before long, she'd see furniture moving in and the blinds would be closed at night to allow for privacy. The tinted windows allowed people to see only shadows during the day, but at night, with the interior lights on, you were your own stage play.

Madison had expensive electric blinds installed before she'd moved in, but she didn't use them often. Instead, she preferred to keep the lights off and sit in her favorite chair to watch the city unfold beneath her. Even better were the nights when electrical storms moved through the French Quarter, putting on a show better than any fireworks display she'd seen. Tonight, the weather was calm but the night lights of the city were bright and festive, especially with the addition of the Christmas decor. She'd changed into her comfortable pajamas as soon as she arrived home from dinner. Now all she needed was a glass of wine and she could curl up in her favorite chair and watch the live show in front of her before she dozed off to sleep.

She started to back away from the window when movement in the apartment across from her caught her eye. A man was opening the door for a woman, who stepped inside, then hesitated, glancing around. The apartment wasn't nearly as nice as Madison's, but the flooring had been updated and a fresh coat of paint had been applied.

She frowned, suddenly realizing that the only item in the apartment was a large blue square in the middle of the dining room floor. Why would someone put a rug in an otherwise empty apartment? Staging for sale required a lot more effort than that, and a better color selection.

The bright blue clashed completely with the cherrywood cabinets in the kitchen behind it.

The man put his hand on the woman's back and guided her from the entry, through the empty living room and into the dining area. As the woman stepped on the rug, the man raised his hand to the back of her neck and jabbed at her. The woman crumpled and fell onto the rug, then lay there motionless.

Madison sucked in a breath. It looked as if the man had stabbed the woman in the neck with something, causing her to collapse. Surely she was wrong. Maybe the woman had passed out and the man had attempted to help her steady her balance before she went down. The man bent over the woman and placed his hand on her neck.

Good. He's checking for a pulse and will call for help.

He reached into his jacket and pulled something out, but it wasn't a cell phone. It was a big, long knife. Even this far away, the glint from the blade was visible. Madison reached for her cell phone on the table next to her chair but grabbed the lighting remote instead. The overhead lights popped on, momentarily blinding her. She dropped the remote, grabbed her phone, and dialed 911. She looked up from her phone in time to see the man pull the knife across the woman's throat. Blood spurted from the woman's neck and Madison screamed in horror.

"911, what is your emergency?"

The operator's voice seemed to boom from the cell

phone, but Madison couldn't speak. Her heart pounded in her chest as blood rushed to her head. She grabbed her chair to keep herself from falling, and the last thing she saw before she lost consciousness was the man in the other apartment, staring across the street directly at her.

2

MONDAY, DECEMBER 21, 2015
Patterson Law Office, New Orleans

SHAYE ARCHER PICKED the pen up off the table and lifted her hand to the document in front of her, but before she could put the pen to the paper, Corrine grabbed her hand.

"Are you sure about this?" Corrine asked. "I mean, really, really sure."

Shaye smiled. "As I've assured you at least twenty times today alone, I am sure."

"But it's your inheritance, too. And if I thought you felt pressured to give it up because of what I want, then I'd never forgive myself."

Shaye locked her gaze on her mother, praying that

this time she'd finally believe what Shaye said and let her sign the documents that Corrine was so worked up over.

"I have a trust fund that ten families could live comfortably on," Shaye said. "If I didn't want to, or for some reason became unable to, I would never have to work a single day. As it is, I have plenty of paid insurance work and more importantly, the luxury of taking cases that help the people who can't afford my service. Some of the same people you're trying to help as well. I have more money than I'll ever need. I have you and Eleonore and Jackson. What more could I possibly want?"

"A metabolism that allowed you to eat all the Danish you'd like and never have to get on the treadmill to pay for it?"

"And if I could buy that metabolism with my inheritance, I might reconsider, but since it's not available on the open market, I'm going to go ahead and sign away my fortune to you so that you can spend it on helping kids who don't have anyone else. Now, can I please do this?"

Corrine blew out a breath and withdrew her hand. "You know I love you more than anyone in the world, right?"

Shaye signed her name on the document. "Of course you do. What's not to love?"

Corrine waited until Shaye put the pen down before throwing her arms around her and clutching her tightly. "This is going to be so awesome. I haven't slept in days, just thinking about all the things I'll be able to do."

Shaye hugged her mother, trying to hold back the

tears that were forming. "Well, go home and get some rest. Those kids need you at a hundred percent. It's time for game face."

Corrine released her and wiped the tears from her cheeks. "I'm having dinner with Eleonore. Would you like to join us?"

"I can't. Jackson is cooking for me tonight and he's being rather secretive about the whole thing, telling me not to bring anything, don't be late. I'm concerned that he's going to make my offer of pizza and beer while helping me put together my bookcases this weekend look a little weak."

Corrine's expression softened and she teared up again, the way she always did when Shaye mentioned her budding romance with Detective Jackson Lamotte.

"I'm so happy for you," Corrine said. "And I love seeing you so happy."

"And if he does anything to mess it up, you'll kill him." Shaye finished her mother's sentiment.

"I'm glad you've been listening." Corrine rose from the table and gathered up the stack of documents. "I'm going to turn all these over to Bill and head out. Drive safe and let me know when you're available to look at those buildings with me."

"Any day this week is fine," Shaye said. "I wrapped up my last insurance case yesterday, and I'm not working on anything else at the moment."

"Good. You should take off until January. Maybe we can work in some last-minute holiday shopping as well."

"I might feel the sudden onset of the flu."

Corrine waved a hand in dismissal. "Why did I get stuck with the only daughter in the Garden District who hates shopping? Don't answer that. I'll call you with a schedule after I talk to the Realtor."

Shaye grabbed her purse and headed out of the law office and into the parking garage. Traffic was heavier now that it was closer to 5:00 p.m., and the drive to her apartment in the French Quarter took longer than the fifteen minutes it had taken on her way to the law firm. Lampposts were wrapped with red-and-green lights and garland, and big red bows were tied at the tops. Shops had Christmas scenes painted on their storefront windows and pretty wreaths hanging on the front door.

The sidewalks were crowded with people carrying shopping bags, smiling with the joy of the season or looking harried for the same reason. Shaye watched as children stopped in front of a picture window with a Christmas train scene in the display and smiled. Corrine was doing an amazing thing. Selling her father's many lucrative businesses and real estate holdings had resulted in hundreds of millions in profit. Profit that legally belonged to Corrine and Shaye, except for the big chunk that went to the IRS.

Shaye had just signed over rights to all of her share to Corrine for use in her new business venture. It was a massive undertaking—a group home for children who needed a place to live while their lives were being sorted through the government red tape, trucks and vans that would deliver much-needed food, coats, and blankets to the street kids who were afraid to do things through the proper channels, and an advocacy firm, complete with attorneys who would fight for the rights of children in the system.

Shaye couldn't even fathom the amount of work it would take to get it all organized and running, but she knew without a doubt that Corrine was the best person for the job. Despite her own enormous trust fund and being the sole heir to her father's fortune, Corrine had never settled for the life of a socialite. She fulfilled her obligations to charity events and appearances in the city, but her passion had been for her job as a social worker.

Unfortunately, recent events, including her father's suicide, had led to her taking a leave of absence and had forced her to consider how she could make the biggest difference. Ultimately, she'd elected to sell everything and cut all ties with her past, hoping to bury the bad memories of her father's sins and ultimate sacrifice. In doing so, she'd created the financial opportunity to do something incredible. Something that Shaye was thrilled to support in any way she could. Some of her recent cases had brought her face-to-face with street kids and their plight. It was heartbreaking, and yet she understood why they didn't trust the system to provide the help they needed. An alternative would help them survive until they were legal adults.

As Shaye pulled up to the curb in front of her apartment, she saw a woman she didn't recognize standing at her front door, just staring at it. The woman was young, midtwenties, with long blond hair pulled back in a pony-tail, no makeup, and wearing sweats, hoodie, and tennis shoes. She looked like a thousand other average people whom most would pass on the street without even taking notice. Shaye, on the other hand, couldn't stop taking notice.

When Shaye exited her SUV, the woman whirled around, and Shaye could practically feel the woman's anxiety it was so apparent in her expression.

"Can I help you?" Shaye asked.

"I...I'm looking for Shaye Archer."

Shaye's curiosity was piqued. Given her appearance in the news headlines for the last several months, it was rare for Shaye to go unrecognized, but apparently not impossible.

"I'm Shaye. What can I do for you?"

"I want to hire you to investigate a crime."

The woman had her full attention. Investigating crime was a job for the police, not a private investigator. Shaye was certain the woman already knew that, which made the situation even more interesting.

"Why don't you come inside and we can talk," Shaye said as she unlocked the front door.

She stood back from the entry and motioned the woman inside. The woman looked at her again, as if sizing her up, then took one hesitant step inside.

"You can have a seat there," Shaye said, pointing to

two comfortable leather chairs in front of her desk. "Can I get you anything to drink? Water? Soda?"

"Water would be nice," the woman said, and perched on the edge of one of the chairs, her back ramrod straight.

Shaye retrieved two bottled waters and then sat in the other chair, hoping the more casual seating arrangement would relax her a bit. The woman opened the bottle and took a drink, and Shaye waited for several seconds to see if she would initiate a conversation. But when none was forthcoming, Shaye took charge.

"What's your name?" Shaye asked.

"Madison Avery."

"It's nice to meet you, Madison. You said you wanted to hire me to investigate a crime," Shaye said. "Have you already spoken to the police?"

Madison nodded. "They said they can't do anything. Maybe you can't, either. Maybe no one can. This was probably a mistake."

"Please tell me what happened and let me decide if I can help you."

Madison took a deep breath and blew it out. "I live in a penthouse unit of a high-rise apartment complex in the French Quarter. Three nights ago, I came home from dinner, turned out the lights, and went to look out the glass wall in my living room. The view is why I bought that unit. When my apartment is dark, the city is so bright and colorful."

"I can imagine."

"Lights came on in an empty apartment in the building across the street. It's for sale, so Realtors have been showing it, but it was almost ten thirty, which seemed strange."

"That is a little later than usual," Shaye agreed.

"A man came in with a woman. He guided her through the living room to the dining area, where there was a blue rug on the floor. I remember thinking it was really strange because the apartment was completely empty except for that blue rug that completely clashed with the kitchen cabinets. Now it seems like a stupid thing to be thinking about, but I didn't know what was going to happen."

Madison's voice hitched and went up several octaves with her last words.

"Your observation was completely normal. Can you tell me what happened next?"

"He...the man, made this motion like he was stabbing her in the neck. I couldn't see if he had anything in his hand—it was too far away—but the woman immediately crumpled onto the rug."

Madison paused for a moment, clutching the armrest of the chair, her gaze dropped to the floor. Her breathing was more rapid than before and Shaye started to worry that she would hyperventilate.

"He bent over her and touched her neck," Madison continued.

"Like he was checking her pulse?"

Madison looked back up at her. "That's what it

looked like, but then he pulled a knife out of his jacket. A really long knife. He grabbed her head with one hand and twisted it to the side, then he slit her throat."

Madison's hands flew up over her mouth as she finished the sentence in an attempt to cover her choked cry. Shaye leaned over and put her hand on Madison's arm.

"That must have been horrible to see," Shaye said.

Madison nodded as she started to cry. "I dialed 911, but before they answered, I passed out."

Shaye reached onto her desk to grab a tissue for the distraught woman. "But they dispatched a unit to your apartment."

"Building security let them in. I was just coming around when they got there."

"You told them what you saw?"

"Yes, and they sent police to the apartment, but they didn't find anything."

"What do you mean?"

"Everything was gone. The man, the woman, the blue rug. There was nothing at all to indicate anyone had been there. Because I insisted that what I'd seen was real, they had a forensics team work the apartment, but they told me they found no evidence that a crime had been committed."

Shaye considered what Madison had told her and weighed it against her impression of the woman in front of her. Madison was clearly stressed and anxious. Either she'd witnessed something horrible or she believed she had. The question was figuring out which one.

"You gave the police a description, right?" Shaye asked. "So that they could check for a woman matching it on the missing persons' list."

Madison looked down at the floor again, a red flush creeping up her neck.

"Madison?" Shaye said gently.

"I couldn't," she said quietly.

"I don't understand."

"Have you ever heard of prosopagnosia?"

Shaye shook her head.

"It's a disorder that affects your ability to recognize faces. It can be a really light case where you struggle a bit to place someone but finally do, or far more severe, like the cases where people don't recognize their immediate family, even after decades of living with them."

"That sounds scary," Shaye said. "I assume you have this disorder."

She nodded.

"How bad?"

"Pretty bad. I might not recognize my own parents in a photograph."

"But you would in person? By voice, I assume?"

"That and by their mannerisms. I'd recognize both of them across a street by the way they walk. Some people I recognize by their hair because it's a specific style and they rarely change it. Tattoos are another way. Clothes are too, although that's harder with young girls as they like to exchange outfits with friends. Smell also works sometimes. That can be good or bad."

Shaye shook her head. "I can't even imagine what that must be like. Something that everyone else takes for granted...and I understand where your problem lies. If you can't describe the woman, then the police have no way of knowing if she matches a missing persons report or not and with no other evidence that a crime occurred—"

"There's nothing they can do," Madison finished Shaye's thought. "Don't get me wrong. I'm sure they did everything they could, but they don't have anything to go on."

Shaye frowned. "That guy took a huge risk doing something like that in plain view of the other building. The police couldn't find any other witnesses?"

"My building is one of those that was recently renovated into condos. The building manager told me I was the first person to move in, and I've only been there a week. And even if there are other occupants now, none of them would have been able to see into the other apartment. My unit stretches the entire length of the building across the front, and it's higher than the building across the street."

"So you were looking down into the other apartment."

Madison nodded. "And they weren't right up against the window, so I don't think anyone lower could have seen them."

Shaye considered everything Madison had told her. There were several more angles of investigation that she assumed the police had covered but probably didn't go to the lengths of explaining them all to Madison.

"Do you remember the name of the detective you spoke with?" Shaye asked.

"Detective Maxwell. He was nice and patient, even though I'm sure my condition sounded weird to him. I don't want to make it sound like I'm unhappy with the police because that's not the case. I understand that his hands are tied."

"But you thought I could do something the police can't?"

"Maybe. I hope, anyway. I have a good job. The money isn't an issue."

Shaye knew a little about Detective Maxwell and even though her relationship with the New Orleans PD was strained, he might be willing to talk to her about Madison's report. And if he wouldn't, there were still a few inquiries she could make—likely the same ones the detective had already made. But the real question was what she could legitimately hope to accomplish. And there was something else about Madison's story that was bothering her, but she couldn't put her finger on it. Something that wasn't quite right.

The young woman was clearly traumatized, which Shaye understood well, but she was also willing to spend her own money on what was likely to be a pursuit without results. And for what? If everything was exactly as Madison had seen it, the woman would be reported missing or her body would turn up. Either way, an investigation would ensue and Madison wouldn't be able to identify her as the woman in the apartment anyway. So unless the police got a confession or were able to track the woman's death back to the apartment, Madison might never know that the murder she witnessed had been solved.

It bothered Shaye to know that the woman might have to live the rest of her life without answers. She had intimate knowledge of how living in the dark felt, but she also didn't want to give the woman false hope by taking the case. It was a complicated situation at best. An impossible one at worst. Yet she felt a level of desperation emanating from Madison that didn't quite coincide with her story.

"Can I ask you a question?" Shaye asked.

"Of course."

"Why are you so determined to have this investigated? The police will work the case from a missing persons report or if they locate the body, so one way or another, someone will be looking for this woman and then her killer."

"What if no one reports her missing? Some people don't have others looking out for them. And what if he dumps the body somewhere that it's not found? That happens all the time in the bayous. I'm sure you know how many people disappear around these swamps every year."

"Yes. Any of those things is possible, and they're probably all things beyond my ability to change. I don't mean to push, but I get the feeling there's something you're not saying. If you want me to help you, I have to know everything."

Madison stared at the floor for a while and Shaye wondered if the young woman was simply going to say "never mind" and leave. Finally, she looked back at Shaye, all color washed from her face, tears streaming down her cheeks.

"The killer saw me."

3

Shaye stared at Madison for a couple seconds, trying to control the spike of fear that coursed through her with the young woman's words.

"You're sure?"

Madison wiped the tears from her face and nodded. "When I went to grab my phone, I hit the remote that controls the electrical systems in my apartment. I accidentally pressed the button to turn on the lights. The entire front of my living room is a giant window. With the lights on..."

"He could see you as easily as you could see him," Shaye finished. "But are you sure he looked up?"

"Yes. It's the last thing I remember before I lost consciousness. I can't describe his face, but I'm certain he was looking directly at me. I think that's why I passed out. I was already horrified at what I'd just seen, but that wave of terror when I realized he'd seen me must have been too much to handle. Or maybe I'm just a wimp."

"Don't do that to yourself. What happened to you was terrifying and your reactions were completely normal. They still are. You have every right to be scared and upset. You witnessed something that we aren't supposed to see and aren't equipped to handle."

Madison sniffed. "Thank you. I've been so angry with myself."

"Why?"

"Because if I hadn't passed out, they might have caught him. But when he saw me, he knew he had to clear out. By the time I came to and told the cops what had happened, it was too late. He'd made it all disappear, and I just looked like some emotional mess of a woman."

"You were distraught. I'm sure Detective Maxwell recognized that fact. He's been doing his job for a while. I've only dealt with him briefly, but he's never struck me as callous or shortsighted."

"I offered to take a drug test. To prove that I wasn't drunk or strung out."

Shaye shook her head. "I'm sorry you thought that was necessary, but I understand how it feels to know something that you can't explain and to have people look at you as if you're deliberately trying to make things harder."

Madison nodded. "That's why I came here. I know your story and I'm really sorry about everything that happened to you. I also knew that no one would understand how I felt as well as you could. You spent years walking the streets of New Orleans, never knowing if the person you'd just passed on the sidewalk was the man who'd hurt you."

"And every man you pass could be the killer."

Shaye's chest clenched as a flood of bad memories coursed through her. Madison was right. Shaye understood exactly how she felt, with one caveat. Even if the killer was identified, Madison still wouldn't recognize him. Not during trial, not if he got probation, never. He could literally show up at her doorstep claiming to be the cable guy ten years from now and she wouldn't be the wiser. Basically, her fear couldn't be completely overcome unless the killer got life in prison without possibility of parole or died.

"Do you have someplace you can go?" Shaye asked. "Family you can stay with? At least for a little while."

"No," Madison said quietly, and stared at the floor again. "My parents...let's just say they're thrilled that I left town. They don't want me back, especially if there's even the remote possibility that I could be involved in something they would consider crass."

Shaye blinked. "We're talking about your safety."

"I'm not as important to my parents as their social standing in Baton Rouge. I was always an embarrassment. I couldn't remember important people like the mayor and the governor and my mother's wealthy friends. They were convinced that I refused to remember people on purpose, just to cause them shame."

"But surely...I mean, doctors must have explained your condition to them."

"They said the doctors were wrong. That I was just slower to develop and I would grow out of it. As I got older and didn't improve, they convinced themselves I was doing it to spite them."

"I honestly don't know what to say, except that I'm sorry."

Shaye might have had one of the worst starts in life that a human being could get, but her life with Corrine contained all the love, support, and encouragement that every parent-child relationship should consist of. The difficulties Madison faced living with the disorder were already monumental in so many ways, but to have her own parents accuse her of faking it went beyond bad parenting. It was abuse.

Madison gave her a small smile. "It's okay. I wanted to be away from them and their lives as much as they wanted me to go. They restructured my trust fund and dispersed it to me on the day I graduated from high school. Lucky me. An eighteen-year-old millionaire."

"So you moved to New Orleans?"

"No. I moved into a little apartment near the LSU campus and went to college. Don't get me wrong, my trust fund was a great way to start out, but it wasn't going to support me an entire lifetime. Between college and buying my apartment, it's mostly tapped out, but that's okay. I wanted to work."

Shaye nodded. It was a sentiment she understood.

"You wanted a career. College must have been difficult given your situation."

"At first, it was really hard, trying to explain to people why I didn't recognize them. People get offended, you know? But finally, one of my teachers suggested I have cards printed up that explained prosopagnosia and let people know what they could do to make it easier for me to be more normal."

"Like what?"

"Simple things really, but stuff you'd never do with people you know. Like telling them who you are every time you run into them. The people I was around the most, I grew to recognize by voice, but it's a big campus and there were a lot of students and group projects and such. I thought everyone would keep away from me—you know, the weird girl with the weird disorder—like they could catch it. But mostly everyone was cool about it."

"That's great. Do you have the same sort of understanding at your job?"

"Yes and no. I'm a programmer, but I'm an independent contractor and work from home. I majored in programming for that reason. The project manager I report to knows, of course, but all of our exchanges are by email or phone except for a meeting once a week at their office in the French Quarter." She sniffed. "He always wears the same suit that day. He's been really nice about everything."

Madison stopped talking for a moment and looked

out the window, then back at Shaye. "I know it may sound cowardly, but I didn't want to work in an office and deal with it every time we had a new employee start. I made it through college but it took a lot out of me, and there, at least, I knew it was only for four years. But this is my career. I didn't want explaining my condition to become a part-time job."

"I understand completely."

"Except you had it even worse in college because your case was covered all over the news and never solved. The amount of questions, insinuations, and strange looks you must have gotten is overwhelming for me to even think about."

"College was tough, but I had my mother and an incredible therapist. You did it all alone, and that's a different level of difficulty that I didn't face. You're stronger than you think, Madison. We all are."

"That's probably true. But still, I took the easiest route with everything that I could."

"What do you mean?"

"Well, for example, even though I could live anywhere with decent Internet, I moved to New Orleans —specifically downtown—because it's a city with a lot of people who didn't know me and that I never had to get to know."

"You could disappear."

"Yes. And my job allows me to mostly be a hermit. Between Amazon and food delivery, there's little reason to have to leave."

"I have hermit tendencies myself. My mother used to make me get out of the house and go shopping with her and when I was older, to charity events, but I'm still not a fan of either. She's still a bit dismayed over the shopping one."

Madison smiled. "I think I'd like your mother, based on what I've read about her."

"And I think she'd like you. So, we have a murder that appeared not to have happened, a victim who appears not to be missing, and a perpetrator who saw the only witness to the crime but that witness can't identify him."

"When you put it like that, it sounds ridiculous and impossible."

"I don't think it's either. I think it's challenging and I can't guarantee success, but I promise you, I'll track down every angle until I've exhausted them all."

Madison's entire body relaxed. "So you'll take the case? Even with nothing to go on?"

"I think there's far more to go on than you think there is."

"But how? I told you everything I know."

"I don't think you did. Don't get upset. I'm not saying you're lying. You just don't process the things you've seen like an investigator does. That's my job. All I need you to do is relax and answer some questions. Do you have time now?"

"Yes. Of course. Whatever it takes."

"Great. Do you like chocolate chip cookies? My mom made some yesterday and I have more of them than I need to eat. So how about a little inquisition and a lot of cookies."

"Cookies sound really good."

Shaye went into the kitchen and grabbed the container of cookies, two small plates, and napkins, then headed back into her office. She placed the items on the desk in front of Madison, then stepped around to her office chair behind the desk.

"If you don't mind," Shaye said, "I'm going to do this from here so that I can type my notes. My handwriting is not the most legible. Please help yourself to the cookies."

Madison opened the container, pulled out a cookie, and took a bite. "Oh my God. These are great."

"My mom loves to bake and she tends to do it more when she's stressed. I've been putting in two extra days a week on the treadmill because of her baking."

Madison's expression filled with sympathy and although she didn't say anything, Shaye knew that the young woman understood why Corrine had been baking more lately. Granted, it was hard to miss unless you never watched the news, signed on to the Internet, or talked to another human being. It was especially hard for Corrine because she was such a private person, but she'd faced the reporters with her usual grace and eventually, they'd drifted away, leaving Corrine and Shaye to rebuild their broken world.

"Okay, let's get started," Shaye said, and created a new document for case notes. "The first thing I want you to do is describe the man to me. I know you can't describe his face, but your powers of observation of other items is sharpened based on your inability to remember faces. I gathered as much from the way you described your methods for recognizing individuals you saw regularly. Start by telling me about his size."

"I can't tell you a lot, but what I saw might narrow it down. Okay, the doorframes of the unit he was in are around seven feet. I know because I saw them moving the refrigerator in. It's hard to know exactly because of the angle, but I'd say he was over six feet but not by a lot."

"That's good. What about weight?"

"Thin, but I'm not sure if it was toned or not because his body was completely covered by his clothes."

"Tell me about the clothes."

"Black slacks, black-button up shirt—the kind you wear on the outside of pants—black raincoat, black shoes and gloves."

Shaye typed the information, making a note that fingerprints were a dead end to follow because of the gloves. She'd figured as much, but knowing for certain saved time.

"What about his hair?"

"Light brown. Not short. Not long. Your average middle-class white guy haircut, I suppose."

"You think he was white?"

"I'm sure of it. It's one of the only things that consistently registers with me."

"Great. Now tell me about his movements. I know

you didn't see much, but was there anything specific you can recall about the way he walked, a limp, a long stride?"

Madison frowned, then slowly shook her head. "Nothing that I can think of." Her eyes widened. "Wait. His hand. He had the knife in his left hand. But I think... no, I'm certain he used his right hand to stab her in the neck with a needle or whatever. If that's what he did."

"So potentially ambidextrous but maybe left-hand dominant since that's the hand he used for the..." Shaye let her voice trail off. Finishing the sentence was unnecessary. "Okay, now tell me about the woman."

"Also white. Shorter than him only by a couple inches but she had on high heels—at least four inches."

"Body?"

"Really thin. Not muscular. Big chest. Long limbs."

"Hair?"

"Long and platinum blond. I mean really long—like halfway down her back."

"Clothes?"

"Cheap." Madison's hand flew over her mouth and her face reddened. "Oh my God. That sounded horrible. Just like something my mother would say."

"But it was your immediate impression and that's important. Tell me why that's the first thing that came to mind."

"The clothes were a little too tight, but not in the way that high-end clothing fits the body. The blouse was silver, sleeveless, very low cut, and made from a clingy fabric like Lycra or spandex. Something that shows every curve. Her skirt was black and so small that it tucked up under her rear instead of hanging straight down. It ended a couple inches below her rear. Her shoes were red and strappy with a tall red heel. They were a little shiny, so maybe satin?"

"What about her coat or jacket?"

"She wasn't wearing one."

Shaye frowned. "Wasn't it raining that night? And it's been chilly lately, especially that late."

Madison nodded. "I'd just gotten in from dinner and my hands were still cold even though I kept them in my jacket pockets. I hadn't thought about it before, but it is strange. Maybe she left her jacket in her car?"

"They might not have arrived by car. In fact, they might not have arrived together at all but met up there."

"If they came separately, wouldn't someone have noticed her car just sitting in the garage?"

"He could have moved it afterward or even left in it. She also could have taken a cab. There's several options, but don't worry. I'll explore them all. Was she carrying a purse?"

"A small black bag with a gold chain. It wouldn't have fit more than an ID, cell phone, and keys. Maybe lipstick."

Shaye typed up Madison's observations and looked over at the nervous girl. "You did great. This is a lot of information and you didn't think you had any."

"It's a lot of information but what good does it do?"

"Well, it gives me an angle to pursue on the victim."

"How?"

"Thin, large chest, cheap clothes, no jacket on a chilly, rainy night, and no one railing against the heavens that she's missing. Meeting a man in an empty apartment late at night. That doesn't bring anything to mind?"

Madison sucked in a breath. "A prostitute? Oh my God. That makes sense and it's sickening. That poor woman. She probably doesn't have anyone looking out for her. It's like her entire existence has been erased."

Shaye could hear the fear in Madison's voice and knew she was wondering what would happen if that had been her. Would anyone have noticed? She'd intentionally separated herself from society and had no apparent relationship with her immediate family. Sooner or later, her employers would go looking for her when they couldn't reach her, but after how long?

"We don't know anything for certain," Shaye said, "but that's where I'm going to start."

"But how?"

"Let me worry about that. Getting information is what I do for a living, and I know more about what goes on down the backstreets of the French Quarter than you would think."

"Okay. Then what do you want me to do?"

"I want you to be very careful. The man you described has an overall appearance that is very average, and the only thing you might be able to pick up on is the left hand usage. So don't let anyone into your apartment unless you know for certain who they are and that they have a valid reason to be there. When you go out, stay in largely populated areas and make sure you're not followed. If you feel uncomfortable, go into a public place—a store or restaurant—and call me. I'll come get you."

Shaye leaned across the desk and looked Madison directly in the eyes.

"Most importantly," Shaye said, "never, ever ignore your feelings, especially fear. Our instincts are there for a reason, and too many times, we forget that. Now it's more important than ever for you to be aware of everything that's going on around you *and* how it makes you feel. Promise me."

"I promise. But I think for both our sakes, I'll try to stay inside as much as possible. I don't think you want me calling you every time I'm uncomfortable."

"You'll know if you need to call me. I have confidence in you."

Madison blew out a breath. "I'm glad one of us does."

4

JACKSON LAMOTTE CHECKED THE FRENCH BREAD IN HIS oven, then moved the vase of fresh roses to his kitchen table. The lasagna he'd made was steaming under aluminum foil on the back of the stove, and a big bowl of Caesar salad was tossed and chilling in the refrigerator. It was the first dinner he'd ever cooked for Shaye, and he wanted it to be perfect. Until tonight, he'd specialized in throwing something on the grill, but he wanted to try his hand at something more intimate. More personal.

Of course, he was probably the only man in New Orleans serving a romantic dinner with every light in the house on, but good lighting was comforting to Shaye. He'd probably never own another candle. The mere sight of them still turned her stomach, and after learning details of what had happened to her during her captivity, he wasn't that thrilled with them either.

Their relationship had moved from friends to more

after her last big case—a kidnapping and murder. Given everything that Shaye had been through, Jackson had wondered if he was going to carry a torch forever for the only woman he'd ever wanted. But her desire for normalcy and her emotional strength continued to amaze him every single day. The fact that she trusted him was so humbling it was almost overwhelming. She was the most extraordinary person he'd ever met.

They were taking things very slowly, but that was fine with Jackson. He had a lifetime to spend with Shaye if she was willing. This dinner was just one more baby step in their relationship. He had just finished taking the bread out of the oven when he heard the knock on the door. He hurried over to open it to a smiling Shaye. He leaned in to kiss her, then stepped back for her to enter.

"Your timing is excellent," he said. "I just took the bread out of the oven and the lasagna is piping hot."

"You're kidding, lasagna? It's smells incredible," she said. "You're going to make my superior ability to call for takeout look underwhelming, aren't you?"

"We all have different things we like to do. I grew up cooking with my mother. I can't say that I'm interested in doing it all the time—at least not to this extent—but sometimes you just want the stuff you had growing up, and a restaurant can't deliver the same experience."

Shaye nodded. "I feel the same way about Corrine's baking. I mean, there are exceptional bakeries in the French Quarter, but there's something about hers that is always better."

Jackson pulled a bottle of wine out of the refrigerator and poured them each a glass. "That is something we definitely agree on, and as I spotted a container under your arm, I find myself hoping that it holds the afore-mentioned baked goods?"

Shaye waved the contained in front of him. "Choco-late cookies with peanut butter chips."

"My favorite."

"I can't bake them myself, but I can call in a favor."

He grinned. "Takeout."

Shaye laughed and he felt his chest constrict. Every burst of laughter felt like a small miracle to him. Now, when he found himself hesitating over taking a new course of action, his inner voice asked "what's stopping you?" No roadblock he could encounter would ever match the ones she had scaled.

"Well, let's get this dinner show on the road," he said. "Because I cannot wait for dessert. Please sit. I'm serving tonight."

Shaye sat at the table and leaned over to sniff the roses. "These are beautiful."

Jackson placed the bowl of salad on the table and took his seat. "They are matched only by my dinner guest."

Shaye blushed and smiled and busied herself by stab-bing her salad. He thought the fact that such a confident woman blushed over a compliment was charming. But then, there wasn't anything he didn't love about Shaye Archer.

You're such a goner.

He smiled. Nothing wrong with being a goner.

"I know you need to get in some greens," he said, "but save most of the room for dinner."

"Please. Only an amateur would load up on salad when there's lasagna and garlic bread waiting in the wings. I'm eating enough to satisfy that nagging voice of my mother in my head and then I'm digging in. The smell alone has my stomach rumbling."

"Mine too. I skipped lunch to make more room and after all the cooking, I'm pretty much starving."

Shaye finished the last bite of her salad and pushed the plate to the side. Jackson stacked their empty salad plates and jumped up to get the lasagna. He pulled the foil back from the top and put the serving spoon in the dish, then carried the entire thing to the center of the table. He snagged the bread and tossed it in a basket before sitting back down.

Shaye cut the lasagna into squares and lifted one onto her plate, then another onto Jackson's. He watched as she took a bite, hoping she liked his mother's recipe as much as he did. The instant the fork left her mouth, her eyes widened.

"Oh my God," she said when she finished the bite. "That is the best lasagna I've ever had."

"Seriously?"

"Absolutely. If the rest of your mother's recipes are this good, you should open a restaurant."

He laughed, pleased that she liked the dish. "I think that might interfere with my police work."

"Corrine would tell you that you could always quit the police force. After all, you're less likely to get shot at if you own a restaurant."

"Probably true. But given how ridiculous customers can be, I'm *more* likely to shoot someone myself."

Her smile faded just a bit, and she asked, "How are things going at the department?"

"Better. People are focusing more on the job again and less on what happened with the chief. There's still a couple of holdouts—old-timers mostly—but the rest don't see a future in clinging to a tainted past."

Chief Bernard, the man who'd been running the department when Jackson was hired, had recently been exposed for his part in the plot to keep Shaye's abductor a secret. He'd been blackmailed, but apparently even Bernard had determined that wasn't a good enough excuse for the things he'd done. He'd taken his own life, and a wake of destruction had swept through the department immediately afterward, many indirectly blaming Shaye for the chief's decision and Jackson for helping her uncover the truth.

Eventually, common sense and reality had sunk in, and the men who were committed to upholding the law returned to thinking logically rather than emotionally, and the chill that Jackson had felt every time he entered the department was mostly gone. Only a couple still held a grudge, one of them his former partner and senior officer, a man who accused Jackson of trying to make him look bad. The reality was, Jackson didn't have to do a thing to make Detective Vincent look bad. He was disgruntled, lazy, misogynistic, and determined to ride his desk into retirement, but it was much easier to blame Jackson than to admit his own flaws.

"They're not blaming you, either," Jackson said, because he knew that was the unspoken part of her question. She felt guilty for the flak he'd endured when her sordid past was finally uncovered, even though she couldn't possibly have known that Bernard was involved or what his exposure would cause. Her own grandfather had covered up part of her forgotten past and Shaye hadn't been aware of his involvement until the very end, when he killed her captor and then himself.

"Maybe not, but they still wouldn't be happy to see me, which sucks because given my profession, it would be nice to have a relationship with the local police that wasn't necessarily adversarial. With one notable exception, of course." She smiled.

Something in her tone sounded more focused than noncommittal. As though her desire for a good working relationship with the police department was something she wished she had right now and for a specific reason. Which could only mean one thing.

"You have a new case," he said.

"I have a lot of new cases. As of an hour ago, three to be exact."

"I'm not talking about the insurance stuff or the

background checks. You could do those in your sleep. You picked up something different."

"Oh, it's different all right. I mean, I've made a bit of a name for myself by investigating the impossible, but the deck is really stacked against me on this one."

"Tell me."

The fact that she didn't even hesitate before launching into the details of her new case was both encouraging and a relief, especially given that it was supposed to be a one-way street. Departmental rules forbade the discussion of an active investigation with civilians, and that point had been doubled down on by the acting police chief, especially with regard to Shaye and more specifically to Jackson because of their relationship. Granted, cops gave information to civilians all the time in order to solve cases, but emotions still ran a little high when it came to Shaye and police business.

He listened intently as Shaye described her new client and what she had seen. It seemed straightforward at first and he wondered why he hadn't heard any buzz about the case. Then Shaye got to the impossible part of her story, and he was so distracted by the number of roadblocks and complications that he stopped eating. He managed to remain silent until she was done, but just barely.

"That is one of the most unreal things I've ever heard," he said. "You have a murder with an eyewitness but no description of the victim or the killer and no forensic evidence."

"I know. Solving this will take extreme luck or maybe

even a miracle, because I don't think skill set is going to be enough."

"Can I ask why you took the case? Assuming your client's observations were accurate, either the woman's disappearance will become a missing persons case or her body will turn up and she'll become a homicide case."

"Unless she's not from the area, the body was dumped in the swamp, and no one is looking for her." Shaye repeated the detailed description of the woman's appearance and told Jackson her theory.

"A prostitute is a really good fit," he agreed, "but unfortunately, opens up a whole other avenue of silence."

"Maybe for cops, but I'm hoping I can get some of them to talk to me."

"They might. A woman—not a cop—and trying to figure out who might have killed one of them. A few might be motivated to give up information they wouldn't spill to the police. But where do you plan on starting?"

"With the parking garage of the building, for one."

"There are girls working the parking garage?"

Shaye laughed. "No. At least, not that I'm aware of. But she had to get there somehow. So unless she walked coatless in the winter rain, took a cab, or rode with the killer, she drove. If she drove, and the killer didn't take her car, it might be flagged for towing. If she took a cab, I might be able to run down the fare. If she walked, then she might work an area nearby."

"That's smart." Jackson shook his head. "Man, I wish

I could help you. It wouldn't take me any time to find out if a car was towed from that building."

"Don't even think about it. I'm paid to do the legwork, and the last thing I want is for you to put your job in jeopardy over my *Mission: Impossible* case. I can run down everything I need to know without you sticking your neck out."

"I know you can, but I still wish I could save you the time."

"Hey, you made me dinner. That saved me the time of ordering and waiting for delivery."

He smiled. "And my food is way better."

"That is absolutely true."

He quickly quashed his aggravation at the hand-tying and turned his attention back to dinner, not wanting to waste time spent with Shaye being irritated over the way things ought to be that were out of his control. But he already knew that at first opportunity, he'd have a little talk with Detective Maxwell. He was a good guy and a solid cop. He wasn't out to prove anything and didn't have a chip on his shoulder about Shaye, so he wouldn't see it as threatening that she'd taken the case. Besides, Jackson could always pitch it as his own concern that Shaye might be walking into a dangerous situation. No one would blame him for wanting to prevent that from happening.

Even though a hurricane couldn't compete with the force of nature that was Shaye Archer.

MADISON HURRIED down the sidewalk toward her building, her anxiety growing with every step. She chastised herself for the millionth time for not getting Uber service, then reminded herself for the millionth time that Uber presented issues as well as walking. Other people didn't understand when she said that. After all, the app sent you a picture of your driver. What could possibly go wrong?

Unless, of course, you didn't recognize faces.

So it was a leap of faith every time she got into a private vehicle with someone. Granted, there probably weren't a lot of people roving around looking for random women and pretending to be Uber drivers, but it was still one more thing outside her control. What she needed to do was find a private driver she could schedule with when driving was a better choice than walking. Maybe she could ask for a recommendation, then get Shaye to run a background check on him, just to be sure.

It would be easier still to simply buy her own automobile, but given that her need for transportation averaged two to three times a month at most, it seemed an unnecessary expense and time consumption with maintenance and everything else that went with ownership. One of the many reasons she'd intentionally moved to the midst of an urban area was the ability to walk to just about everything. Besides, owning a car meant walking through parking lots, and sometimes they came with their own sets of issues.

Under normal circumstances, walking wouldn't bother her, even at night. She'd bought an apartment in a well-trafficked area, and that was especially true now with even more people flooding into the French Quarter to make their holiday purchases. But tonight, everything seemed off. Everyone looked sinister whether they fit the description of the killer or not. Suddenly it felt as if everyone were looking at her when before, she'd always felt as though she'd disappeared in the crowd.

The skin on the back of her neck prickled and she slowed and glanced around, the feeling of being watched overwhelming. But no one stood out. People moved by in all directions, seemingly intent on getting to a shop or their car or home. No one paused to stare at her. No one slowed their step when she did. Instead, people just swerved around her and kept walking at their original pace. Nothing looked out of place, but everything felt that way.

You're freaking yourself out over nothing.

And she could have bought that. After all, she was no action hero who played off things like witnessing a murder. She was your average introvert who was normally never a part of something like this. Dealing with people had always been stressful enough. Knowing that someone walking the same streets with her was a killer was so much worse.

And then there was what Shaye said. It would be far

easier to dismiss her unease if Shaye hadn't specifically told her not to ignore those feelings. And her reasons had made sense. Certainly *Homo sapiens* had advanced far beyond their primitive ancestors, but those safety nets built into humans were no less relevant now than they were thousands of years ago. In fact, they might be more important now when the threat could blend in with everything else, unlike a lion or tiger.

She quickened her pace until she was just short of jogging and was completely out of breath by the time she entered her building. James, the security guard who worked nights, was standing at the desk in the center of the entry, where he had a full view of anyone entering the building or attempting to access the elevators. Madison knew for certain it was James working because the building management required them to set out a name placard on the front desk when they went on shift. That way, new tenants could get to know the men and women protecting their investment.

"Good evening, Ms. Avery," James said with a warm smile. "It looks like it might storm out there."

She nodded. "That's why I was hurrying but apparently, I need to put in some more time on the treadmill. I'm a bit winded."

"I sold my treadmill when I retired from the police force. Put it all in a garage sale and decided if I couldn't maintain decent shape with diet and a bit of exercise, putting on a few pounds wasn't the end of the world."

Madison stopped next to the security desk, curious

about the older gentleman in front of her. "I didn't realize you were a policeman."

He nodded. "Did my duty for the navy, then put in thirty years with the department in Lake Charles. My wife and I always loved New Orleans, so we moved here when I retired. Got us a little place near the French Quarter, and I picked up this job for some spending money and to get me out of my wife's hair for a bit."

"And how's the weight thing going?"

"Gained ten pounds and not a pound more. This city is dangerous with the food, but if you walk most everywhere, it's manageable, especially if you don't eat all the fattening stuff late at night."

"The food is definitely the best," she said. "Hey, James, I'm pretty sure someone was following me earlier. It was probably nothing but if you see anyone strange hanging around, would you let me know?"

"Following you tonight?" His tone got serious.

"Yeah. I think. I mean, it could have been my overactive imagination, but I just had this weird feeling."

"You're smart to listen to that feeling. You don't know how many victims I've taken statements from who ignored that feeling and ended up in the police station. I used to wonder how many more ended up in the morgue. I'll keep an eye out. If anyone is hanging around the area for too long and doesn't look like they have business here, I'll check it out. Probably a pickpocket, especially given the time of year. But it's smart to be safe."

Madison nodded. "Someone else told me the same

thing. I'm sure you're both right. Well, I'm going to get upstairs and watch a movie. Have a good night, and thanks for looking out for me."

"I'm happy to. You have a good night too, Ms. Avery."

Madison walked past the front desk and back to the elevators. She stepped inside and pressed the button for the penthouse floor. As the elevator rose, some of her anxiety slipped away. If someone had been following her and was foolish enough to lurk around, James would notice. She had seriously lucked out with him. Not only retired, but a retired cop. Too old and the wrong build to be the killer, and had put in so many years at his job that he'd definitely notice something odd.

All she had to do was never leave her apartment again, and she'd be perfectly safe.

She opened her door and stepped inside but didn't turn on the overhead lights. The lights under her kitchen cabinets offered enough glow for her to traverse the living room and move into her bedroom, where the shades were down and would probably remain that way. She grabbed her nightclothes and changed, then ran a brush through her hair and put it up into a ponytail. When she was done, she studied her face in the mirror. It was an ordinary face, something else that disappointed her mother. She knew about the ordinary face and the disappointment because she'd overheard her mother say both to a friend. It had hurt then, and if Madison was being honest with herself, still smarted now.

She understood that she wasn't the problem. That her parents' all-consuming desire for status with their high-brow friends overrode compassion, even for their own child. Especially when that child didn't measure up on any level they considered important. But it still stung. She reached up to brush her eyebrows in place, then stopped herself. Her parents' standards weren't important. Not to her and not to her life.

She headed into the kitchen and poured herself a glass of wine, then turned off the cabinet lights and walked to the picture window in the living room. The lights from the outside provided just enough of a dim glow that she could see where she was walking, but without interior lights on, she knew that no one could see her inside her fishbowl. Still, she felt exposed standing in front of the window, and grabbed the remote to lower the blinds.

Feeling her way to her chair in the now pitch-black room, she sat and picked up the remote for the lights, turning them on to a low setting. Her hand shook slightly as she traded the lighting remote for the television one. She needed a distraction, and reading was beyond her current concentration level. She'd find a movie—something funny—and finish her glass of wine. Then hopefully, she'd be calm enough to sleep.

But even as she made those plans, she already knew it was going to be a long night.

HE WATCHED from across the street as she entered her building. The quickness of step and the way she glanced around told him she was uneasy. When she turned her head his direction, he could see the fear in her expression. He ducked behind a lamppost and waited until he was certain she had entered the building before slipping into the shop behind him so that he could study the building from the inside of the store. Well away from the watchful eyes of the nervous woman.

He hadn't realized the building across the street had occupants, and that was an enormous miscalculation on his part. Even when the lights in her apartment had popped on, it barely registered because he was so intent on his work. And such careful work it had been...except for that one mistake.

The woman had ruined his fun. He'd picked the apartment for his game because of the exposure. It was like being on stage except the heavens were his audience. A place where God himself could see what he had created. Could see all the intelligence and cunning of the one made in his image. Then the woman had made a fool of him and all his careful planning. Had ruined his opportunity to show himself in all his glory before the creator. Losing that had been a terrible blow, but he had an even bigger problem.

The woman had seen him. He was certain. All day, he'd monitored the local news, waiting to see an artist's rendition of his face or his companion's. But nothing had been mentioned at all and that confused him.

After he'd disposed of the body, he'd returned to the area and driven by on a cross street. Two police cars and a CSI van were parked in front of the building. The CSI team didn't worry him. He knew how to avoid leaving evidence. And besides, the apartment was full of hair and skin cells from the constant trail of contractors, real estate agents, and home buyers. Unless that DNA was in the system, they wouldn't have anything to match it to without a body or a suspect.

And he didn't plan on giving them either.

The lack of news reports told him that the police had dismissed her claim, but that didn't mean he was safe. He had no desire to creep around the city, constantly on the lookout for the woman, worried that she might spot him and call the police or get a picture of him that would be flashed on every news station in the state. No, the woman was a big problem.

A problem he intended to correct.

5

Shaye was up early and out the door to meet her mother's real estate friend, Monique. The woman was a bit nervous about the reason behind Shaye's desire to see the apartment, but was also perturbed enough by Madison's story that she wanted to help.

"You don't have to come inside," Shaye said as Monique hesitated in front of the door.

Monique shook her head and removed the key from the lockbox to unlock the door. "I need to do this," she said as she opened the door and stepped inside. "I know you suspect that woman was a...uh, working girl, but that could have been me or any other Realtor. It's the one thing we fear the most. I mean, we try to verify as much as possible before showing a property, and I would never

53

show anything late at night, but the risk can't be eliminated."

"I'm sure you do everything you can to mitigate risk, but if you're ever uncertain, please don't hesitate to call me. I'm happy to play security for a showing."

Monique smiled. "My husband usually gets saddled with that job, but if he's out of town on business and I run into a situation I don't want to get into alone, I might take you up on that."

Shaye nodded and checked out the doorframe before stepping inside the unit. Nothing on the door indicated forced entry, but then she hadn't expected it to. If there had been any indication of such, the cops would have discovered it and the investigation would have taken a different turn, at least for a while longer. But without forensic evidence, especially a body, it was hard to make a case for allocating already-stretched resources to an investigation based on one witness. Especially when that witness couldn't provide a description of the victim or the perp.

Shaye stepped inside and glanced around the large open space, then walked into the dining area where Madison had indicated the crime occurred. Squatting, she studied the hardwood floor, running her hand across the surface, but there was no way the new finish had come into contact with anything wet, especially blood. There would have been stains, or if it had been scrubbed, signs of discoloration. But the smooth, shiny surface showed no signs of damage.

She rose again and scanned the room. Madison had said a large blue rug covered the floor, but Shaye was fairly certain that wasn't the case. The shade of blue that Madison had described was a popular one for tarps, and a tarp would have prevented blood from seeping onto the hardwood floor where a carpet would have allowed some to leak out. Luminol would have picked up even a drop and would have been used by the crime scene unit right after vacuuming.

She walked over to the window and looked up at Madison's apartment. The height of the penthouse afforded her a perfect view directly down into this unit. Given the placement of the tarp, Madison would have had a clear line of sight to what had happened.

The problem was how to prove it.

"Tell me about the lockbox system," Shaye said. "How does it work?"

"We all register with our credentials," Monique said, "then we use a phone app to request access to the key chamber."

"So it's Bluetooth?"

"Exactly. The box unlocks, we use the key, then replace it when we're done. The listing agent can pull a report of the date, time, and showing agent for each entry."

"Do you have the listing agent's name?"

"I figured you might need it, so I brought you his card. I had one on file."

"Do you know anything about him?"

"I've worked with him on a couple of deals. He's young, talented, and more than a little full of himself."

"And I'm sure he'll be thrilled to hear from me."

"Possible murder in a seven-hundred-thousand-dollar listing...yeah, he's not going to be happy at all."

"Better to work with me than the police. At least I can offer some discretion."

"But for how long? Look, if you believe this woman, then I have no doubt she saw what she says she did. And when it all unravels, no one will be able to keep it a secret."

"Good. Things like this shouldn't be hidden away. Everyone needs to know what kind of people walk among us."

MADISON JUMPED when her cell phone rang. Her concentration had been bad for days, and she had to get this last bit of programming done before the release to testing next week. She'd finally regained some of her stride and was surprised to see she'd been at it for two hours straight when she checked her phone.

She tensed a bit when she saw the number for building security.

"Ms. Avery?" the security guard asked.

"Yes."

"You have a guest downstairs. Her name is Shaye Archer. Is it all right for me to send her up?"

Relief swept through her and she relaxed her death grip on the phone. "Yes. Thank you."

She headed to the front door, a million thoughts racing through her mind. Shaye had just agreed to take her case yesterday evening. It wasn't quite noon. Had she discovered something already? She froze.

Oh my God. What if she changed her mind?

Madison shook her head. No. She wouldn't allow her thoughts to go that direction. Shaye had told her she'd take the case and had provided her with a contract specifying services to be provided. Madison had written her a check for the retainer. It was a done deal. Well, everything but the investigating part.

Knocking at the door broke her out of her semitrance and she took the last couple steps toward the door. Before she could check through the peephole, a voice sounded outside.

"Madison? It's Shaye Archer."

Even though she'd already known that Shaye was on her way up to her apartment, and the only way up was through security, it was still comforting to hear Shaye's voice. Looking through the peephole would tell her very little, and she didn't know anyone in New Orleans well enough to recognize them using other cues.

She opened the door and waved Shaye inside. "Thank you for stating your name."

"Of course," Shaye said. "We should probably pick a word or phrase that can distinguish me."

"I recognized your voice pretty well."

"Yes, but someone could record my voice or mimic me well enough to fool you since you haven't known me very long. A word known only to the two of us would eliminate that possibility."

Madison stared. "Oh. I hadn't even thought of that."

"Of course you hadn't. You're not supposed to have to think of things like that, but for now, you do, so we might as well make it as easy as we can."

Every time Madison started to question her own judgment or mentally chastise herself for the things she hadn't considered, Shaye was there to remind her that it wasn't her skill set and wasn't supposed to be. It made her feel less inept and reinforced her belief that going to Shaye had been the right decision.

"How about Casper?" Madison asked.

"Who's Casper?"

"No. I mean for our code word. But to answer your question, he was a white cat that I had for twelve years. He died a couple years ago from cancer, and I keep saying I'm going to get another but I haven't been able to yet."

"Casper is perfect, especially since it's not a word that would come up in random conversation."

"Great. So did you find out anything?"

Shaye's demeanor so far had been observant but relaxed, and Madison wasn't sure whether that was good or bad.

"Nothing to speak of, but I'm just getting started," Shaye said. "I toured the apartment across the street and have the information for the listing agent, but since I was here, I thought I'd take a look at the apartment from your vantage point...just to make sure there's nothing I've overlooked."

"Oh, of course." Madison walked through the living room to the glass wall directly in front of her recliner. "I was standing here," she said, and pointed to the area next to the end table.

Shaye stepped into the area she'd indicated and looked down at the apartment across the street. With the sun shining bright overhead, the mirrored glass didn't allow them to see inside, but Shaye would be able to tell from the angle that Madison was correct about the visibility from her unit.

"Were the lights on before the man arrived?" Shaye asked.

"No. I would have noticed. He turned them on when he got there."

Shaye nodded and looked around the apartment. "You have a beautiful place. I can see why you chose it."

"Thank you. I really love it, or at least, I used to. Nothing feels the same now."

"Don't give up on it. You picked this place for a reason and that reason hasn't changed."

Madison nodded. "I'm surprised you didn't go for something like this. I mean, I've seen your mother's house in one of those home and garden magazines and it's gorgeous. And this building is so secure."

"I looked at a couple of units similar to this but not

nearly as elegant, but the view that you love is exactly the reason I didn't pick one of them. I've lived my entire life under a microscope and I didn't want to be on display. It works for you because you're comfortable in the dark, but that's something I haven't mastered yet."

"Oh! I'm so sorry. I hadn't even thought about the light."

"Please don't apologize. You couldn't have known, and I have no trouble telling people my limitations. A few years ago, I might have felt differently, but after everything that's happened, I've found a lot of freedom in not caring what other people think."

"That sounds like something I need to do."

"It takes some time to retrain your thoughts, but it's worth it." Shaye looked back at the apartment building across the street. "I'd like to come back sometime, if that's okay, and see it after dark."

"Of course."

"Do you have any plans for tonight?"

Madison almost laughed. "No. I'm not much of a party girl."

Shaye smiled. "Even a hermit needs an occasional breath of air. And I think you're safe out there as long as you're smart about it. Stay in well-lit areas with lots of people around. Basically, everything smart women already do, just take it up a notch. This time of year, it's easy enough to stay in a crowd all day and a good part of the night."

"I guess that's the upside of no friends, family, or

physical contact with coworkers. My Christmas list is really short."

"Mine too, which is good given how much I hate shopping. If I get done with the other things I need to do, I might stop by tonight. Is nine too late?"

Madison shook her head. "I'll still be up. I'm not much of a sleeper lately."

Shaye squeezed her arm. "It will get a lot easier once you have answers."

"And if you can't find any?"

"It will still get easier. It just takes longer. I'll text you either way about tonight."

Madison nodded and walked Shaye out. She locked the door and pulled the dead bolt after Shaye left and leaned against the door, looking across her living room and out at the city. It had already been four days since her life had been turned upside down. Since then, it hadn't gotten easier. In fact, it felt as if everything had gotten more difficult.

But if anyone knew how to handle the unknown, it was Shaye Archer.

Madison just prayed she could summon the amount of strength Shaye had.

JACKSON RETURNED to his desk following a briefing on a new case and saw Detective Maxwell headed for the break room. He grabbed the coffee mug from his desk and followed the detective down the hallway, hoping for a chance to speak to him privately. He'd maintained a calm demeanor the night before when Shaye had described her latest case, but the truth was it had him kind of spooked.

Shaye had already gone through seven different levels of hell, and much of it in just the last several months. The last thing he wanted was for some killer who couldn't even be identified to find out she was investigating and fixate on her. If there was any chance of turning it into a police investigation, then Shaye could back off the case.

You can't protect her from everything.

He shook his head. Those words had been recycling through his thoughts since last night. Not that he hadn't thought them before now, but it had been a while since they'd been cropping up every hour or so. Still, Shaye had chosen her path, and even if she'd taken up cake decorating instead of returning to investigating, she would still have some level of risk simply because of who she was and the money she had access to.

But none of that logic was about to stop him from mounting his white horse and riding into the break room.

Maxwell was pouring a cup of coffee when Jackson walked in. Fortunately, the room was otherwise empty. "You got a minute?" Jackson asked.

"Sure. What's up?"

"It's about a case Shaye took on."

"Oh, man, I can't give you information for her. If the

brass finds out, I'd be demoted or worse. I like Shaye but I got a kid on the way and another that needs speech therapy."

"I would never ask you to do anything that would risk your job. Shaye might contact you, but the information is for me and strictly off the record."

Maxwell frowned. "You trying to get the jump on one of her cases?"

"Actually, I'm hoping she'll drop it altogether, but if you ever tell her I said that, I'll deny it like crazy."

Maxwell's expression cleared. "I see. You're afraid she's about to walk into it, and you're hoping I tell you exactly what she might be walking into."

"Yeah."

Maxwell shook his head. "Dude, you got it bad. Not that I blame you. She's a looker and a class act. The way she's handled everything that happened to her...you know it wouldn't have gone down that way with most people."

"And that's exactly why I'm trying to prevent a sequel."

"I hear you. So what case is she getting in the middle of?"

"That's just it. It's not a case here. You took a call the other night where a woman said she witnessed a murder in an apartment across the street but it was clean by the time you got there."

"Oh man, that was a weird one. Yeah, the woman said she saw the murder and described everything about it except what the perp or the victim looked like. She has some disorder that she can't see faces or something. I've never heard of it but I looked it up. Apparently, it's real and seriously fucked up. I can't imagine living like that."

"But you had the apartment processed?"

Maxwell nodded. "Came up clean. The place had been updated to sell so all the flooring was new. Trust me, there was no blood. No sign of forced entry. Plenty of hair fibers, but the apartment's for sale. Between contractors, Realtors, and potential buyers, probably twenty people or more a day pass through there."

"No security cameras? Guards?"

"Nada. I knocked on doors but most everyone was in for the night. No one saw or heard anything."

"Is the unit below that apartment occupied?"

"It was leased, but the tenants moved out the week before."

"So no one would have heard walking." Jackson shook his head. "What was your take on Madison, the witness? You think she imagined it? Had a nightmare, maybe?"

Maxwell shook his head. "I believed her."

Jackson blew out a breath. It wasn't what he wanted to hear. He'd hoped Shaye's compassion for Madison had caused her to miss something in the woman's story or demeanor, but if Maxwell had bought it as well, then it was likely that Madison Avery had witnessed a murder.

"Shit," Jackson said.

"Sorry, man. I know you were probably hoping I'd say it was all the ravings of a lunatic, but the reality is, I think she really saw something. Maybe it wasn't as serious as she thought. Maybe when the perp realized he'd been seen, he stopped the attack and got the woman out of there. Or maybe it wasn't an attack at all but some kinky sex thing and they didn't want to get arrested for trespassing."

"You checked missing persons?"

"As much as I could. All I had was a description of the clothes and the hair but those didn't fit anyone in the database. Look, the truth is, I wanted to spend some more time on it...poke around for another day or two and see if I could come up with anything, but the brass nixed it. Said I had real crimes with real clues. Bunch of asshats."

Jackson nodded. He couldn't have said it any better.

"I've got to head out, but if Shaye comes up with anything I can run with, tell her to let me know. The thought of someone like that walking around doesn't sit well with me."

"Me either. Thanks."

Maxwell headed out and Jackson poured himself a cup of coffee. He was about to head back to his desk when his cell phone signaled a text.

Meet me in the parking lot.

His curiosity was piqued when he saw the text was from Detective Elliot.

Elliot was one of the detectives working on the Clancy files. John Clancy had been the catalyst that had set off all of the departmental drama earlier that year. He was a human trafficker who had been at work in New

Orleans for years, and Shaye had been one of his "products." Elliot had been tasked with attempting to identify those sold and the customers. People who'd lost loved ones to Clancy needed to know what had happened. Needed closure. That's what they were hoping to provide.

In addition to Clancy's files, Elliot was also reviewing journals kept by Emile Samba, the man who'd purchased Shaye from Clancy and held her captive for seven years to use in satanic rituals. Detectives speculated that because Emile had lived in more than one city, he was likely responsible for more than one murder. They were hoping his journals would reveal other sordid crimes from Emile's past that they could put a solved stamp on and give other victims' families some answers.

And there was one more issue Jackson and Shaye thought Elliot would find answers for.

When everything went down with exposing Emile, and Bernard's and Pierce's suicides, Shaye and Corrine fled New Orleans in order to recover without the prying press looking in their windows. When she returned, Shaye was in a better mental place than Jackson expected, given everything that had happened, but her memory was still returning in pieces, each piece exposing another horror that she had to process.

The last big reveal had been a doozy.

From reading the police reports and her medical file, Jackson knew that Shaye had been pregnant while she was held captive, and her physiology showed all the signs of having given birth. But given her age and the circumstances of the pregnancy, no one expected that the child had survived. But Shaye was convinced otherwise.

She'd finally remembered the labor, the birth. And she'd remembered her baby crying.

Jackson had been so overwhelmed with anger, grief, and sympathy that he hadn't even known which to address first. Sympathy had won out, and he'd assured Shaye he would assist her in whatever route she wanted to take. Anger had settled in as soon as he was alone, and he'd punched a hole in his bedroom wall before breaking down into tears over a life that no child should ever have to endure.

Shaye had been adamant about not sharing that information with anyone—not even Eleonore and Corrine—so Elliot wasn't in the know, but because of Jackson's relationship with Shaye, the kind detective was feeding him information as he came across something new. And because Jackson wasn't cleared to work on the Clancy files or Emile's journals, and never would be as long as the brass had issues with Shaye, Elliot usually gave him information after hours and away from the department. The fact that he wanted to speak to Jackson on the clock was both intriguing and troubling.

Something was definitely up.

6

SHAYE LEFT MADISON'S BUILDING AND HEADED BACK across the street. She wanted to check all access points to the other building and locate a manager who might be able to provide her more information about the structure and those who had regular access to it. But before she started down that avenue of thought, there was an appointment that she needed to make. She pulled out the business card Monique had given her for the listing agent and dialed.

"Hi, my name is Shaye Archer," she said when he answered. "I'd like to make an appointment to discuss real estate in the French Quarter."

"Of course. Yes, Ms. Archer. I'm available this afternoon at one thirty, if that works for you. If not, I can rearrange—"

"That won't be necessary," Shaye said. "One thirty is perfect. Should I meet you at your office?"

"My office is fine or if it's more convenient, I'm happy to meet you somewhere...one of my properties, perhaps?"

"Your office is better. I'll see you then."

She slipped her cell phone into her pocket and sighed. That conversation was not going to be fun. Clearly, Trenton Cooper had known immediately who she was and by default, also knew how deep her pockets were. He'd be trying to sell her everything from a castle to his own socks if he thought he could make it happen.

The front entry to the building was propped open and two men were hauling in a large crate that, given its size, was probably a refrigerator. She waited as the two men negotiated the entry, then stepped into the lobby area and looked around. The building, while nice, was not nearly as elegant as Madison's, nor did it have the amenities, such as a security guard. The elevators were to the left and a hallway branched off to the right, so she headed that direction, hoping to find an office with a human being manning it.

At the end of the hall was a door with the word "Management" stamped on the outside. She knocked and heard a man's voice inside yelling for her to enter. She opened the door and scanned the cramped, stuffed office, but didn't see anyone.

"Hello?" she said as she took a step around a stack of boxes and sidled by three old televisions. The room couldn't have been bigger than fifteen feet square but looked like one of those hoarders shows. She spotted three huge office desks in the room but only one chair, and every square foot of the surface space and most of the floor was stacked with boxes, appliances, or decor. There was a narrow path to one desk that continued on toward a door in the back of the room, so Shaye took another step down the path to the desk and called out again.

There was a loud thump and then some grumbling and finally, a young man popped up from the floor behind the desk, rubbing his head. "Sorry," he said. "I've been looking for a screw I dropped and had just zeroed in on it. I didn't want to come up without it."

He put a small screw on a stack of paper on the desk and looked over at Shaye. "How can I help you?"

"Are you the building manager?"

"Hardly. Catching him in this place is like spotting a unicorn. The owners have a contract with one of those big commercial management firms. Dude's got like ten buildings in New Orleans that he has to keep up with."

"So you are..."

"Oh, sorry. I'm the maintenance guy. I mean, I only do simple stuff. I don't have the licenses to do electrical or elevators. We have companies we use for the hard stuff. I'm mostly fixing drywall, replacing lightbulbs, a new light switch, touch-up paint, that sort of thing."

He didn't look at Shaye while he was talking, choosing instead to focus on one of the many piles of boxes on the floor. It was clear that he was uncomfortable, but that could be his norm. Plenty of people suffered from social anxiety.

"My name is Shaye," she said, and stuck out her hand.

He glanced up at her, then rubbed his hand on his pants before giving hers a shake. "Jason Parks. I'm sorry for all my rambling. Is there something I can help you with? Are you new to the building?"

"I'm not a resident, but I'm looking into an apartment for a friend. Would you mind answering some questions?"

"Sure. I mean, if I know the answers."

"Thanks." She smiled and he blushed, then looked at the floor again. Aha. Jason Parks was shy, especially if a girl was nice to him.

He shoved his hands in his jeans pockets and looked up at her, keeping his head lowered. "What do you want to know?"

"Does the building have security cameras?" She hadn't seen any indication of a security system, but it didn't hurt to verify.

"No, ma'am. A lot of the residents keep asking, but the manager says it's not in the budget."

"Is there a card or password to operate the elevator?"

Jason shook his head.

"So anyone can walk into the lobby and take an elevator up to an apartment?"

"Yes. There was some talk about getting one of those card-key things for the elevators, but then no one could make deliveries unless we had someone working the lobby to let them up so they never did anything about it.

But all the units have individually keyed locks and dead bolts on the inside."

"How often do you change the locks?"

"We rekey them as soon as someone moves out, then rekey them again when someone new moves in. I thought it was a waste of money, but the manager told me the lawyers said we had to, so I call the locksmith out for move-ins and move-outs. Not my money, I guess."

"What about you?"

"What do you mean?"

"Well, I assume you have access to all the units, right? I mean, in case there's a leak or something and no one is home."

"Oh, sure. We have keys to all the apartments."

"Where do you keep them?"

Jason frowned. "Your friend wants to know where I keep the spare keys?"

"My friend wants to be certain that the number of people with access to her home is limited. In other words, are the keys lying around somewhere in this mess or are they secured somewhere safe that a stranger couldn't access?"

"Got it. Yeah, they're in a safe in the back room. It's one of those digital ones. Me and the manager have combinations, and it knows which one was used. I have to keep a log of every time I go into the safe and for which key and why."

"So you would be the one to let in contractors and repairmen if the unit is unoccupied or no one is home?"

"Yes, ma'am, but they only get into the occupied units if the owner cleared them with me or if it's an emergency."

"And you never give them the key and let them go up on their own?"

Jason's eyes widened. "No way! My grandma lives in a high-rise. I'd be mad as heck if someone handed out a key to her apartment to just anybody with a business card with a contractor logo. If residents want contractors to have their own way in, then they can get copies of the keys made and hand them out themselves."

"So the only way someone can access a unit is through you, the owner, or a Realtor through the lockbox system."

"Yes, ma'am. The building might not have a bunch of fancy security cameras and stuff, but it's not like people can just walk inside a residence. I think your friend would be fine here. It's a good neighborhood. Lots of shops and restaurants but far enough away from the craziness of Bourbon Street."

"Is there anyone here at night? In case something breaks?"

He shook his head. "There's a number they call and if it's an emergency, the service calls me."

"And you're here during the week until five?"

"Six usually. Supposed to be five but there's so much to be done, I never get out on time. Could stay here twenty-four hours a day if they'd approve the overtime and still wouldn't be caught up."

"Were you working late Friday night?"

"No. Actually got out of here by five thirty." He smiled. "Beer and pizza night."

"Well, I hope they get you some help soon. Thanks for the information."

"No problem."

Shaye left the makeshift office and headed back toward the lobby. Jason seemed sincere enough, but the reality was he could also be the perpetrator. He had access to the apartment and intimate knowledge of when it would be empty. He could have easily set up a dolly and crate in the apartment or hallway beforehand and used it to transport the body out of the building. If someone happened to leave their unit that late, they wouldn't think anything of the maintenance person moving a large item.

It was risky to do such things at your place of employment, but the kind of people who did these things usually fancied themselves smarter than everyone else. They never thought they'd get caught. Although he was definitely uncomfortable talking to her. That could be shyness or something else entirely.

She paused in the lobby and considered going upstairs to question the other residents, but it was likely most of them were at work and besides, she had that appointment with the Realtor at one thirty. She'd just make a quick pass through the parking lot and see if it yielded anything of interest, then head to her next appointment.

A breezeway led from the building to the detached

parking, and when she saw the management company sign on the wall of the structure, she realized it was managed by a different company than the building. She saw a booth at the exit and headed that direction, excited when she saw someone moving inside. An attended booth might mean information.

She stepped up to the window and took note that the young man inside the booth fit Madison's description. She smiled at him and he gave her an uneasy look.

"Can I help you?" he asked.

"Hi, my name is Shaye Archer. I'm a private detective working on a case and wondered if you could help me."

"Oh, I'm Danny Suarez. But, uh, I'm just the parking attendant. If you need to speak to a manager, he won't be here until this afternoon."

"That's good to know, but I'd still like to ask you some questions, if that's all right."

"Okay."

"How does the parking garage work? Does everyone pay daily or do some have a pass?"

Danny looked somewhat relieved that her question concerned the parking. "You can buy a monthly or yearly pass. People who live in the building in front of it get a discount. A bigger one for the yearly pass. People who work in the office building across the street get a discount too, but they usually buy the monthly one. Probably smarter since you never know when you might be out of a job."

"That's true enough. Have you worked here long?"

His response had contained just enough disappointment that she figured Danny had been on the receiving end of the job loss game before.

"Only a couple of weeks. I worked at a restaurant before, but I wasn't too good at it. All those orders and people were always complaining. This doesn't pay so great, but it's a lot less stress."

"I imagine restaurant work would be taxing. So if someone went into the garage just for the day, but never came out, would anyone know?"

"Yes, ma'am. When we do shift change in the afternoon, our hours overlap by forty-five minutes. One of us does a sweep of the parking garage and makes sure all the day passes are for that day."

"And what happens if they're not?"

"Then we call the towing company and they come get the car."

"Great. Have you had any cars towed recently?"

Danny nodded. "Had a truck towed last week. Guy came down here two days after yelling up a storm. I haven't heard that much cussing since I had that restaurant gig."

"Any others that you can think of?"

"Not that I know of, but I don't work every day."

"I understand. Which towing company do you use?"

"Mitchell's Towing. I don't have a card or anything but I can give you the phone number."

"That's okay. I can look them up. Thanks for your help, Danny."

"Sure," he said, still looking slightly confused.

Funny, Shaye thought as she walked away. Danny hadn't asked what kind of case she was working on. He didn't strike her as the most confident or competent of employees, and given that he hadn't been on the job long, that could have been the reason for his discomfort. Or he could have recognized her from the evening news and that might have put him on edge as well.

Either way, she'd do a quick check on Danny Suarez when she got home.

───

HE LOOKED up at the windows that encompassed the penthouse suite, wondering if she was in there, looking out at the city. He'd taken to his computer to see what he could find out about her, expecting to find little. Most people were exceedingly average and aside from the usual nonsensical social media pages, the Internet didn't yield anything of relevance for the vast majority.

But this time was different.

The Internet revealed quite a lot about Madison Avery. Her rich, privileged upbringing among the elite of Baton Rouge. Her trust fund left to her by her maternal grandfather and her graduation from the university with a computer science degree. But two things had been the most interesting. One was the article that covered the strange malady that affected Madison. The other was the pictures of Madison with her family, in which she was always slightly set apart from her parents and sister.

The one who didn't fit in.

The damaged one.

He understood not fitting in. And he understood damage in a way that most people never would. But Madison's problem was both fascinating and thrilling. Fascinating because he couldn't imagine not recognizing someone he'd met. His mind recorded every detail about people and he could recall those details even years later.

Thrilling because she was the perfect prey.

———

MADISON CHECKED her clock for the hundredth time but it was still lunchtime. And since her growling stomach wasn't going to be fooled by the passage of time and her pantry was still bare due to her lack of grocery shopping the week before, she was going to have to either order in or go out. She looked outside at the clear sky and bright sunlight. It was a crisp fifty-five degrees outside and sunny. The kind of weather she'd normally love walking in. Throw on a pair of jeans, a nice sweatshirt, and a good pair of running shoes and head into the sunlight and all the holiday activity. But now, Madison was scared to leave. Scared that the man who'd seen her would be lurking in the shadows, just waiting for his opportunity to pounce.

You can't hide forever. And it might be forever.

Her mind was solid on the subject, but fear was a strong opponent to logic. Madison knew that Shaye might not find anything. That the police might never know a crime had occurred. That she'd have to spend the rest of her life wondering if the man she was standing next to on the street corner was the man who'd run a knife across that poor woman's neck without so much as a pause.

But behind that fear was an even scarier emotion—the feeling of being trapped.

The day she'd moved out of her parents' home and into her tiny apartment across from the college campus, a huge weight had lifted from her. She'd felt free for the first time in her life. Free to wear what she wanted, do what she wanted...never asked to perform for her father's associates. And always failing those performances by not being able to tell one black suit from another.

She'd been trapped then. Held in a gilded cage, provided with the very best of everything. But much to her parents' dismay, no amount of money could fix what was broken. As soon as Madison's younger sister, Janine, had grown old enough to cling to daddy's arm, making the perfect family picture, Madison had been relegated to her bedroom during parties. Given "permission" to skip the events since her parents knew she didn't really enjoy them.

That much was true, but it wasn't the reason she'd been allowed to skip. The real reason was because her parents didn't want her downstairs embarrassing them.

Now that Janine was older and trained, like a dutiful daughter, it was no longer necessary to push Madison at people and cover for her social issues. So she'd stayed in her five-hundred-square-foot suite, with everything a girl could want, and she'd wished she were anywhere but inside those four walls.

Now she was placing the same restraints on herself.

This is ridiculous.

She jumped up from her desk and went into her closet, yanking sweats and hoodie from hangers before grabbing her tennis shoes and heading back into her bedroom to change. She refused to be held captive again. She'd change clothes and go out to lunch. Nothing fancy, given her choice of wardrobe, but a shrimp po'boy could be had almost every block and plenty of the restaurants were mom-and-pop shops where everyone was dressed down. She'd blend right in.

Ten minutes later, she exited the building and headed up the street where she saw the biggest crowd of people. None of the streets were empty, but if she stayed around clumps of shopping women, it left little opportunity for the wrong person to accost her. She fell in step behind a group of young women, probably college age, who were Christmas shopping and talking about boys. She felt a tug at the excited conversation and wondered what it would have been like to have a normal existence. To date someone and actually recognize him on the second date.

She'd tried a few times, but the last had ended with a frat boy playing a bad joke on her and substituting his roommate on their second date just to see if she'd notice. The fact that she'd had a crush on the boy forever and had practically memorized every hair on his head meant she'd caught on to the prank as soon as the roommate tried to pass himself off as her date. She'd run from the fraternity house, crying, and had refused all attempts by the guy to contact her. The flowers he'd sent to apologize went right into the Dumpster behind her apartment.

After that, she'd given up altogether. What was the point? Even if she met someone who could understand her condition, would he want to cope with it every day? Something as simple as changing his haircut might guarantee that the woman he shared his bed with could potentially pass him on the sidewalk without so much as a flicker of recognition. And she didn't even want to think about the difficulties children could present. When she was in school, girls were always swapping clothes. All it would take was one time of trying to leave the schoolyard with the wrong kid and everyone would brand her a freak, or even worse, a child abductor.

Logic told her that those situations were not overly possible and even if something like them happened, they could easily be explained, but she didn't have the energy to run the risk. So for now, she'd have to settle for romantic comedies on cable and listening to college girls lament their love lives.

It wasn't great, but it was a better life than the woman who'd been killed.

At the end of the second block was a sandwich shop

that Madison had been in once before. It was no surprise that she didn't recognize any of the staff, but she did remember that the shrimp po'boy had been excellent. So she parted ways with the college girls and stepped inside. An older man behind the counter told her to take any empty seat and a minute later, a harried-looking middle-aged woman came over to take her order.

She glanced around the shop, checking out the other patrons, and her gaze locked onto a young man in a back booth. He was the right height, the right build. His hair color and cut matched that of the attacker.

Calm down. He looks like every other average white guy in that age group.

Then he lifted his sandwich...with his left hand.

7

Madison sucked in a breath and reached for her water, frustrated that her hand shook as she brought the glass up to her lips. The guy looked up from his sandwich and caught her gaze. He smiled, and she swung her head around so quickly, she dropped the glass. It crashed onto the floor and splintered into pieces. Madison jumped up from her chair, already apologizing to the waitress as she ran over with a rag.

"Did you cut yourself?" the waitress asked.

"No. I'm fine. It just slipped. It's my fault. Let me pay for it."

"It's no biggie, honey. Just a glass. Do you want to move to another table so I can sweep this up?"

Madison shook her head, her anxiety shooting into space. "I'll just take my order to go. I'm so sorry."

She hurried up to the counter, where the man behind

it was wrapping her sandwich. He handed it to her along with a punch card.

"Fifth sandwich is on us," he said. "But you look like you're having a bad day, so I punched you out early."

"Oh, but I can't—"

"No arguing," he interrupted. "It's my business. If I want to give you a sandwich, ain't nobody telling me I can't. Merry Christmas, miss."

The desire to pay the man for the sandwich warred with the desire to flee back to the safety of her condo. It only took a second for fear to win out, and she thanked the man profusely before hurrying out.

Even though she knew it was calling attention to her, she practically jogged back to her building, bumping into people and apologizing as she went. By the time she reached the lobby of her building, she was flushed and winded, and the sandwich gripped in her hand had been squeezed so hard in the middle that it now resembled a dumbbell.

"Are you all right?" the security guard called out.

Madison looked over and was relieved to see Wanda walking toward her. Wanda was a retired firefighter and a baker of pies. She also had long wavy hair that was bright red. There was absolutely no way she was the killer.

"I'm fine, Wanda," Madison said. "Thanks. I think I just outdid my fitness level."

Wanda scrunched her brow and looked closely at Madison's face. "You sure that's all? You look awfully flushed and your hands are shaking."

"I think some guy tried to steal my wallet on the corner." Madison made up the first lie she could think of that would explain her anxiety.

"Did you get a good look at him?" Wanda asked. "You want me to call the police?"

"No. He disappeared into the crowd before I got a look." She took a deep breath and tried to calm herself. "And now that I think about it, he could have bumped against me accidentally. I think all this talk about pick-pockets and burglaries this time of year has me on edge."

"You need to stop watching the news. It can give you a nervous breakdown. I stopped about five years ago and haven't had to take my blood pressure medicine ever since."

"That's good advice. Thank you for checking on me. I'm going to head upstairs and have my lunch."

Wanda patted her on the shoulder. "You take care now."

Madison forced herself to walk calmly to the elevator but as soon as she was inside, she hit the button for her floor several times, counting the seconds until the door closed on the lobby floor and reopened at the penthouse level. Since there was no one to see or judge her panic, she ran down the hall to her door. She punched in the entry code and practically tackled the door open before running inside and whirling around to slam it shut and pull the dead bolt.

She turned once more, her back against the door, and

slid down onto the floor, wondering if she'd ever feel safe again.

TRENTON COOPER WAS everything Monique had described him to be. From the first moment Shaye set sights on the Realtor, she knew he was going to be difficult and she wasn't going to like him. He stepped out of his office and into the reception area the moment she entered the real estate office, completely bypassing his administrative assistant and rushing to introduce himself. He then directed the assistant to bring in refreshments and ushered Shaye into a plush office, complete with antique furniture that Shaye knew had cost a fortune.

Trenton Cooper was making lots of money and wanted everyone to know it.

"I was so pleased to get your call, Ms. Archer," he said as he took a seat across the desk from her. "I hope I'll be able to help you. Are you looking for something in the city—a penthouse, perhaps? Or maybe a plantation so you can escape to the country. I've just purchased a small one myself and on the rare occasions that I can leave my business for a day, I have to admit that I'm enjoying fishing."

"That's nice," Shaye said, trying to imagine the very sleek Cooper, in his custom-made suit, sitting on a hot, mosquito-infested deck trying to catch bass, but the image never came. "I'm afraid, though, that it's not that kind of visit."

She pulled out her card and handed it to him. "You probably already know I am a private investigator. I'd like your help on a case I'm currently working."

He frowned. "A case? I can't imagine how I could help with anything you're investigating."

"It concerns a property you hold the listing for."

He immediately shifted to his "what my attorney advises" face. "If this is about an insurance claim on one of the properties, I can't speak to you without the full consent of the seller."

"It's not about insurance. It's about a crime."

His eyes widened. "What crime? The police haven't contacted me. Which property?"

Shaye gave him the address. "Last Friday night, a woman was attacked in that unit. A woman who lives across the street saw the attack but passed out as she was calling the police. By the time units got there, the apartment was wiped clean."

"Well, surely, the woman who saw it identified the victim, or the woman who was attacked reported the crime?" He rubbed his jaw and Shaye could tell he was flustered.

"I'm afraid the police have been unable to locate the victim or the perpetrator," she said.

He narrowed his eyes at her. "Which is why I have you here asking me questions and not the police. How do I even know a crime was committed? Maybe this woman was drunk and imagined everything. You say there's no evidence. How is that possible? I watch those shows on television. There's always something left behind."

"The perpetrator is very good. Very clever. The ones who get away with it for a long time usually are."

"No one's so good they don't leave a hair behind."

"I'm sure the CSI unit picked up plenty of hair and other items. After all, the unit is for sale so any number of people have passed through it recently. I imagine some of your hair could have been picked up in that sweep."

She'd said it intentionally, hoping to get a reaction from him. His jaw clenched and his expression shifted from disinterest to aggravation.

"Look," he said, "I don't know what you want from me, but I'm not about to let you start a media circus over the word of one crazy woman. That condo is a big commission and I've got a buyer ready to pull the trigger."

"I'm not trying to affect your sale. I'm simply looking for answers that I think you can provide."

"Like what?"

"Someone entered the unit around ten thirty that night. Unless they have a key, the only way they would be able to do that is by accessing the key in the lockbox. I understand the system provides you records of every entry that identify the Realtor requesting access."

"Yes, it does." He turned to his computer and tapped on the keyboard. "The woman probably saw someone showing the apartment, assuming she saw anything at all.

This will settle things up quickly, and then all this talk about a crime in my property can be shoved back under the bedcovers or into the whiskey bottle, which is where this woman should have left it."

He watched the screen as a list loaded and put his finger up to the screen, scanning the listings. Shaye was looking at the screen from an angle, so she couldn't make out the entries, but his finger stopped in the middle of the page and he frowned.

"Something wrong?" Shaye asked.

"No. Nothing," he said, and looked back at her. "No one accessed the condo."

"Really? Because your expression says differently. Look, Mr. Cooper, I know I have no legal grounds to demand the information, but the police do. I can stir things up until they decide to take a second look simply in order to make me go away. But that second look would probably require them to label the apartment as a potential crime scene, which means no one could enter. And then there's that ugly yellow crime tape they put up keeping people from entering."

The look he gave her left no question what he thought about her and her veiled threat. But he must have decided she was the lesser of evils because he hit the Print button, then grabbed the printout and pushed it across the desk to her.

"There. It shows no access at the time you're interested in. Just as I said."

Shaye lifted the paper and read the entry. "The last

access was at 5:00 p.m. that day. By Maria Foster. Do you know Ms. Foster?"

"Only what she reported on her showing, and I assure you, nothing was wrong with the unit or I would have heard about it."

"I assume since it's your listing, you have a spare key and can enter anytime without going through the lockbox."

"Yes. But I don't like what you're implying," he said, growing increasingly agitated. "If someone was in the unit that night, it wasn't me. I left the city that afternoon for my plantation. At ten thirty I was sitting on my dock catching speckled trout."

"Do you have anyone who can back that up?"

"No, Ms. Archer, I don't. The point of a getaway property is to get away. If I wanted to sit around listening to other people talk, I would have stayed in New Orleans."

"So the lockbox and your spare key are the only ways you know that someone could get into the unit."

"Building maintenance has a key, but they're supposed to be locked in a safe. Maybe you should be talking to him. He's an odd duck, roaming the building at all hours of the day and night. I've often wondered if he's not living in the vacant units. But then, a psychotic mainte-nance guy isn't a big story like the rich taking a fall. And that's what you specialize in, right?"

Shaye bristled but forced herself to remain calm. He was trying to provoke her. The question was why.

Because he was angry about being questioned and wanted her to be angry as well, or because he was trying to divert her attention away from him?

"I specialize in the truth," she said. "No matter whom it involves."

"New Orleans's white knightess in shining armor. How lucky we are. Look, Ms. Archer, I think your client is batshit crazy and imagined the entire thing, but even if she didn't, I assure you that my hobbies don't include attacking women. And even if I was foolish enough for them to, I would never be so stupid as to do it in my own listing. Especially *that* listing."

"So what you're saying is that if you were going to commit a crime in one of your properties, you'd take the commission into consideration first."

"Yes. That's exactly what I'm saying. I think we're done talking, Ms. Archer."

Shaye rose from the chair and headed out of the office. That had gone about as well as expected, except for one thing: the printout she still had in her hand contained every showing of the unit since it was listed two weeks before. There were only twelve of them and three were repeat agents. It might not produce anything, but it gave her another avenue to investigate.

And then there was that one last thing.

When Cooper shook hands with Shaye, he'd extended his right hand, but when he'd handed her the printout, it had been with his left.

JACKSON SPOTTED Detective Elliot in the rear of the parking lot, leaning on the fence and smoking a cigarette. He was half-hidden by a white van and the hanging limbs from a cypress tree, and it took a minute for Jackson to locate him. He frowned as he made his way over. He'd met with Elliot for an information exchange several times, but the other detective had never been this secretive until now. Jackson's back tightened as his mind filled with a million horrible things that Elliot might have to tell him.

Elliot nodded and stubbed out his cigarette on the metal fence post as Jackson approached. "Thanks for meeting me out here."

"I almost didn't see you."

Elliot glanced over the parking lot. "Yeah, that part was intentional. Look, I got something to tell you, and I had to make sure no one overheard. I was gonna wait until tonight and go to your house, but I have dinner at my mother-in-law's tonight and if I miss, my wife is gonna flip."

"It's no problem. What do you have?"

Elliot looked down at the ground, then around the parking lot again, then pushed himself off the fence.

"Whatever it is," Jackson said, "you might as well spit it out. It can't be any worse than what I already know."

"If this job has taught me anything, it's that things can always be worse. Until this morning, I thought you might have heard the worst of it, but now I'm not so sure. I got to this entry in Emile's journal and when I thought about the implications, it hit me like a ton of bricks."

Despite the cool weather, Jackson's hands felt clammy. He knew what was coming. Knew that the only thing that could make a hardened detective like Elliot that nervous was the secret that only he and Shaye shared.

"The entry talked about selling an infant," Elliot said. "Not much detail, just that an attorney handled it and he got ten thousand cash out of the deal. I know Samba was one of Clancy's customers, and I'm sure he figured out just how profitable the business was, but what the journals don't cover is where he got an infant to sell. Then I remembered Shaye's medical records and I almost lost my breakfast."

Elliot stopped talking and drew in a deep breath, staring directly at Jackson. Then his eyes widened. "You knew," he said. "You knew this was possible."

Jackson nodded. His stomach hadn't stopped clenching since Elliot had begun talking. It was one thing to know. It was completely another to have confirmation. And this kind of confirmation was a whole other level of horrible.

"Shaye's memory still isn't complete," Jackson said, "but she remembers the birth, and she said she heard the baby crying. They told her it was stillborn, but she knows that's not true."

"Jesus, Mary, and Joseph. I swear to God, if I had one impossible wish granted, I'd ask for that worthless piece of shit to be brought back to life just so I could kill him again."

"Me too."

"Even though it sounds underwhelming, I'm sorry, Lamotte. I can't even imagine..."

"Me either. Was there anything else to go on? Anything that might help identify the attorney?"

"No. And I scanned forward about six months." Elliot shook his head. "You know what kind of attorney does that sort of transaction, and he won't be advertising it. The only other facts I can give you are the date and the sex of the child. It was a girl."

Jackson's hands clenched until he felt his short nails digging into his palms. "You're sure."

"Definitely. That asshole said clearly that if the infant had been a male child, he would have kept him for sacrificing. Eighteen years I've been at this job, and I've seen some horrible things, but I've never seen anything like this. I wish I hadn't now."

"Yeah. Me too."

Elliot clasped his hand on Jackson's shoulder. "If there's anything I can do. Anything. You just have to ask. I've got a twelve-year-old daughter. When I think..." His voice choked on the last words.

"I know you've got to report everything to the brass, but if you could keep the conclusions you drew to yourself, at least for now, I'd appreciate it. Shaye hasn't told anyone else about her suspicions. Not even her mother. She wanted more information before she put that burden on her family."

"Well, she's got that information now. Damn it. Of course I'll keep my ideas to myself, but I'm not the only one familiar with Shaye's medical file. It's bound to come out, sooner or later."

"I know."

Jackson was afraid later was going to come a lot quicker than any of them wanted.

8

CORRINE POURED HOT CHOCOLATE INTO TWO MUGS and headed into the living room. It was a chilly night and while a glass of wine sounded good after a stressful day, a cup of hot cocoa sounded even better and had the added benefit of being on the list of things Eleonore could drink. She plopped into the recliner next to Eleonore and stuck her feet in front of the fireplace.

"If you're going to keep the house this cold," Eleonore said, "you should at least put on socks."

"The heat dries out my sinuses, and I hate wearing socks. Going barefoot is the one unrefined indulgence I allow myself."

Eleonore raised an eyebrow. "Have you forgotten how long I've known you?"

"Okay, so there might be more than one, but this is the one that irritated my father the most. I like to think that somewhere he's suffering for all the secrets he kept and can see my bare feet."

Eleonore frowned. "You remember what I do for a living, right? I've tried not to get all doctorish, but I really wish you'd talk about everything. If you're not comfortable doing it with me, then at least let me give you a referral to someone I trust."

Corrine sighed. "What makes you think I'd tell a stranger things I haven't told you? You and Shaye are the only people I trust absolutely. It's not that I'm keeping things from you. It's simply that I'm still not sure how I feel about certain things, so it's hard to convey."

"Not to beat a dead horse or anything, but sorting out how people feel about things is kinda in my wheelhouse."

Corrine smiled. "I'm a horrible pain in the ass, aren't I?"

"Well, that's not a medical diagnosis..."

Corrine tossed a pillow at her friend and missed her by a good foot.

"You do suck at throwing things," Eleonore said. "That's pretty official."

"Sometimes, I start to say something, and then I'm afraid if I get started, I won't ever stop. Every waking moment I jump from sad to angry to depressed to outraged, then back to sad. It's exhausting, but I can't seem to hit on the one emotion that fits properly."

"You're making this too easy. You can't hit on one right emotion because there's not one right emotion. Your situation is very complex. Hell, I still haven't sorted out how I feel about all of it, and I'm supposed to be the expert. If you had it all figured out, I'd hang up my notepad."

Corrine took a sip of her cocoa and stared at the fire for a bit. "For a long time—probably the first month—I hated him. I mean really and truly hated him. I'd think about all the secrets and lies and my entire body would stiffen so hard that my muscles cramped. I ground my teeth so badly at night that I broke two crowns. When Shaye would walk down the cliffs to the ocean, sometimes I'd go inside, close all the doors and windows, and scream as loudly as I could."

"Why did you feel you needed to hide your feelings from Shaye?"

"Because what I was dealing with was nothing compared to what she was dealing with."

"So you think suffering has rank?"

"Doesn't it?"

Eleonore shook her head. "No matter what happens to someone, at that exact moment, something that could be construed as worse is happening to someone else. That doesn't lessen our own heartache. It doesn't diminish the fact that right then, you're dealing with one of the worst things that's ever happened to you."

"Ugh. Why do you have to be so rational?" She held up her hand. "That's rhetorical."

"Regardless, I will allow you to play the mother card on not sharing with Shaye. For now. But you have no excuse for not talking to me. Yes, I'm close to the subject matter, but it's not my family. It's not my past."

"What the hell are you talking about? You *are* family. You've been with me longer than my own mother was. You've been with Shaye one week less than I've been. You had a relationship with my father from the day he hired you. This absolutely happened to you too. I'll grant you that you don't have the guilt of being a blood relative on your plate, but I'll trump it with the guilt you're feeling because you think you should have seen something beforehand and had us all prepared."

Eleonore frowned. "Maybe we have known each other too long. You're right, of course. My first thought was what did I miss? What did I fail to see that might have helped avoid so much heartache? And you know what I did about it?"

"What?"

"I *talked* to someone."

"Seriously?"

"What? You think shrinks don't need help too? We might have the answers for other people, but we still need help sorting out our own stuff. The most important thing a mental health professional can know is when they need help themselves. Anything else is hypocritical."

"Huh." Corrine slumped back in her chair and curled her legs up under her. It had never occurred to her that Eleonore would seek help for herself. Aside from the drinking problem, Eleonore had been the one person Corrine had known who always had everything together, always had the answers. But the reality was, Eleonore was human, too. Maybe a little superhuman, but even a superhuman needed help sometimes.

"Who do you talk to?" Corrine asked. "The same guy that helps with your drinking?"

"No. The therapist I talk about my alcoholism with is a specialist in addiction. This was outside of his realm. But I have a colleague from medical school who specializes in family issues, particularly extreme issues that produce emotions outside of the norm."

"He's here, in New Orleans?"

"No. Boston. We Skype once a week. More at first because I had a lot to say and I wandered off topic a lot. Now my thoughts are more organized."

"And you tell him everything?"

"I tell him everything that concerns me and my emotional state. I don't share anything about you or Shaye outside of what he could learn from the news."

Corrine waved a hand in dismissal. "Oh, I never thought you'd tell our personal business. I guess I've just never thought about you seeking that sort of therapy for yourself. See, sometimes you still surprise me."

Eleonore shrugged. "I know my limitations. I tried to handle it my way but when I picked up the bottle again, I knew I needed more than what I and my addiction therapist could provide."

"Fine. You've convinced me. But I want to be official. That way I'll stay focused. So let's make an appointment and I'll go to your office for a session, just like all your other clients."

"Good. Then I can bill you just like all my other clients."

Corrine laughed, then the real reason for her malaise crept back into her mind and she sobered. "I think Shaye is hiding something. I know you can't tell me what you guys talk about, but you'd tell me if something was wrong, right?"

"Yes. And even if confidentiality didn't apply, I couldn't tell you what is going on with her right now anyway as she hasn't spoken to me about it."

"But she's keeping up her sessions?"

Eleonore nodded. "I'm just agreeing with you that she's distracted by something she's not yet talking about."

Corrine bit her lower lip. "If she's not talking about it to you, it's bad."

"Not necessarily. Shaye is an adult now. She's trying to handle more on her own. Perhaps she's simply seeing if she can sort things out herself without relying on my help. If it looks like whatever she's mulling over starts to burden her, then I'll press her on the matter."

"You don't think there's anything wrong between her and Jackson, do you?"

"No way. She lights up if I just say his name. That man is the third-best thing that ever happened to her, and if he keeps it up, he might knock me out of second place."

Some of the tension in Corrine's shoulders dissipated. "I didn't want to like him—cop and all—but it's impossible not to. She's happy with him and it's genuine. More importantly, she trusts him, and I was afraid that was something that might never happen."

"It's a good thing, and he's very smart about the relationship. He gives her space to let him in rather than pushing. He accommodates her quirks without question or hesitation. And he protects her without being overbearing. I think she made an excellent choice. I don't think we could have done better if we'd built a man from scratch."

"If we could build perfect men from scratch, we wouldn't be sitting here drinking cocoa."

"I'm pretty sure the perfect man has already been built. She's called 'woman' but you keep turning down my offers of marriage."

"You snore. Besides, I don't want to live with anyone who might want to borrow my shoes."

Eleonore laughed. "One day, Corrine. One day the right man will turn up in your life, and you'll be completely dumbstruck by it. I, for one, can't wait to see it."

"Really? And you're what—gunning to be the cat lady?"

"I'm allergic to cleaning litter boxes. But I'm open to the idea that there's a man somewhere who could tolerate all my bad habits and still want to be around me for extended periods of time."

"You make it sound so romantic."

"Romance and love are two different things."

"So true. Well, for the moment, we can be happy that Shaye has both."

Eleonore lifted her cocoa in salute. "Here's to it lasting."

SHAYE SPENT the rest of the afternoon talking to residents in the apartment building where the murder occurred and then headed back to her apartment to do administrative work on the case. Three couples resided on the same floor as the empty unit but none of them shared a wall, and none saw or heard anything. The rest of the interviews went along the same lines—no one heard anything at the time of the murder, and the only people they saw in the building that night were other residents. One resident thought he saw Jason that night, which didn't fit with his claim that he'd left work at five thirty, but the resident also agreed that he might have been wrong as he'd only seen the person in question from the back.

The manager of the tow truck company told her no vehicles had been towed for over a week, so that eliminated the car as a means of identification. Given how careful the killer had been about everything in the apartment, she doubted he would have overlooked the problems a vehicle with an expired parking ticket might create, but it was still a box that needed to be checked off. Now she would move forward under the assumption that the victim had ridden with the killer to the building or had been close enough to walk.

She'd also run background checks on Trenton Cooper, Jason Parks, and Danny Suarez. Cooper had a clean record and had indeed purchased a small plantation earlier that year, but a quick satellite view of the place showed her that it would be easy for him to be in residence and for no one else to know. The property was in the middle of a ton of wooded acreage, and the lake that butted up against it only had a couple of houses with direct access. And even if someone had seen Cooper in town that day, it still didn't mean he didn't drive back to New Orleans that night. His home in New Orleans was a historical in the Garden District, not too far from Corrine's. Shaye made a note to ask her mother if she knew the Realtor.

The only tidbit of dirt she could find was an accusation of abuse by a woman who claimed she used to date the Realtor, but she couldn't offer any proof and had no injuries, so no charges could be pressed. A tiny article with the story appeared in a local newspaper, but it was the only black spot she could find. Still, a woman with an abuse claim was interesting. She'd checked the woman as well and found she'd gone on to marry a local doctor. If the other angles of investigation didn't yield a solid lead, Shaye planned on arranging a chat with Cooper's accuser.

Parks, the maintenance guy, had some minor items—a

DUI and petty theft—but they were a couple years back and it looked as though he'd been clean since then. But the check had yielded one curious item. Parks's address was listed in a rundown area of the Seventh Ward. The property was registered to a Cora Parks, his mother. But Cora Parks had passed away a year ago and the property had been condemned by the city shortly thereafter. Which made her wonder where Parks lived now. Perhaps Cooper's insinuation that the maintenance man was living in empty units wasn't a big stretch.

Danny Suarez had a sealed juvenile record, but based on his adult one, Shaye had a good guess as to what it might contain. Suarez was a confirmed pothead. Either the parking lot company didn't test or Suarez was a pro at getting around such things. He lived with his parents in a middle-class area of Uptown. Shaye wasn't ready to eliminate anyone from her suspect list completely, but she put Danny at the bottom. She'd never known a pot smoker who had a rage issue. Most were too chill to do more than change the television channel. Not saying it couldn't happen, but she wasn't betting money on this time being the case.

She saved her notes on the three men and leaned back in her chair. On paper, Cooper and Parks were both decent suspects. Both had access to the apartment and neither had an alibi for Friday night. Means and opportunity were covered. The problem was motive. Based on all the reading she'd done on serial killers, Shaye knew there was no one kind. They didn't share the same motivations and thought processes any more than the average sane individual did. And doctors had mixed opinions on how their minds got to that point and whether or not they could be treated.

Shaye believed serial killers fell into two camps—those who were born and those who were created. Based on the case studies she'd read, she absolutely believed that some people were born without a conscience. John Clancy might have been one of those people. The way he'd callously sold human beings, even young children, knowing full well what was likely to happen was something that most people didn't have the stomach for. Maybe there was something in Clancy's past that had stripped him of his feelings, but maybe he'd been that way since the day he took his first breath.

Other serial killers were made, usually by extreme abuse most often suffered at the hands of their parents or someone connected to them. If the abuse allegation against Cooper was true, then it might indicate a problem with women. Everything Shaye could find on Parks indicated he'd lived with his mother in less than optimum circumstances. And she'd died recently. It could have been the catalyst that sent him over the edge. So motive could be as simple as some emotional damage that tied directly to women. Prostitutes were easy targets, so perhaps it was simply an efficient choice.

The problem she had was that for either of them to choose a location for a murder that would be tracked directly back to them was the height of stupidity. That didn't automatically mean they were innocent. If private investigating had taught Shaye one thing it was that most criminals either weren't that bright—and thank God for that—or were so egotistical they thought they wouldn't get caught.

So the only thing she had to go on was her gut, and right now, it wasn't telling her anything one way or another. She'd found Parks pleasant enough, if not a little nervous, but that could be for a number of reasons that had nothing to do with being a murderer. Cooper was every bit as defensive and abrasive as she'd expected him to be, but being a douche wasn't a crime.

She glanced outside as the last of the sunlight disappeared and the streetlights blinked on. Time for the next round. She opened her desk drawer and pulled out her nine-millimeter. When she'd first started investigating, she'd been assigned mostly insurance cases and hadn't bothered with a gun. But now she didn't leave home without it. Her martial arts training was great, but it wasn't a good defense against a bullet. And these days, it seemed that everyone was carrying.

Tonight, it was especially important that she stay alert because the area of town she was going to wasn't exactly the shopping district. But she needed to figure out who the victim was and without a body, she had to find someone who knew the woman was missing. If the victim was a working girl and Shaye could find her regular area, then other girls might have noticed that she wasn't around.

She shoved her gun in her waistband, grabbed her car keys, and headed out. There was a lot of ground to cover and no way she could get to it all in one night, but she was going to talk to as many people as she could. Hopefully, one of them would know something.

The first area was a couple blocks from the apartment building. She started there using the theory that the woman had walked to the building or the perp had picked up a victim close to the building to minimize the potential of being seen with her. Cameras were a growing part of every urban area, and the smart move would be to avoid as many as possible if he'd picked the woman up in his automobile.

At the first location, she found two women who were willing to talk, but neither of them could think of anyone they knew fitting the description Shaye gave and who had recently gone missing. Shaye thanked them for their help and headed to the next stop.

Three hours later, she pulled up to what would probably be her last round of the night. It had been a long day. She was getting tired, and the areas she was covering were the kind of places you needed to visit when you were firing on all cylinders. Tired was weak, and the slightest sign of weakness was an opportunity to become a victim.

There were two women standing in front of a bar at the last location. Shaye parked in the first available spot on the street and made her way back to where the women were standing. One was a tall, curvy black woman. The other was blonde and white and stick-thin. They both gave her wary looks as she approached. She pulled out her ID and showed it to them, but they barely glanced at it.

"You 5-0?" the blonde asked.

"She's private," the black woman said. "But they all in bed together."

"I'm not in bed with anyone," Shaye said. "I'm working for a private client who witnessed a woman being attacked last Friday night."

The black woman lifted an eyebrow. "Sounds like a job for the cops...oh wait, they don't actually *do* anything."

"The police did investigate," Shaye said, "but by the time they arrived, the crime scene had been cleaned."

"So what do you want from us?" the blonde woman asked. "If that woman got hurt and wanted the cops to know about it, she would have told them herself."

"Not if she wasn't able to," Shaye said.

The blonde woman's eyes widened. "You think somebody got killed?"

"It's possible," Shaye said. "But no body has turned up and no one has filed a missing persons report for someone fitting the description of the victim."

The black woman stared at her for several seconds. "So you out here walking the streets at night because you think one of us got capped? You trying for sainthood or something? Wait...I know you. You're that rich white woman that crazy man held hostage. You busted that asshole selling kids."

The blonde woman whipped around and stared at Shaye. "It *is* you. I didn't recognize you with the ball cap. Didn't read your ID."

Shaye hesitated for a moment, wondering whether her identity helped or hindered her ability to get information out of the two women. Finally, honesty won out. "Yes. I'm Shaye Archer."

The black woman nodded. "Name's Shonda. This is Louise."

Louise's eyes widened. "You gave our real names."

"It's okay," Shonda said. "She ain't trolling the streets trying to bust us for something. If she said a girl was hurt then I believe her. What can you tell us?"

Shaye gave them Madison's description of the woman. As she talked, they glanced at each other and Louise bit her lower lip.

"That sounds like Carla," Louise said, shooting Shonda a worried look. "I told you she didn't go back to Rattler."

"Well, how was we supposed to know that?" Shonda asked. "That fool been back and forth with that asshole for a year now."

"Carla fits the description I gave you?" Shaye asked.

"Oh yeah," Shonda said. "Down to that outfit. I helped her pick out them shoes. I ain't got the balance for those high heels, but Carla was graceful like."

"When was the last time you saw her?" Shaye asked.

"That night about ten," Louise said. "We was all working."

"Did you see who she left with?" Shaye asked.

"No," Louise said. "Shonda and me both had regulars come by. By the time I got back, Carla was gone. Shonda came back after that. Since Carla never came back that night, we figured she'd either hooked a live one or called it quits. It was a slow night."

"And you never saw her again after that?" Shaye clarified.

They both shook their heads.

"Does she have a cell phone?" Shaye asked.

"One of them prepaid jobs," Shonda said. "I called the number but it doesn't go through. Lots of times, she didn't have the money for service."

"Did she have a car?" Shaye asked.

Shonda snorted. "Can't afford no car on what we make. We use the bus. If it's a good night, we take a cab home. If not, it's a long walk in uncomfortable shoes. I gotta ass you can bounce quarters on, though."

"Not me," Louise said. "I just got blisters."

"I'd probably have blisters as well," Shaye said, and pulled out her phone to make notes. "What can you tell me about me about Carla? Do you know her full name?"

"Carla Downing," Louise said.

"Where did she live?" Shaye asked.

"She usually stayed at the Franklin Motel when she and Rattler was on the outs," Shonda said. "I didn't ask, but I assumed she was there this time."

"Did you try calling the motel for her?" Shaye asked.

"I did," Louise said, "but some guy told me they can't give out information about their guests. I didn't figure it would make a difference if I went there."

"Probably not," Shaye said. "What about this Rattler? Do you know his real name? Can you tell me where he lives?"

"Don't know his real name," Louise said. "Everyone calls him Rattler on account of the snakes. He's always got one wrapped around his arm. Real creepy."

"He's straight up crazy is what he is," Shonda said. "I don't know where he stays. Somewhere in the Ninth Ward is all I know."

"Does he have a job?" Shaye asked.

Shonda snorted. "If you call slinging coke for the Gravediggers a job, then yeah."

Shaye stiffened. Everyone in New Orleans had heard of the Gravediggers, mostly from the evening news. And none of it was good. They were the most violent motorcycle gang in the city, and there was no shortage of bodies attached to the members.

"What does Rattler look like?" Shaye asked.

"Besides creepy?" Louise asked. "Tall, skinny, brown hair. Nothing to look at really."

"That's true enough," Shonda said. "If he didn't have that snake, probably no one would give him a second glance."

"What about tattoos?" Shaye asked.

They both nodded. "He got them on both arms,"

Shonda said, "and something on his back. I only seen part of it at the top of his shirt."

"None on the face?" Shaye asked.

"No," Louise said, "although it might be an improvement."

"Ha," Shonda said. "Ain't no improving on that one. He's bad straight to the bone. I always said things was gonna end bad for Carla if she didn't leave that one alone."

"She said she was done with him for real this time," Louise said.

"She been saying that ever since the night she hooked up with him," Shonda said.

Louise frowned. "I know, but this time felt different. There was something about the way she looked and sounded that made me think maybe it was true this time. You think he killed her?"

"I don't know what happened," Shaye said, "but I'm going to try to find out."

"But he look like the guy your witness saw, right?" Shonda asked.

"My witness didn't see much," Shaye said. "He was tall and lean with brown hair, but he wore pants and a coat, so she couldn't see his arms. She can't describe his face, so it leaves things a little open on that end."

"A tall, lean white dude with brown hair," Louise said. "You just described half the men walking around New Orleans."

Shaye pulled out her phone and brought up the

pictures she'd captured and saved earlier of Cooper and Parks. "Do you recognize either of these men?"

They leaned in and studied the photos, but both shook their heads.

"Is one of them the guy that did it, you think?" Louise asked.

"Both of them had access to the apartment and don't have an alibi for that time, but I have no way to connect them to Carla."

"Us working girls got a pretty good memory for faces," Shonda said. "You need to so you can avoid the creeps. I ain't seen either of them around here, but whoever picked Carla up Friday night did it while Louise and me was gone."

"Or she called it quits because it was slow, and he got her on her way home or at the motel," Louise said.

Shaye nodded and studied the two women for a moment, an idea that had been festering in her mind popping back into play.

"You don't know of anyone else who's missing, do you?" she asked.

"This ain't exactly government work," Shonda said. "Nobody sticks around any longer than they have to. Why? What you think happened?"

"I don't know for sure," Shaye said, "but if the man my client saw managed to collect a woman without being seen and clean a crime scene so that police didn't find a trace of anything, then it's hard for me to believe it was his first time."

Louise's hand flew over her mouth. "Oh my God."

Shonda frowned. "There was a girl named Mitzi, used to work a couple blocks from here. I seen her in the coffee shop sometimes, but I ain't in a month or so."

"What did Mitzi look like?" Shaye asked.

"White, blonde, tall, thin," Shonda said.

"Like Carla," Louise said.

Shaye's mind screamed at her that she'd known, but she forced herself to remain focused. It was only one other woman, and there might be an explanation for her disappearance that had nothing nefarious attached to it. Plenty of working girls were blonde.

But her gut told her differently.

"Do you know anything personal about Mitzi?" Shaye asked.

Shonda shook her head. "We just chatted about things that didn't matter, really. There's another girl that works that area, though. Brandi. White, brunette, and got a mole on her cheek. She might be able to tell you something."

"I really appreciate you talking to me," Shaye said.

"What do you think is going on?" Louise asked.

"I don't know," Shaye said, "but I want you two to be very careful, especially you, Louise."

Louise sucked in a breath. "Because of my hair. Shit. I just did it blond because they make more money."

"I'd get a wig if I was you," Shonda said.

Shaye pulled out her wallet and handed them both a

hundred bucks. "Maybe take the rest of the night off and grab a bite to eat. See about that wig in the morning."

Shonda stuffed the money in her cleavage and pulled out a card. "That's my cell phone. If you find out anything…"

Shaye shoved the card in her pocket and handed Shonda and Louise one of her own. "I'll let you know as soon as I do. Please be careful, and if you see or hear anything suspicious, let me know."

"We will," Shonda said. "And I'll ask around. See if there's a recent shortage of blondes. I know a lot of people well enough that they'll talk. Definitely they'll talk to me before they talk to you."

"I really appreciate it."

Shonda nodded. "You all right. Most people wouldn't bother with any of this."

Shaye smiled. "That's my job."

Shonda snorted. "You ain't fooling nobody. You ain't got to work. You out here because you have to be. Some people got the calling. My grandmama worked relief in Africa for thirty years. I seen the difference between a job and something you ain't got no choice but to do."

"Well, let's just hope my calling makes a difference," Shaye said.

"Already has," Shonda said. "That monster Clancy is dead."

9

SHAYE LEFT SHONDA AND LOUISE AND HEADED BACK TO her car. It was too late to go by Madison's place. She'd intended to go home after this stop, but since Shonda had indicated that Brandi worked only a couple blocks away, she decided to make a pass in that area and see if she could spot her. It was a quick drive two streets over and she slowed to a crawl, looking for a woman who might be Brandi. This street was a little busier than the other had been so she had to take it slow to get a good look at everyone. Finally, she spotted a brunette in a low-cut silver dress and red high heels leaving a convenience store with a pack of cigarettes in her hand.

Shaye pulled to the curb in front of the store and exited the vehicle. The woman had stopped next to a lamppost and was lighting a cigarette. She narrowed her eyes as Shaye approached.

"I'm just having a smoke," the woman said. "I ain't breaking any laws."

Shaye showed the woman her ID. "I'm not a cop. I'm a PI. Are you Brandi?"

The woman's eyes flickered and Shaye knew she'd found the right person, but she didn't answer straightaway. "I might know Brandi," she said finally.

"I got your name from Shonda," Shaye said. "I'm not looking to cause you any trouble. I'm working a case and Shonda thought you might be able to help me out."

"Don't see how. Don't know nothing about nothing and wouldn't tell it even if I did."

"Did you know a girl who worked this area named Mitzi?"

Brandi took a puff on the cigarette and blew it out. "Maybe. Why? What's she done?"

"Nothing that I'm aware of. I'm afraid maybe something was done to her. I understand she hasn't been around in a while."

Shaye finally had Brandi's full attention. "What do you mean done *to* her?"

"I'm investigating an attack on what I think was a white, blonde working girl. Shonda said she hadn't seen Mitzi in a while and thought you might know where to find her if she left on her own accord."

Brandi glanced up and down the street, then leaned closer to Shaye. "I ain't seen her in a month. She don't have no phone so I went to the apartment she rented. Damn landlord wouldn't let me in to look. One of her neighbors said they hadn't heard a peep from her unit though, and the walls is thin. Really thin."

"Do you think she could have left town? Maybe gone back home, wherever that is?"

"Her stepdaddy turned her out when her momma died. She was thirteen. She ran clear of him a couple years later. The only reason she'd ever go back to that town is to spit on his grave when he dies."

Shaye nodded. "Can you think of anywhere else she might have gone?"

"No. She didn't have no other family that I know of. And even if she was cutting out, she would have told me."

"Did she have a boyfriend?"

Brandi shook her head. "I don't even think she liked men much. But they pay the bills, you know?"

"Can you tell me the address of her apartment? Maybe I'll have better luck with the manager."

Brandi gave Shaye the address. "He's a real piece of work. Told me he'd let me in for a blow job."

Anger coursed through Shaye and paying the apartment manager a visit moved up to priority one on her list of things to do the next day.

"Any other girls who've stopped showing up for work lately?" Shaye asked.

Brandi stared at her for a moment, then shook her head. "Not that I've heard, but I don't talk much. You think you got some kind of Jack the Ripper thing?"

"I'm not sure what's going on." Shaye pulled out a

business card and handed it to Brandi. "But if you hear anything about other girls missing—even rumor—please call me. I promise I'm not going to cause any trouble for you."

Brandi took the card and tucked it in her tiny purse. "Yeah, all right."

"And please be careful."

"Who are you working for, anyway? The cops?"

"No. Just an average woman who witnessed something horrible and wants justice."

DESPITE THE FACT that it was close to midnight, Jackson was parked in front of Shaye's apartment, waiting on her to return. He'd known her plans for the night and although he'd tried to convince her to let him come along, she'd insisted that even the sight of him would close up any mouths that might have otherwise spoken. He didn't like it but he couldn't argue with her when she was right. Working girls could spot a cop ten blocks away. He'd insisted on regular contact, so he'd known when she was about to conduct her final interview and would be heading home. That's when he'd set out for her place.

She wasn't expecting him. If he'd insisted on talking to her in person when she finished up work, she would have known something was up. Something so big it couldn't wait until the next day. And wondering could have thrown her off her game at a time when he needed her to be focused on everything around her and not what he had to say. So he'd decided to let her focus on her work tonight and meet up with her when she was done. She'd been out later than he'd thought she would be, which meant either that she'd found a line to work or that she hadn't found anything and had refused to stop trying until she'd exhausted her options.

The headlights from her SUV flashed onto the street a couple minutes after he arrived. He watched as she parked behind him and got out of her vehicle. He stepped out of his truck and walked over to her. She gave him a smile but he could see the unspoken question in her eyes.

She kissed him, then motioned to the door. "I know you're not here to tuck me in, but whatever it is will have to wait until I change. Then you can fill me in over a beer and cookies."

"Best offer I've had all day."

Shaye smiled. "That's not exactly a compliment given what you do for a living."

Inside, he headed straight for the refrigerator while Shaye went to change. She looked tired and worried, and the last thing he wanted to do was add to all of that, but no way was he going to keep what he knew from her. Not even for one day. Their relationship was built on trust—something Shaye had for very few people—and he wasn't going to do anything to compromise it.

But he wasn't looking forward to the conversation. To be honest, he hadn't really decided how he felt about the information, which left him with no earthly idea how Shaye would receive it. Part of him wished there was nothing to be found about the baby. With no avenue of investigation, Shaye would have had to let it go, and part of Jackson thought that might be better. But the other part of him understood that not knowing was a form of torture all in itself.

But what if the unimaginable happened? What if Shaye found the child? What then?

He wasn't sure Shaye knew the answer and he couldn't even begin to offer one up. Which left him filling the role he most often filled with Shaye—supporting whatever decision she made. He hated that he couldn't contribute more, that he couldn't share some of her burden, but for the life of him, he couldn't figure out a way to do it.

Shaye came back into the kitchen wearing shorts and a T-shirt. Even though it was chilly outside, her apartment was always toasty warm. Jackson had joked once about her utility bill but instead of laughing, she'd gone quiet, then explained that she'd spent so many winters shivering in that crypt that she refused to be cold in her home. It was a stark reminder to him that no matter how much Shaye had healed, there were things that she might never be able to shed.

Shaye flopped onto the couch as Jackson headed into the living room and placed a container of cookies on the coffee table in between the bottles of beer before sitting next to her on the couch. Shaye took a sip of beer, then leaned back and looked over at him.

"Tell me," she said. "By the look on your face, I know it isn't good, so rip the Band-Aid off."

Jackson blew out a breath. "I talked to Elliot today."

Shaye stiffened. "He found something?"

Jackson nodded and told Shaye about the entries in Emile Samba's journals. Shaye listened in complete silence, but Jackson could tell by the way her jaw clenched that she was angry. When he finished, he studied her for several seconds.

"Are you okay?" he finally asked. "I'm sorry. I shouldn't have laid this on you tonight. It could have waited."

"No. You made the right call. This wouldn't have been any easier to hear in the morning or a week from now. That's all Elliot found?"

"Yeah. He scanned ahead a good bit to see if there were any other mentions, but that's it."

"It's not surprising. Once he exchanged the baby for the money, he was done. It probably never crossed his mind again."

The anger and bitterness in her voice made his heart clench, and he reached over to take her hand. "He was a monster. A psychopath. Nothing he did has any relevance as to your worth or that of the child."

Shaye squeezed his hand. "I know. Eleonore has spent a third of my life drilling that into my head. I accept it mentally although I can't help the disgust I feel. But emotionally…"

"I understand. When it's something this big, it's hard to separate the head from the heart. I don't even know that it's possible."

"I have to find that attorney."

Jackson held in a sigh. He'd known it was coming and understood the reasons why it had to happen, but he was still afraid of what the eventuality would be as the weeks, then months, ticked by without a single lead. She'd handled so much already. Could this be the one thing she wasn't ready for?

"You know better than anyone the difficulties," he said.

"I do, but I have to try. I'm not going to make this my life's work. I'll do the things I would for any client asking for the same service. If it doesn't yield anything, then I'll file it all away to revisit if something new gives me another angle to pursue."

He knew she believed what she was saying, but he also knew that once Shaye started down that road of pursuit, it would be much harder to file it away than she thought. He'd known detectives who couldn't let go of a case. That one case that they never really closed the door on, even though it cost some of them their families, their health, and in a couple cases, their jobs. And in every instance, Jackson absolutely understood their reasons, but he couldn't help but feel bad about the lives ruined by their dogged pursuit of a question with no answers.

"I'll support you and help you with anything you want to do," he said. "You know that. But I feel like I had to say that. You've had so much to deal with lately. Disappointment is far too trite a word for what you've experienced. I just don't want any more heaped on you."

She let go of his hand and slipped her arms around him. He pulled her in close until she was nestled against him and kissed the top of her head. If only he could hold her right there, on that couch forever, protecting her from all the bad things out there for the rest of her life. But he knew he couldn't.

Because once Shaye Archer was determined to do something, it was all over but the worrying.

He roamed the house, his eyes looking past the peeling wallpaper and tattered furniture. At one time, this had been home. Now it sat, decaying a little more each day.

Just like the bodies he'd disposed of.

He headed down the hallway, his footsteps heavy on the rotting floors, and made his way into her room. Rats had shredded the end of the quilt, probably to build a winter nest, and a thick layer of dust covered every surface, but otherwise, it looked as it had when he'd lived here. He peered in the closet and saw her favorite pink dress hanging there, and he flashed back to the day that had changed everything.

The day he'd learned the truth.

All those years he'd believed her lies. Believed that his father had left them because he didn't want a child. Believed that she did her best to take care of him. But none of it was true. His mother was the reason his father left. She was a whore. Maybe she didn't walk the streets selling herself like the others, but a nice dress and an expensive haircut didn't make her any different or any better. In fact, it made her worse. At least the others weren't hypocrites.

He walked over to the dresser and picked up a picture. All of the rage he'd felt the day he'd learned the truth came racing back into his body, knotting every muscle. Making it hard for him to breathe. The fake blonde hair. The thick makeup and tight clothes. Decent women didn't look that way. Good mothers definitely didn't. But she'd paid for her lies. One bad batch of cocaine was all it had taken to rid himself of the worst thing that had ever happened to him.

But then she'd come back. He saw her everywhere. On every street corner.

And now, in a penthouse apartment.

10

JACKSON STRETCHED his arms out from under the blanket that covered him and lifted himself into a sitting position. He'd spent the night on Shaye's couch. She had a guest room, but he preferred staying where he could see the front door and figured Shaye probably preferred it as well, even though she would never admit she was nervous about being there alone. She also had a king-size bed that could easily accommodate both of them, but that was territory they hadn't gotten into yet and definitely one of those areas where he would wait for her to make the first move. Or at the very least, give off signals that were the equivalent of holding a neon sign above her head.

He would be the first to admit that he wanted her that way, but why wouldn't he? She was the most incredible woman he'd ever met and beautiful to boot. And if he was being honest with himself, his feelings grew deeper with every moment he spent in her company. He'd never fallen like this before, and he knew this was different. Special. And he was prepared to do anything required not to screw it up.

He heard water running in her bathroom and a minute later, Shaye trudged into the living room and leaned over to kiss him, her breath smelling of spearmint. "Coffee?" she asked.

"Please." He rose from the couch and headed into the guest bath to brush his own teeth and see if anything could be done about couch hair. He kept some bathroom items and spare clothes at her house—her suggestion—and it came in handy because then he didn't have to go home to get ready for work.

A little water and his brush managed the worst of his hair problems and he went ahead and dressed for work. It was already 7:30 a.m., and although they didn't have a set time to report to work, his senior partner preferred to start early and hopefully clear the way to regular dinner times. The reality was the hours were whatever was required to solve the case. So no one said anything if you weren't at your desk by 8:00 a.m. or some other arbitrary time someone deemed the start of the workday.

He headed back into the kitchen, and Shaye pushed a cup of coffee across the counter to him. "You're not going to sit?" he asked as she opened the refrigerator.

"I was thinking about breakfast," she said.

"You can think about it all you want, but it's not going to make food materialize in that refrigerator."

She pulled a bag of strawberries and a carton of skim milk out and sighed. "I'm really horrible at domestics. My mother just about has apoplexy every time she looks in there. Last time I had ketchup, salsa, six bottles of beer, and what was left of a pizza that should have been thrown out days before."

He smiled, easily able to picture Corrine's dismay. Her own kitchen was always stocked with the ingredients needed to whip up a gourmet meal at a moment's notice, and Corrine was a good enough cook to pull it off.

"In your defense," Jackson said, "Corrine does have someone who does all her grocery shopping for her."

Shaye put the strawberries and some protein powder into a blender and poured the milk over it. "You're sweet to defend me, but she offers to have them do my shopping all the time. I'm the one turning it down because I know exactly what would happen. I'd have an entire pantry and refrigerator of food go bad because I wouldn't prepare it in time. It's best if I just ruin a thing or two at a time."

"Hey, whatever works," he said as she fired up the blender. "I'm good with strawberry protein shakes for breakfast. Helps balance out all that pizza and takeout Chinese."

She poured the shakes into glasses and took a seat next to him. "You working on anything big?"

"Nothing that we have solid leads on. We've got a

couple of things we're assigned to but right now, we're down to beating bushes and hoping something turns up. What do you have planned for today?"

"First up, I'm paying a visit to Mitzi's pervy landlord and seeing if he wants to pull the same crap on me that he did on Brandi. I'm guessing not."

"He better not. If he even hints at it, you call me. I have no trouble hauling him in. A night in jail might get him to rethink his policies."

"It would probably take more than a night. Guys like that have been doing that sort of thing forever. They just never get called on it."

"I'm sure."

"After that, I don't know. Depends on what I run down at her apartment. I'll try the hotel where Carla stayed when she wasn't living with Rattler, but I want to pay Rattler a visit first and see what he has to say about his missing girlfriend."

"Be careful dealing with him. The Gravediggers are the most violent gang in the city. He won't like being questioned, even though you're not a cop."

"I'm going to try the friendly approach, maybe flirt with him a little."

Jackson stared at her in dismay until she broke out in a smile.

"You should see the look on your face," she said.

"I was trying to figure out something to arrest you for until you came to your senses."

"Don't worry. I don't plan on doing anything to piss

off the Gravediggers. It will just be a friendly conversation about his girlfriend. Honestly, I don't like him for this. If Carla was the only girl missing maybe, but it feels like something more than a simple domestic."

He nodded. "What Madison saw was far too elaborate for the Gravediggers. They would have simply put a bullet through her head and dumped the body."

"Exactly. But it's an avenue I have to travel to be certain it's a dead end."

"Are you going to Rattler's house?"

"The only address I could come up with is a bar the Gravediggers own. It has apartments above it so I figure some of them might live there. Maybe I'll get lucky and he'll be all hungover and talk to get rid of me."

"Will you do me a favor and text me when you get there and when you leave?"

"Of course. My phone will be on at all times. If you get worried, just track me."

"I don't like invading your privacy that way."

"First off, I'm giving you permission because I don't hide anything from you. Second, if I thought you wanted tracking privileges because you didn't trust me, that would be a whole other story. You want access because you're worried and you want to be able to help if needed." She smiled. "I like that you worry. Just a little, mind you, because worrying isn't all that fun."

"Well then, you should be thrilled. Because I'm going to be thinking about that conversation with Rattler until I know you're back in your SUV and at least ten blocks from the bar. Are you sure you don't want to hire some backup?"

She raised one eyebrow. "And by backup, you mean a bodyguard. You sound like my mother."

"She's a smart woman. And no, I don't mean a bodyguard. Okay, maybe I do, but here's the thing. I don't go into situations alone. I have Grayson and we report to dispatch so they know what's going on. You're one woman, and while being a woman doesn't make you any less capable, it does make you a more likely target."

She leaned over and kissed him. "You're a good man, Jackson Lamotte. But I'm not going to be someone's victim again."

He knew she meant it. But sometimes people didn't get a choice.

MADISON PULLED on black slacks and a turquoise sweater. It was chilly out, but the sweater and her leather jacket should be fine for the trip to the office. The dress code at corporate was business casual, but Madison always made it a point to dress slightly better than what was called for. As a contractor, she felt it was smart to portray a professional image. It set her apart from the regular employees and reminded the client that she wasn't one of them.

With her first contract, Madison had tried to blend in with the corporate culture of the company that'd hired her, but it had led to management feeling a familiarity for her and authority over her in areas that they didn't have grounds for. Since then, she'd kept everything different enough from the standard that management didn't lump her in with their employees, but not so different that they wouldn't hire her again or recommend her to other businesses.

Brett, the manager she reported to, didn't have the characteristics that usually led to the problems she'd experienced in the past, but she'd decided on a method for conducting her contracts and since it seemed to work, there was no sense abandoning it, because things might turn out okay this time. Besides, if she didn't wear her two whole pairs of slacks sometime, they might not ever wear out. And despite her savings and good salary, she wasn't a spendthrift. Clothes got replaced when they wore out or went so out of style that people might stare.

She grabbed her jacket and purse, took one last look at her hair in the hall mirror, and headed out of her unit. James's nameplate was on the security desk when she stepped into the lobby and she gave the guard a wave. "How are you this morning, James?"

"Doing well, Ms. Avery. It's a fine day for a walk. Are you going to do some shopping?"

"Business meeting, I'm afraid. But maybe I'll get some in afterward."

She didn't bother telling him she had no one to buy for. That wasn't the sort of thing you unloaded on a person you barely knew.

"Would you like me to call you a cab, or are you doing that Uber thing like all the other young people?"

"Actually, I'm going to walk. The office is only four blocks away, so when the weather is nice, I like to get in a little exercise and sunlight."

"I don't blame you. Have a good day, Ms. Avery."

"You too."

She headed outside and paused to scan the sidewalks before setting off toward her client's building. Everyone appeared to be going about their business. No one paid attention to the average woman standing there. She waited to see if anything triggered her, but all she felt was the cool winter breeze blowing across her cheeks. Taking a deep breath, she took off down the sidewalk.

As she walked, she scanned the people bustling around her. Old, young, pretty, not so pretty...what would it be like to actually remember them once they were out of sight? How many faces did a normal person retain every day? One? Two? Only those that they interacted with on some level? She knew that if people like her existed, then the opposite existed as well—people who never forgot a face. That would come in handy, especially if you were in a sales profession. People liked to be remembered. It made them feel important.

As she crossed the street a block away from her building, the breeze blowing across the back of her neck felt colder and she stiffened. Someone was watching her. She slowed down, pretending to gaze into a storefront window at an art display, but she was using the reflection in the glass to study the street behind her. Slowly, she panned from right to left, searching for the source of her discomfort. Then she locked in on him.

He was across the street and a little ways down from her, leaning against the wall of a store. He wore jeans with a hole above the right knee and a black New Orleans Saints hoodie. His tennis shoes were red and white. No one else would have given him a second glance, but she knew he was watching her. Was it the killer? Or was it just some random creep staring at strangers?

She turned away from the display and started walking again, this time checking her watch and increasing pace. If anyone were watching, they'd assume she was hurrying to make an appointment. Not that it mattered what anyone thought, but she didn't want to let him know that he could unnerve her. As she approached the area directly across the street from where he was standing, she glanced over.

He was gone.

She let out a big gush of air and slightly slowed her pace. Between fear and walking so fast she was practically jogging, her breathing had become erratic, and she drew in several long breaths and slowly let them out.

You panicked.

Once again, she chided herself for overreacting. She couldn't keep letting this happen or it would affect her health, physically and mentally. When Shaye told her she'd know if she was in danger, Madison had been skeptical but had wanted to believe her. After all, if anyone knew about the dangers of the unknown it was Shaye Archer. But at the same time, Madison knew that she didn't trust herself. That after a lifetime of living with some sort of fear, her thoughts would create things that simply weren't there.

When her breathing was back to normal, she picked up the pace a little again. She wasn't in any danger of being late, but it certainly wouldn't hurt to be early. She stopped at the next street corner and waited for the light to change so she could cross over the main street to the other side.

And that's when she saw him again.

She didn't recognize his face, of course, but the clothes were the same, down to the hole in his jeans. And he was staring directly at her. This time, leaned against a lamppost and smiling. The Walk light came on, and the people surrounding her started walking, jostling her as they moved past.

He stared at her the entire time, the smile never leaving his face, his eyes locked on hers. Then when the traffic light changed, he lifted his hand, one finger extended, and drew it across his neck.

11

Madison choked back a scream and launched forward into the street as the light changed to green. A car slammed to a stop just inches from her, the driver yelling and shaking his hand at her. She mumbled an apology as she continued across, ignoring the horns, and didn't stop running until she reached the other side of the street. She fled into the first open storefront she found, then hid behind a display, sneaking peeks at the street.

He was gone.

More than ever, she wanted to lock herself in her condo and never leave again, but she knew that wasn't possible. The meetings were mandatory. She could reschedule, but for when? She had no guarantees that the killer would ever be caught, and while her trust fund had covered the cost of her condo, she needed to work to pay for normal living expenses.

She pulled her phone out of her purse and accessed the Uber app. A minute later, the information about her car and driver popped up on the screen. Relief engulfed her as she saw the smiling face of a young black man on the screen. She clutched her phone and waited until a blue sedan pulled up to the curb outside the store. The Uber sticker was on his car window and a young black man stepped out of the vehicle. She slipped her phone in her purse and hurried outside.

"Madison Avery?" the young man asked.

"Yes."

He opened the car door and she practically dived inside. As he slid into the driver's seat he turned to look at her. "You realize you're only going two blocks, right?"

"Yes. I was walking but I twisted my ankle and I have a meeting that I need to get to. I didn't think I could make it on time limping."

He nodded. "I just wanted to make sure. Didn't want to take advantage of you."

"I appreciate it," she said, but her attention wasn't on the courteous driver. It was on the outside of the car. Where was he? Did he see her get into the car? Was he following her? Traffic was heavy and the car wasn't moving very fast. But surely if he was following the car she'd see him, right?

A couple minutes later, the car stopped in front of her client's office building. She thanked the driver as she jumped out of the car and practically ran inside. It wasn't until she was behind the tinted doors that she looked out at the street, scanning it up and down for the killer. She gave it four passes before deciding he wasn't there.

But that didn't mean he wasn't lurking just out of sight. Waiting for her.

What did he want? If he'd simply tried to kill her because of what she'd seen, she'd understand that. Not that she was asking for a bullet through the head from a block away, but that would make sense. This didn't make sense at all. Why taunt her? What if she'd dashed into that store and called the police? Granted, he'd disappeared, but the cops could have searched the area.

Call Shaye.

Her hand shook as she lifted her phone, but then she noticed the time. Her meeting started in five minutes, and she had to try to compose herself beforehand or she risked looking like a basket case in front of her client. The job she was currently working on would wrap up soon but there was another with this same company in the pipeline, and it was a job she hoped to have the inside track on. Flaking out this late in the game wouldn't improve her chances at it.

She shoved the phone in her purse and hurried to the bathroom. Maybe some cold water on her face would help and she could grab a bottled water from the café in the lobby before heading up for her meeting. In the meantime, she'd concentrate on breathing slowly in and slowly out. With any luck, her racing heart and shaking hands would calm before she had to speak.

THE OAKWOOD ESTATES APARTMENTS didn't contain a single oak tree and would never pass as an estate. The building was constructed from crumbling brick that had seen too many hurricanes and even more years of neglect. Shaye parked in front of the sign that indicated where the office was located and headed up the sidewalk. The place was quiet for 10:00 a.m., but Shaye guessed a lot of the residents were more of the night sort of crowd.

She followed the sidewalk through a breezeway and spotted the office off a courtyard that was overgrown with weeds and now appeared to serve as a trash heap for the residents. Apparently, the only thing the manager actually managed was collecting rent...probably in whatever form he could get it.

She pulled open the door and stepped inside. The office reeked of stale coffee and cigarettes, and she felt her eyes tear up as she coughed. The front room had a single desk with a telephone on it and paper scattered everywhere. A door was located behind the desk but was drawn almost completely closed.

"Hello?" she called out.

"Leave the money on the desk with your name on it," a man's voice called out from the partially closed door.

"I'm not here to pay rent. I'm here to speak to the manager."

The man cursed, then she heard things banging

around. "What now?" he yelled as he flung open the door.

"Are you the manager?"

He gave her a long look up and down and immediately his attitude changed. "Are you looking for a place? I've got a one-bedroom opening up as soon as I can get the stuff cleared out. Should only take a day." He smiled. "I can make you a really good deal...if you're willing to negotiate."

The overwhelming desire to punch him dead in the face and return home to shower came over her, and she struggled to maintain her professional demeanor.

"I'm not interested in an apartment," she said, and pulled out her business card. "I'm interested in a tenant."

He took the card and stared down at it for a moment, then his eyes widened and he shuffled a bit. "Hey, I was only joking about that negotiation thing."

"No, you weren't, and you weren't joking when you made a lewd suggestion to a friend of Mitzi's when she came here looking for her a couple weeks ago."

"Mitzi? Is that what this is about? What in the world is a classy broad like you doing trying to run down some whore? Your man hire her services? Maybe that's why she cleared out."

"So she's gone? Since when?"

"This ain't kindergarten. I don't take roll call. She pays every two weeks and I never got the last payment. I been watching, but she ain't been back far as I can tell."

"You're sure?"

"Ain't nothing gone from her place. Not that there's much to collect, but all her clothes are still hanging in the closet. Same dirty laundry in the basket on the bed. Ain't none of it moved since the first time I went to check it out."

"Is everything still in the unit?"

"Yeah. I mean, I was gonna clear it out as soon as I found someone to take the place, except for the furniture. It ain't that great but if somebody ain't got nothing, it's better than sitting on the floor."

"You know there are laws concerning how you have to treat abandoned property, right?"

He snorted. "I guess she'll just have to sue me."

"I have a better idea. How about I pay up her rent and you let me take a look in her apartment."

"You got a warrant?"

"I'm not a cop."

"So what's your beef? That furniture ain't worth fifty bucks."

"My beef is that the woman is missing, and I'm interested in finding her. Why is none of your business."

He scowled a bit, but the offer of easy cash was too much for him to ignore. "Hey, you want to pay two hundred bucks to look at some furniture that belongs in the dump then I ain't got no problem with it."

Shaye pulled the cash out of her purse and handed it to him. He counted it out, then reached into the desk next to him and handed her a key.

"Unit 12," he said. "Across the courtyard on the

bottom floor."

"Thanks." She took the key and left the office, unable to look at his smug face any longer. He had no right to sell or give away Mitzi's things. Not without going through the proper court procedure, and it killed her to hand over money to the perv, but it was the quickest way to get what she needed. If she left without accessing the unit, she had no doubt he'd clean it out and then anything that might help her case would be long gone.

She walked around the courtyard until she found the apartment and opened the door. The manager had been right about the furnishings. They were few and hanging on by a thread. A stained brown couch that sagged in the middle sat against the far wall, a packing crate next to it serving as an end table. A folding table and two metal chairs stood in the nook area of the kitchen. A coffeepot stood on the counter along with a dish towel. Two unwashed dishes were in the sink.

A hallway off the kitchen led to a tiny bathroom and a small bedroom, and that was the sum total of it. She started with the bedroom closet, but the few clothes hanging there didn't yield anything of value and the one shoe box on the shelf contained a pair of spiked-heel shoes and nothing else. She made a note that the shoes didn't appear to have been worn, then turned around to check the rest of the bedroom. It was a short search. The nightstand didn't have any drawers, and a glass with a small amount of brown liquid was the only thing on it. She took a whiff. Whiskey.

There was nothing under the bed or in between the mattresses, but then if Mitzi was hiding anything, she probably wouldn't put it in the first place a burglar would look. She headed into the bathroom next. There was a small cabinet for the sink, but the only thing in it was hair products and a cosmetic bag that contained only cosmetics. The mirror was one of those medicine cabinet kind but didn't hold anything out of the ordinary. When she closed the cabinet, it jiggled and she paused.

She put both hands on the side of the cabinet and pulled it gently from the wall. It moved easily then held, probably secured at the top. She leaned over the sink and lifted the entire cabinet up, surprised at how light it was, then placed it on the floor. When she looked back up at the wall, she smiled.

Bingo.

Mitzi's hiding place was behind the cabinet. An envelope had three hundred dollars in cash, and a plastic baggie held white powder. She placed both items on the counter and shook her head. Sometimes people got a line on a better deal. And if that had happened to Mitzi, Shaye could understand leaving the furniture and even the clothes, assuming the new gig was something other than hooking. But no way would she have left the cash or the drugs.

Mitzi was officially missing.

And she'd bet her PI license that Mitzi and Carla had met the same outcome.

JACKSON EXITED the car and looked over at his senior partner, Detective Grayson. Their working relationship had started off great, with Grayson actually requesting Jackson to work with him. But when the big fallout happened around Shaye, and Grayson realized that Jackson had initially suspected he was in on the cover-up, things had gotten tense for a while, even though Grayson had admitted from the beginning that he would have suspected himself as well. Over time and after many apologies, Grayson had gradually let it go and their relationship, while not as good as it was in the beginning, was settling back into something reasonably comfortable. More importantly, they were 100 percent focused on the job again, and that meant solving more cases.

Grayson pointed to a path that led to Lake Pontchartrain. "It's down this way."

"A floater? Why did we get the call?"

"ME says it's murder. Probably a body dump."

"Must be recent or he couldn't have made that determination on site. Wouldn't be enough left."

Grayson nodded. "Guess we're about to see."

The path wasn't an official Recreation and Parks installation, so it wasn't paved or even groomed. More likely, locals used it to access a favorite fishing spot. The end of the trail opened onto a small cleared area with an embankment sitting about six inches above the water. A man with a ball cap sat on a stump. The fishing rod and tackle box next to him and the paleness of his face let Jackson know he'd been right on at least one count.

Grayson glanced over at the man, then looked back at Jackson. "Let's get the story from the ME so he can move the body, then we'll talk to the fisherman."

"Definitely not the catch he expected."

They approached the ME and her assistant and nodded. The body had already been bagged and was ready for transport.

"What do we have?" Grayson asked.

"Female Caucasian," the ME said. "In her twenties. Her throat was slit."

"That's COD?" Grayson asked.

"I can't be positive until I do the autopsy. It's possible the killer could have slit her throat and then tossed her and she drowned before bleeding out. Either way, it's a homicide."

"Any idea on time of death?" Grayson asked.

"I can't be specific yet until I run some tests and account for the temperature of the water, but my initial estimate is three days or more," the ME said. "However, I don't think she was in the water that long. My guess is she was dumped sometime in the past twenty-four hours, but since I have no idea when she was removed, that might be hard to pin down."

"What do you mean?" Grayson asked. "The fisherman didn't pull her out?"

"No," the ME said. "Sorry, I thought you knew. It

looks like an animal dragged her out of the water, probably to feed. Could have been a gator or something else."

"How bad is the predation?" Jackson asked, his instincts kicking into overdrive. The slit throat and potential time of death had set off alarms.

"Not horrible. Most of the fingers are still intact, so I can run prints. The damage was predominantly to the internal organs."

"I'd like to take a look," Jackson said.

"Of course," the ME said, and motioned to her assistant to unzip the bag.

Grayson narrowed his eyes at Jackson. "You got something in mind?"

Jackson nodded. "And I'm hoping I'm wrong."

The assistant pulled back the bag and Jackson leaned over for a closer look. The damage was fairly extensive and he blanched involuntarily. Her own mother wouldn't have been able to identify her the way she was now, but the long platinum-blond hair snaking around her corpse was still there. The remnants of a silver top clung to her chest and around her neck.

"Was she wearing shoes?" Jackson asked.

"One," the ME said, and motioned again.

The assistant unzipped to the bottom of the bag and exposed the woman's feet. A red high-heeled shoe held on to her ankle by one thin strap.

"Thanks," Jackson said. He motioned Grayson to the side.

"What's up, Lamotte?" Grayson asked. "Based on

your expression, it's nothing good."

"Let's get the story from the fisherman first," Jackson said. "He's not going to have much to tell, and the poor guy probably needs a stiff drink or two. What I've got will take a while, and you might need a drink of your own when I'm done."

Grayson closed his eyes for a moment, then looked back at Jackson. "Please tell me that this does not involve Shaye Archer."

"I wish I could."

HE WATCHED her enter the building, practically running from the cab. It gave him a rush that he'd never experienced before. He'd always thought that the killing hit the peak of his emotions. He regretted killing his mother with drugs, and he wouldn't take the easy way out again. But he was making up for it now. All that adrenaline and those few seconds of fear when the whore knew she was going to die. The feel of his knife, cutting through her throat like butter. He was never as hard as he was then, and the sexual release afterward was so intense it felt like shock waves through his entire body.

But this...this slow teasing was the foreplay he'd been missing.

And he'd been missing a lot.

When he'd slid his finger across his throat and all the color had disappeared from Madison's face, his cock had gotten so hard it had been painful. He'd fought the urge to enter the nearest restroom and give in to the overwhelming desire and forced himself to watch from a distance as she got into the car. Because of the holidays, traffic was clogged more than usual, and he'd managed to follow. He was some distance away when it stopped, but close enough that he'd seen which building she'd run into.

Figuring he had some time until she exited, he ducked into the nearest convenience store bathroom. His swollen cock was the first thing he needed to attend to. He'd grabbed it and closed his eyes, picturing her terrified face, and in two jerks, his body exploded with release. He collapsed back against the wall and kept his eyes closed as the spasms rocked his body, his cock still twitching in his hand until it finally went limp.

He opened his eyes and smiled.

He'd thought Madison's seeing him had been a really bad thing. Not just because she'd interrupted him during the best staged event he'd ever put together, but because of the threat of being exposed. Of being caught. But instead, it had given him a new life. A new thrilling avenue that the other way didn't offer.

Now he just had to determine the extent of his range.

He opened his backpack and pulled out a pair of sweats, a T-shirt, and blue tennis shoes and swapped them out for the clothes she'd seen him wearing. Time to see if Madison Avery was really as face blind as the news story claimed.

12

SHAYE PULLED UP IN FRONT OF THE BAR THAT THE Gravediggers owned. It was on a corner in an area of the Ninth Ward that was known for its violent crime. Mostly due to the Gravediggers, if one believed the rumors. Actual arrests were in short supply, but that wasn't surprising. In these types of areas, eyewitnesses didn't exactly grow on trees.

Even though it was only 11:00 a.m., a row of motorcycles was parked on the sidewalk in front of the building and loud music blasted from inside the bar. Since most of them probably had unconventional employment, Shaye didn't think anything of the small crowd. Unfortunately, it meant she had more of them to contend with than she was hoping for. Still, she wasn't a cop and didn't pose a real threat, so maybe she could locate Rattler and call this line of inquiry closed.

As she stepped inside, her eyes immediately watered

from the thick smoke that filled the room. She blinked a couple of times and spotted the bar off to the right and headed that direction. Three men sat at one end, and she took a seat closest to the exit. The rest of the patrons were playing pool or sitting at tables. Everything but the overly loud music had ceased as soon as she'd walked in.

"You lost, sweetheart?" the bartender asked.

"I hope not. I'm looking for Rattler."

The bartender raised one eyebrow. "You don't exactly look like the type of woman Rattler goes for."

"What kind is that?"

"The kind with no standards," one of the guys sitting at the bar said, and all of them laughed.

"I'm not looking for a date," Shaye said. "I just wanted to ask him some questions."

The bartender shook his head. "We're not big on answering questions around here. You the cops?"

"No. I'm a private investigator."

"Really? And what exactly would a private investigator want with Rattler?"

"I'm trying to locate his girlfriend Carla."

The bartender looked over at the three men. "Any of you seen Rattler's old lady lately?"

The men all shook their heads.

The bartender turned back to Shaye. "Rattler and Carla wasn't really a solid thing, you know? She was gone more than she was around. What's she done?"

"Nothing that I'm aware of, except go missing. I was asked to look into it."

"By who?"

"Friends," she said, not about to give him the real story.

"You mean other whores? How'd they scratch up enough money to hire you?"

"How they're paying isn't important, but they are paying, so I'm trying to do my job. Can you tell me where to find Rattler?"

"You found him," a voice sounded behind her.

She forced herself to remain calm and turned around to face the man behind her. He was about six feet two and thin with brown hair and tattoos up both arms. Shonda had been right that the only thing about him that stood out was the boa constrictor wrapped around his left arm. If he had on a long-sleeved shirt and no snake, people would pass Rattler on the sidewalk without a second glance. And Shaye was betting he knew that, which was exactly why he had the snake.

"Hi," she said. "I'm a private investigator, and I've been retained to locate your girlfriend Carla."

"She ain't my girlfriend."

"Okay, but you lived together, right?"

"Not lately." He narrowed his eyes at her. "What's this about? She got some rich uncle that died or something? Because I might take her back if she's got some money coming."

"No rich uncle that I'm aware of. Just some concerned friends. They haven't seen her since last week."

"You want me to believe some whores hired a PI because Carla took a powder for a couple days? They ain't got the money, one. And two, even if they did, the last thing they'd spend it on is running down Carla. The girl's a flake. Here, there, she never stayed anywhere for long. What's this really about?"

"Exactly what I told you, whether you choose to believe it or not. I'm just asking some questions on behalf of some concerned citizens."

"Whatever. Look, I told you I don't know where Carla is and don't care besides. Girls like her are a dime a dozen...literally. If she done got herself into trouble then that's no surprise, and it ain't on me."

"What kind of trouble might she get into?"

"What?"

"You said if she'd gotten into trouble then it wasn't on you. I presumed you had an idea what she might have gotten into."

He shrugged. "She was a hooker and an addict. Do you really need to know more than that?"

"When was the last time you saw her?"

"I don't know. Maybe three weeks ago." He looked over at the bartender. "When was that night we had boiled crawfish? That's the night Carla blew out of here pissed over something."

"It was about three weeks ago," the bartender said. "We don't keep no calendar in here."

"And no one saw her after that night?" Shaye asked.

The bartender shook his head.

"Look," Rattler said. "She got pissed. She left. She does it a lot. Why a bunch of whores got their G-strings in a bunch over it, I don't know. Probably she'll come crawling back when she's out of cash and can't give a blow to get some blow. And if she doesn't, so what? It's not my problem. Now, you being in the bar is dragging things down, and that *is* my problem."

"I'm leaving," Shaye said.

"Good," Rattler said. "I don't want to see you around here again."

Shaye headed out of the bar, fighting the overwhelming urge to jog back to her car. She'd deliberately avoided giving her name, hoping that no one would recognize her. Kidnapping wasn't something she worried about on a regular basis, but a certain element might see her as an easy payout, especially since they weren't aware that she had a very anxious cop who knew her exact location and was waiting for her to check in.

She jumped in her SUV and drove away, waiting until she was completely out of the Ninth Ward before pulling over to send Jackson a text.

Am done with Rattler. Safely back in 7th Ward.

She watched the screen until she saw Jackson had read the text, then pulled away. He might not have time to reply. A couple seconds later, a simple "Good!" came through. She'd looked up the address for the Franklin Motel before she'd left that morning, so she punched it into GPS and guided her SUV in that direction. As she drove, she mulled things over.

Rattler was clearly dangerous based on his ties to the Gravediggers alone. And Shaye had no problem believing he'd tuned Carla up more than once. She didn't even have a problem believing he could kill someone. But had he killed Carla?

Her gut and his repressed curiosity told her he hadn't.

He'd engaged her for longer than she'd expected he would if he'd had anything to do with Carla's disappearance, and she sensed he was trying to get information out of her. If he'd killed Carla, she would have expected him to be defensive and strong-arm her out of the bar as soon as he knew why she was there. Probably threaten her.

His build was right and the ordinary brown hair, and the coat would have prevented Madison from seeing the tattoos, so that worked. But if the killer had been wearing a snake, Madison definitely would have noticed that. No. Rattler didn't feel like her guy, but she was reluctant to dismiss him altogether. Instead, she'd just put him in reserve and do some general poking around into the Gravediggers.

But first, she'd check out the motel. The lack of solid leads was expected but a tiny bit disappointing. Some days she wished being a PI was like what you saw on television, where the clues just popped up in time for them to solve the case before the hour of airtime was up. But real life was rarely that way. Sure, sometimes you got lucky, but most of the time it was a long grind to figure out anything difficult.

The Franklin Motel looked as she'd expected. It was

two stories and had probably thirty rooms...the kind you could rent by anything from an hour to a month. A few cars that should probably have been totaled years ago were scattered across the lot in front of rooms. A late-model pickup truck that looked a bit better than the rest of the offerings was parked at the back of the parking lot in front of a single-story section of the building.

The Vacancy light flashing in the window told her that was the place she needed to be, so she pulled through the lot and parked. An older, beefy guy glanced at her as she walked in the door, then looked back down at his paperwork scattered across the counter.

"Got a good weekly special right now," he said.

"Thanks, but that's not why I'm here."

He looked up at her, this time for long enough to get a good look, and his eyes widened. "You're that Archer girl."

She nodded and extended her hand. "I'm Shaye."

"Ray," he said as he shook. "Well, you sure as heck don't need any rooms I'm offering, so I can't imagine what I can do for you."

"I'm looking for a woman who stayed here some-times, maybe recently. Her name is Carla Downing."

"Yeah, sure. I know Carla. She shows up every couple months for a week or so. Most of the time with a black eye, but she always seems to go back."

"Has she been here recently?"

He nodded. "Checked in about three weeks ago. Paid

a month in advance this time. Told me she was making some changes."

Shaye's pulse quickened. The month wasn't up. Was it possible that Carla was tucked into her motel room, nursing an injury? Maybe from Rattler or maybe from a john? It was an unfortunate and normal part of the job.

"Is she still here?" Shaye asked.

He frowned. "Far as I know, but I haven't seen her for a while."

"Do you mind if I go check? I just need her room number."

"You're not going to cause any trouble for her, are you? Carla's got her issues but she's not a bad person, and the kind of people I got staying here usually don't want to be found."

"I'm not here to cause trouble. Exactly the opposite. I'm here because I'm afraid something happened to her. I'm sorry, but I can't tell you more than that."

His eyes widened. "Shit. I haven't seen her in days. Let me grab my keys."

"That would be great," Shaye said, relieved that he was taking her seriously and wanted to check her room. She still held on to the tiniest sliver of hope that Carla would answer the door, but she didn't really think that was going to be the case. At least she'd be able to check out Carla's room with the manager. See if there was anything that indicated who she might have been with that night.

Ray grabbed a set of keys from a drawer and hurried

around the counter. "Her room is at the end of the motel. That's why I didn't see her often. Well, that and our work schedules aren't exactly the same, if you know what I mean."

"Did she ever bring clients to the motel?"

"Ha. Clients. That's rich. Bunch of scumbags taking advantage if you ask me, but I guess the women don't feel like they have many options. I never saw Carla with a man, but then it's not good business to take 'clients' to where you stay."

"No, I suppose it's not."

"This is the one," he said, and pointed to the door. He knocked and they waited several seconds, but no sound came from inside. He knocked again. "Carla, it's Ray. If you're in there, I need to talk to you for just a sec. It's important."

Nothing.

He gave Shaye a worried look and shoved the key in the door. Given the type of establishment he ran, she knew the thoughts running through his head. Ray had probably seen more than one dead body, and he was hoping he didn't add another to that list today.

"Carla?" he called out as he opened the door and stepped inside.

It was a small room with only the bed, nightstand, and dresser with an old console television on top of it. Folding doors were on the opposite side of the bed, probably housing a closet, and there was a door at the back of the room that Shaye assumed was the bathroom. Ray looked at the door and hesitated a second before heading that direction. He poked his head inside the doorway, then let out a relieved sigh.

"There's no one here," he said as he turned back around and looked at the room again. "In fact, it doesn't look like anyone's been here recently. Usually when Carla's been here for a while there's pizza boxes and Chinese food containers all over the place."

"Do you have housekeeping?"

"Sure, but on the weekly and monthly rentals, it's just once-a-week cleaning."

"When would they have cleaned here last?"

He rubbed his chin. "Saturday."

"So that's four days, at least, that she hasn't been back to her room."

"Something must have happened, right?" Ray now sounded as worried as he looked. "Carla knew I'd refund her if she left early. I've done it before."

Shaye pulled open the closet and pointed. "Even if she'd gone back to her boyfriend, she would have taken her things. Her clothes are still here and I'm going to guess you saw personal items in the bathroom."

He nodded.

"Then we have to assume that she meant to come back and didn't. You said you've never seen Carla with a man?"

"No, but like I said, our paths didn't really cross much outside of her paying up rent. And sometimes if I had to cover the night shift I'd see her leaving."

"Do you have a regular night manager?"

"Got two. One that covers from nine p.m. to five a.m. Sunday through Thursday and a weekender."

"I'd like to come back and talk to both of them if that's all right."

"Sure. You think they might have seen something?"

"I hope so, because I'm running out of places to look."

He frowned. "It's hard to find out things with these sort of people. They're, uh, transient. Don't make friends easy and don't trust no one. Apt to disappear at the drop of a hat. Maybe you see them again. Mostly you never do."

Something about his tone led Shaye to believe that Ray was speaking from personal experience rather than just generally. "Sounds like something you've dealt with before."

"Yeah, my mother wasn't exactly reliable. Drugs, you know? And men. She cut out for the last time when I was ten. I haven't seen or heard from her since."

"I'm sorry. That must have been rough."

He shrugged. "Had a girlfriend way back when who started down that road. I cut her loose right quick. No interest in reliving the worst part of my childhood as an adult."

"I can appreciate that."

"My pops was decent, though. He didn't know nothing about taking care of a kid and he was hard as nails, but he did his best. My life isn't grand, but I've never used and I've always had a job and a place to live. Bought this place right after Katrina. It's not fancy, but it's a living. I figure we've all got our cross to bear. You more than most. It's what we do after all that's been done to us that matters."

Shaye smiled. "Yes, it is. Thank you, Ray. You've been a big help. Do you mind if I poke around in Carla's things? You're welcome to watch."

"Nah," he said, and handed her the room key. "Just lock it when you leave and drop the key back at the office in the mail slot. I've got to run to the post office. If you find out something, will you let me know?"

"Of course, and thanks again."

He gave her a nod and headed out of the room. Shaye went through the room as she had Mitzi's, checking everywhere for Carla's hidden stash. She found it in an envelope taped to the back of the dresser. No drugs, but it held six hundred dollars cash.

Once again, even if Carla decided to ditch the clothes and buy a new toothbrush, she wouldn't have left the cash behind. There were only two reasons why the money was still here and Carla hadn't been back to collect it—she was scared to or she was unable.

Unfortunately, Shaye was betting on unable. And in the worst way possible.

He waited next to a lamppost outside the building,

watching the doors for Madison to exit. He was fairly certain he hadn't been in the store long enough to miss her but for all he knew, she might take another exit. Or she might go into the parking lot behind the building with someone else and leave that way. It had been an hour since she'd gone inside. He'd give it another thirty minutes, then he'd switch to plan B and wait down the block from her building to avoid the risk of being seen by the security guards who worked there. Madison would definitely report what happened today, and they'd be on the lookout for anyone loitering.

Another twenty minutes passed, and he was about to call it quits when he saw her rush out. He hurried away from the lamppost just as a car with an Uber sticker pulled up to the curb. Madison was practically running down the steps as he rushed forward, then turned his head at the last minute and crashed into her.

"Oh," he said, putting his hands on her arm to steady himself. "I'm so sorry. That's totally my fault."

She looked at him, her expression troubled but no different from when she'd exited the building. "That's okay," she said, and hurried to the car. She jumped inside without so much as a backward glance. He watched as the car drove away, his smile growing larger the farther it went.

Unbelievable.

He'd done his research and knew that the disorder she claimed to have was a real thing, but he hadn't really believed it was possible. What a delight to find out it not only existed but that she had it. And not a mild case of it, either. She'd looked straight at him and hadn't known he was the same person who'd taunted her earlier. All because he'd changed his clothes.

It was fate.

He'd spent his entire life being invisible—to his mother, to society—and now he'd met someone to whom the entire world was invisible. She was meant for him.

And she would be his finest work.

13

MADISON CLENCHED HER HANDS AS THE BLOCKS slowly went by. It seemed as if she'd never get home. The traffic, the people...all clogging up the Quarter and driving her blood pressure up another level.

She'd managed to stay calm and focused for the meeting, and for that, she was grateful. All her years of managing her disorder and she'd never wanted drugs, but today, she would have traded a year's salary for a Xanax.

What was she going to do?

Sure, she could lock herself in her apartment for the rest of the day, and the next day and the next, but she couldn't stay there forever. Her job required weekly meetings, and she couldn't afford to piss off clients and get a bad reputation. Right now, she was working strictly by referral and that was a great thing. If she had to do a big sales pitch for every assignment, it would mean all kinds of hurdles that she had been lucky enough to avoid since her first year hunting for clients. She had a bit of a name in the tech community, and it was a good one. The last thing she wanted to do was damage it.

No, that wasn't exactly true. The *last* thing she wanted to do was die.

When she put it in perspective, her career didn't seem as important. She could always relocate, but the thought of doing all of this over again was so overwhelming she didn't even know where to begin. Tears spilled out of the corner of her eyes, and she struggled not to cry. Just a few more minutes and she'd be home. She could collapse on the couch and wail to her heart's content.

"Here you are," the driver's voice cut into her thoughts. "Sorry it took so long. Streets are crowded."

"No problem. Merry Christmas," she said and jumped out of the car.

She practically ran into the building and Wanda looked up in surprise as she hurried across the lobby.

"Are you all right, Ms. Avery?" Wanda asked.

"I'm not feeling well," Madison replied, looking down at the floor so that Wanda couldn't get a good look at her face.

"I'm sorry. Let me know if you need anything."

"Yes. I will. Thanks." Madison barely slowed as she crossed the lobby and hurried for the elevator. She bolted inside as soon as the door opened, almost knocking over a woman in a dress and high heels.

"Hey," the woman said as she stepped out of the elevator and turned around to glare at Madison.

"I'm sorry," Madison said. "I have to get home."

The woman was still standing there frowning as the door closed, and Madison pressed the button over and over, begging the elevator to pick up speed. Everything seemed to be running in slow motion—the car, the elevator. When the door opened on her floor, she sprinted down the hall and punched in her door code, barely waiting for the click before shoving the door open and barreling inside.

She whirled around and slammed the door shut, then drew the dead bolt into place. She dropped her purse and laptop bag next to the door and ran for the kitchen, her hands shaking as she poured herself a shot of the whiskey she'd received as a gift from a client, but had never tried. She hoped it was as good as he'd claimed.

The liquid burned going down her throat and her eyes watered, but she took a second gulp, then set the glass down and clutched the cabinets to keep from swaying. If she didn't calm down, she was going to pass out. Closing her eyes, she drew in a deep breath and slowly let it out, then repeated the process again. She opened her eyes and poured another bit of whiskey, this time sipping it rather than taking it in gulps.

Her body started to warm, and her heart rate slowed as the alcohol moved into her system. She waited until her hands were almost steady again, then pulled her cell phone out of her pocket and sat on a barstool at her kitchen island. She'd loaded Shaye's number as first in her favorites so she could dial it quickly if she needed to. Hoping, of course, that she never needed to.

Her hands still shook a bit as she went to lift the phone, so she placed it on the counter and hit the Speaker option instead. It was going to be hard enough to explain to Shaye what happened without rambling incoherently. Holding the phone meant focusing on her hands and her voice, and right now, she didn't think she had the capacity to do both of those at the same time.

When Shaye answered, all her emotions started to bubble over.

"It's Madison," she said, trying to keep her voice steady.

"Are you okay?"

"No. I'm so not okay."

She took a deep breath and blurted out everything that had happened, her voice increasing in speed and volume as she talked until at the end, she was practically shouting.

"I don't know what to do," Madison said, choking on the last couple words.

"Take a deep breath and try to calm down," Shaye said. "I know it's hard, but do your best. I'll be there in ten minutes. Okay?"

A tiny bit of relief trickled through her, and she nodded before remembering that Shaye couldn't see her. "Thank you so much. I didn't know what to do."

"Don't worry about that. We'll figure it out when I

get there. Just stay put and focus on your breathing. I'll be there soon."

The call disconnected, and Madison lifted the whiskey again and took another sip. The help it had provided before had disappeared completely during the phone call as fear took over, but now that she was concentrating on breathing again, she could feel her stiff muscles loosening ever so slightly. She checked her phone. Nine more minutes until Shaye got there. Nine more minutes for her to hold things together before dumping all of her problems onto a woman who was essentially a stranger and then asking her to solve them.

Nine more minutes to convince herself that there was even a solution.

———

JACKSON WAITED until they'd finished with the fisherman and were back in the car before filling Grayson in on who he thought the victim was and how it all tied into Shaye's latest case.

"You gotta be kidding me." Detective Grayson stared at Jackson, clearly irritated.

"You don't know how badly I wish I were," Jackson said.

Grayson sighed. "Yeah, I suppose you do. The brass is going to have a shit hemorrhage."

"The brass is going to have to figure out a way to deal. The bottom line is that as long as Shaye pursues cases that we refuse, we're going to keep crossing paths when things escalate. And trust me, she has no intention of giving up her work. The brass can be as pissed as they want to be, but they can't stop her from doing the job clients hire her to do."

"No, but they can make things damned impossible for you, which makes things damned impossible for me."

"I'm sorry about the position it puts you in. I've been thinking about that a lot, and if you want to request another partner, I would understand. Completely."

Grayson shook his head. "I requested you because I think you have the potential to be one of the finest detectives in the department and because our investigative styles complement each other. I don't want a change. We'll just have to deal with whatever comes down the pike. And you have to make sure you're so clean they could eat lunch off of you."

"I don't think we'll have to worry about this one directly," Jackson said. "I assume Maxwell will catch the case, being that he took the call when Madison reported it."

"You don't want to request a shift?"

"Of course. But that's because I'd like to find this predator before Shaye runs into him. And if she knew that, I'd be in trouble so deep I might never get out of it. So I'm going to do the right thing, even though it's killing me, and let Maxwell handle it."

Grayson nodded. "Okay. I'll pass up what we know. If the brass wants Maxwell to jump back on it, I'm fine with that. Not like we don't have four open cases to work right now."

"Thanks. And Grayson, thanks for sticking with me. Not a lot of people would."

"A lot of people have no backbone."

SHAYE DISCONNECTED the call and put her SUV in drive and headed down the street, mentally calculating the quickest route to Madison's apartment. Her hands clenched the steering wheel as she drove, and she felt her jaw flex before realizing she needed to take a deep breath as much as Madison did.

This was so bad.

The risk that the killer would come after Madison had always been there, but without a police investigation, Shaye was hoping that he'd decide it wasn't worth pursuing, as witness testimony wasn't enough to make a case. There were simply too many instances of witnesses falsely identifying the alleged perpetrator for a prosecutor to hinge a case solely on eyewitness testimony, especially only one eyewitness who saw the crime across the street. Even if Madison didn't have a visual impairment, it would be a hard case to make without any specific identifying markers on the accused.

But this. This was completely out of left field. In all of the ways Shaye imagined the situation could escalate, she'd never included stalking and taunting Madison on the list. It spoke to a whole other level of evil, and Shaye would be the first to admit that it scared the hell out of her. What kind of mind came up with this sort of thing? And what would he do next? She had to figure out a way to protect Madison, but there was a huge sticking point.

For how long?

Even if Shaye managed to identify the killer, without more evidence, there was a good chance he would walk anyway. And there was nothing she could do about Madison's disorder. Shaye had lived for years with the uncertainty and fear that her captor would come for her, but as more and more years passed, she finally believed that he'd either died, moved away, or decided that her loss of memory kept him protected.

She stiffened. Maybe that was part of the solution. Her memory loss had been blasted on every news station around the country, making it common knowledge, so her captor had known he was safe. If she could find a way to bring Madison's condition to the killer's attention, maybe he'd make the same choice to slip into the shadows, knowing he could never be identified, especially since the police weren't investigating.

The problem, of course, was figuring out a good reason for news stations to jump on such a story enough for it to spread and not just have one of those public awareness two-minute spotlights right before commercial that most people had already wandered out of the room for.

Her cell phone rang, and she saw Jackson's name

come up on her SUV's display. She pressed the Answer button, wondering why he was calling while on the clock. He sometimes texted her, but actual phone calls were rare when he was working.

"What's up?" she asked.

"Can you talk?"

"I'm driving, but I have you on Bluetooth. What's wrong?" The combination of the timing of the call and the tense sound in his voice were dead giveaways that something wasn't right.

"A fisherman found Carla Downing on the edge of Lake Pontchartrain this morning. She'd been pulled from the water, probably by an animal."

Her stomach rolled. "You're sure it's her?"

"Her prints were in the system for a prior."

"Well, then I guess I'll give up that one percent chance I thought she had of still being alive. I appreciate you telling me."

"There's more."

He went silent for a bit, and Shaye wondered if the call had dropped.

"It was her," he said. "The woman Madison saw was Carla. Most of the clothes were still intact. The blouse, skirt, shoes...everything was just as Madison described it."

"Was her throat cut?"

"Yeah. The ME will have to do the autopsy, but given the length and depth of the cut, I don't think there's any way she was alive when she went into the water."

"Are you on the case?"

"No. I told Grayson about Madison, and he agreed that it was Maxwell's case."

A momentary rush of disappointment coursed through her when she heard that Jackson wasn't on the case, but she knew his job was more secure if he wasn't working a case that she was involved in. She had no doubt he'd do what he could to assist and keep up with the investigation, but this way, he couldn't be accused of using the department to help her clients. After all, Madison had called the police department and given them the opportunity to launch an investigation before she'd contacted Shaye. She didn't think for a minute that the brass would give a damn about the distinction, but she didn't care. The facts spoke for themselves.

"I'm on my way to Madison's place right now," she said. "Something happened."

She told Jackson what Madison relayed to her earlier, and he cursed.

"He's playing with her," Jackson said. "You know how dangerous that makes him."

"I do, and I'd be lying if I said it didn't scare the crap out of me, but she's terrified and I have to do something. I just haven't figured out what."

"Send her to Europe with a new identity."

"Don't think the extreme hasn't crossed my mind, but it still wouldn't solve the bigger problem."

"I know," he said quietly. "The never-ending fear every time she sets foot outside her apartment."

"Yes. Is Detective Maxwell going to contact her soon?"

"I just spoke with him, and he was on his way to call her. There's a good chance you two will cross paths at her place here shortly. I'd bet he wants to go over everything with her again, and in light of this new development, I'm glad you're going to have police resources on this."

"Me too."

She knew he was hoping she'd drop the case now that the police were involved, but she couldn't do that to Madison, and she knew he was aware of that as well. She'd started this journey, and if Madison still wanted her to stay on the case, then that's exactly what she'd do. Even if Madison didn't want her to investigate any longer, she couldn't abandon her. Not now.

"Thanks for letting me know," she said. "I'm sorry if this causes you any grief."

"Don't you worry about me. Worry about Madison and watch your back. I don't have to tell you how bad this new development is. Are you working tonight?"

"I don't think so. I need to see what Madison wants to do and see what Detective Maxwell has to say, but I think I'm going to need to regroup."

"Mind if I come by after work to help?"

"I'd love for you to. I don't have homemade lasagna, but I can order up Chinese and I do have raspberry tarts."

"Corrine?"

"Yeah, she's going to bake me into a bigger size if her

foundation doesn't get up and running soon. I keep coming home to new Tupperware containers on my kitchen counter."

"I should be off on time. I'll let you know if that changes. Gotta run."

The call disconnected, and she stared out the windshield and blew out a breath. The fact that Carla was dead wasn't really a surprise, nor was it that Madison had been accurate in her description of the event. Shaye's opinion of her was that she was highly reliable, albeit frightened and stressed. But with Carla's body being found, Madison was even more of a threat than before. Now the police would launch an investigation. The story would be on the news, and no way would the police want everyone to know that their only eyewitness wasn't reliable.

She parked in front of Madison's building and hurried inside. The security guard was a woman this time, and Shaye gave Madison's name and waited while the woman called up to get the okay. A couple seconds later, she hung up the phone and looked at Shaye.

"Is she all right?" the guard asked. "She came through here earlier like a tornado and white as a sheet."

"She's not feeling well," Shaye said, figuring it was the closest to the truth she could manage without betraying a confidence.

The guard nodded. "You let me know if she needs anything."

"I will. Thank you."

Shaye hurried to the elevator and up to Madison's floor. She must have been standing at the door because it opened before she even knocked. As soon as she stepped inside, Madison pushed the door shut and threw the dead bolts, and then she flung her arms around Shaye and began to cry.

Shaye held the girl as she sobbed, feeling helpless that she couldn't have done anything to prevent the situation and didn't know how to make it better now. Right now, all she could offer was comfort, and what Madison needed were answers. It was a couple minutes before the sobbing subsided and Madison let go of her death grip and took a step back.

"I'm so sorry," Madison said. "I didn't mean to fall apart on you like that."

"Please don't apologize," Shaye said, guiding Madison into the living room and onto the couch. "You've had two terrifying experiences. I'd be more worried if you were calm and collected."

"Yeah, I guess at least I'm still firmly rooted in reality. Of course, the reality is I'm totally fucked, but I'm definitely grounded in it."

"We're going to figure this out. I'm not leaving here until we have a plan."

Madison looked at her, and the relief in her expression was apparent. "So you're not dropping the case? When Detective Maxwell called and said he needed to talk to me again, I figured that meant they were going to investigate."

"They are, but I can't tell you anything else. I need you to hear it from him so that I don't get the person who told me in trouble. But that doesn't mean I can't continue with my own work. If you want me to, that is."

"Of course I want you to. I'm glad the cops are going to do something, but the more people on this the better. I can't live like this, knowing he could be standing on the corner every time I exit my building and I wouldn't know. I can't hide in here forever or I risk losing my contract and reputation, and I can't leave and start over for the same reason."

"Can you take a vacation? Just a couple of weeks and maybe we could figure something out?"

She shook her head. "I'm scheduled to deliver the project by year-end. It's all but done except for some tweaking. I've been working on this for six months. The client is happy, and I think I'll get a referral to another company project out of it. If I bail now, they'll lose a lot of money because they've scheduled all their other upgrades around this one. I know it sounds stupid, worrying about my job when this guy threatened me, but if this ever ends, I still have bills to pay."

Shaye squeezed her hand. "I understand. We'll figure something out, okay?"

Madison's cell phone rang, and she pulled it out of her pocket. "That's fine," she said and sat the phone down on the end table. "Detective Maxwell is on his way up. Is he going to cause you problems?"

"I don't think so. And besides, I have information

he's going to need. As far as I'm concerned, his main job is finding the killer. Mine is making sure you're safe. Two different focuses, just with some intersecting lines."

A knock sounded at the door, and Shaye jumped up to get it. Detective Maxwell didn't look surprised when he saw her.

"Ms. Archer," he said and nodded.

Shaye motioned him inside. "Can I get you something to drink, Detective?" she asked.

"A glass of water would be nice. Are you staying for this?"

"If you don't mind. Madison needs the support, and I also have some information for you."

Maxwell nodded and headed into the living room, taking a seat in a chair next to the couch. Shaye hurried into the kitchen to retrieve a glass of water for Maxwell and noticed the glass on the counter next to a whiskey bottle. She poured a bit more of the whiskey and took both glasses into the living room before taking a seat next to Madison on the couch.

Maxwell waited until she was seated, then looked at Madison. "Ms. Avery, I'm here because there's been a development. A fisherman found a young woman in Lake Pontchartrain this morning who fits your description of the woman attacked across the street."

Madison's eyes widened. "Was she...was her..."

"Her throat had been cut," Maxwell said. "I've opened a homicide investigation and wanted you to be aware. I also wanted to see if there's anything else you remembered about that night. Anything at all that might give me a direction to pursue."

"I told you everything," Madison said, "but Shaye has been investigating."

Maxwell looked over at Shaye. "Have you discovered anything?"

Shaye filled the detective in on the conversations she'd had and her search of both Carla's and Mitzi's rooms. Maxwell sat focused and silent until she finished.

"There's another woman missing?" Madison asked.

"Maybe," Shaye said, not wanting to upset Madison even more than she already was. "I don't know for certain."

She looked at Maxwell, and he gave her a slight nod. "There's a bigger problem though," Shaye said, and motioned to Madison. "Tell him what happened to you today."

Madison took a deep breath and began to recount her story. Her voice was shaky, and the panic she felt came through as the story progressed to the finger across the throat part. Shaye watched Maxwell's expression as Madison talked, and although he did a good job of containing his feelings, she saw his jaw flex and knew that he was as deeply disturbed by this development as she was.

When she finished, Maxwell leaned forward. "I know you're frightened," he said, "and I don't blame you. I believe there is a specific threat against you. I can request an increase in police presence in the area. More patrols. More eyes on your building."

He leaned back again and blew out a breath. "I'm going to be honest with you. I have no idea how long it will take to find this guy, which makes it completely unrealistic to ask you to stay inside your unit until it's all over. But I will ask you to make changes to your routine, especially if it involves walking in areas that aren't crowded."

"I don't have to leave very often," Madison said, "but I have a meeting every week with my client, and I'll probably have several next week because I'm delivering the product."

"At the same time and location?" Maxwell asked.

"The regular meeting is. The rest, I don't know."

"See if you can change the time of the regular meeting, at least. If he can establish a set time and place for your movements, he has a far better chance to come at you. But he can't sit outside of your building 24-7 waiting for you to appear. Not without someone noticing."

Madison nodded. "I can do that."

"Do you walk to that meeting?" he asked.

"I used to, but I won't anymore. I used Uber to get home."

"And you're okay with that?" he asked.

Madison looked down at the floor for a moment, then shook her head. "I check the car for the sticker and make sure the make and model is right, but I probably wouldn't know if the driver was the man shown on the app unless there's something specific about his hair."

"I have a solution for that," Shaye said. "Corrine and I use a car service sometimes. One owner and she's the driver. She's driven employees from my grandfather's corporations for years. I trust her, and she has long black hair and a butterfly tattoo on the back of her left hand. She'd be easy to identify and happy to help. You'd just need to plan a little ahead so she's available."

Madison's relief was apparent. "That sounds perfect. Thank you."

Maxwell rose from the chair. "I promise you that I'm going to put all my effort into this. Given the threat on your life, it will be the only thing I'm working on. I'm in between partners right now, but I'm sure I can get some more resources assigned. If you think of anything else or see anything else, call me. Do you still have my number?"

Madison nodded.

"Then I'm going to get back to the office and get all this down."

Shaye rose and followed the detective out of the apartment. "I don't want to step on your toes," she said, "but Madison has asked me to stay on the case."

"I figured as much, and given the situation, I don't blame her. The truth is she could use someone looking out for her, and you know better than most what that entails. I can't promise you that I'll keep you updated because my hands are tied by the brass, but I'll share what I can, especially if it's relevant to Ms. Avery's safety."

"And if I find out anything else, I'll contact you immediately."

"I'd especially appreciate it if you hear any more from the working girls. They're not likely to talk to me. This other girl who's missing, Mitzi. Do you have a description?"

"Yes. Tall, blonde, and thin."

He frowned. "And Madison not only witnessed the murder, she fits the profile. I really hope this isn't what it looks like. This town doesn't need another serial killer."

"I agree, but I'm not optimistic."

"Neither am I. Take care, Ms. Archer."

Shaye nodded and watched as he walked down the hallway toward the elevators. She had every intention of taking care. Of herself and of Madison.

She just had to figure out how.

14

Jackson looked up as Detective Maxwell stopped by his desk. "Take a walk with me," Maxwell said.

Jackson popped up from his chair and followed Maxwell down the hall and into the break room. His current cases were at that point where it was all online research, phone calls, or random interviews, and they only required one person to do them. Grayson had been out all afternoon on interviews, and Jackson had stayed back to handle the online research and phone calls.

Some days one of them felt more confined in the office, and that's the one who took the legwork. Today it was Grayson, which was fine with Jackson. It left him readily available for an emergency phone call should one arise, and centrally located in the French Quarter where he could get most places quickly. And it allowed him to work on his side project—creating a list of birth records for the time frame surrounding the sale of Shaye's baby.

Then he'd create a list of adoption records and they'd have a starting point.

In the break room, Maxwell started a new pot of coffee and waited until two other cops cleared the room before speaking.

"I just interviewed Madison Avery," Maxwell said. "I assume you know what happened to her today?"

Jackson nodded.

"And that Shaye intends to remain on the case?"

"I didn't expect anything different."

"Neither did I, but I have to tell you, this one worries me. I know she's dealt with some harsh stuff...is she ready to do it again? Because this guy, taunting Madison on the street like that. That's a whole different level."

"I know, and I've been grinding my teeth ever since Shaye told me what happened, but on that end of things, there's nothing I can do. Shaye is determined to help Madison, and I get it. Shaye spent a lot of years walking the streets of New Orleans not knowing if she was standing next to the man who abused her. She's not going to let another woman go through that. Not if she thinks she can make a difference."

"I get it. And I don't blame her. I just wanted to make sure everyone was on the same page as to the severity of this."

"Oh, I'm definitely there."

Maxwell nodded. "I've already asked for additional resources. I haven't had a new partner assigned, but the brass agreed to give me two men gunning for a detective badge to help with the legwork. And they also said they'd increase patrol presence around Madison's building and maintain a unit within five minutes or less for a week. After that, it will be a day-to-day decision based on need."

Jackson felt a bit of tension leave his body. "That's something, at least. I didn't figure they'd do anything."

"Ha. Well, you can thank Shaye for that one. When I told them the target was a client of Shaye's they jumped right on the additional help bandwagon."

"They don't want her making them look bad."

Maxwell grinned. "And I figured that would be the case, which is why I made sure to mention it."

Jackson smiled, his respect for the young detective shooting up another notch. "Well played. And I appreciate it."

"I know how worried I'd be if it was my lady in the middle of this. Hell, shit like this makes me really glad she's a florist. Anyway, I just wanted you to know that I'm doing everything I can to keep Madison safe and track down this psycho before he can terrorize her again."

"Let me know if you need anything. Even off the record."

"I will, and thanks for trusting me with this. Grayson could have pulled rank since you guys got the call on the body."

"We both know that would have caused problems this

department doesn't need, but I'll be the first to admit it's killing me."

Maxwell patted him on the back. "I'm going to find this guy. And I'm going to take him down."

He poured his cup of coffee and headed out of the break room. Jackson leaned back against the counter, his mind overloaded with all the potential scenarios running through it, and none of them good. He believed Maxwell would do everything possible to find the killer.

He just hoped everything possible was enough.

***

SHAYE CLOSED her laptop and looked at the television. The news had come and gone with no mention of the investigation but she still hadn't decided whether that was a good thing or a bad thing. Probably it didn't matter in the big scheme of things at all, but she wondered if an open investigation would push the killer to close in on Madison quickly. Perhaps force him to take a chance he wouldn't otherwise. That risk might be the opening they needed to catch him, but she hated to think of Madison as a sitting duck.

So she'd gone through all the facts with Jackson earlier that night and they'd talked them through until they were both hoarse. Unfortunately, the identity of the killer hadn't magically appeared for either of them, nor had an easy way to track him down. Normally when someone was murdered, you tracked backward to identify the people who had access to them, but with the victims being working girls, it made things difficult as it was an anonymous cash sort of deal, and the streets they chose to work tended to be camera-free. Even looking based on proximity was an issue because a man cheating on his wife with prostitutes would drive across town for such a transaction to ensure he wasn't spotted by anyone he knew.

If the girls she'd already talked to had any idea who Carla was with that night, they would have shared it with Shaye. But he'd been smart. He'd probably waited until Carla was alone and then made his move when no one was watching. The question was, had he picked Carla specifically, or had he set up the apartment, then gone looking for a victim? If Carla was a random selection based on opportunity, it made identifying her killer next to impossible. Especially since he was smart enough to leave no forensic evidence behind.

Stalking Madison was the one mistake he'd made. He was exposing himself in a way that wasn't necessary. If he'd simply taken a shot at her, Shaye would have understood, but this toying with her made no sense. Every time he was within eyeshot of her, he ran the risk that she saw him and called the police. At least, that should be his line of thinking as he didn't know about Madison's disorder.

Or did he?

She frowned. Was she making an assumption that was incorrect? Property records were public, so finding out her name based on her apartment address wouldn't be difficult. She grabbed her laptop and did a search for Madison Avery. There were several articles about her parents and their charitable and political contributions and events, and then she saw it...a small article in the health section of a local newspaper about living with prosopagnosia. She sucked in a breath.

He might know.

And if he did, that changed everything. Because if he knew she couldn't identify him and was toying with her anyway, then this wasn't about eliminating a witness.

It was about finding a new victim.

Shaye pulled on her tennis shoes, jumped up from the couch, and grabbed her keys. She had planned on taking the night off and getting some sleep as she'd been short on it the night before, but no way would she be able to sleep now. Not with that thought racing around her mind. First, she'd go talk to the night manager at the motel and see if he could provide her any information, then she'd see if she could find Shonda and Louise again. She knew Detective Maxwell would try to talk to them eventually, but doubted he'd head there tonight. So far, Carla's murder wasn't public, and Shaye didn't want Shonda and Louise finding out that way. It was best if they heard it from her.

The streets were starting to empty out so the drive to the motel went quickly. The only sign of activity Shaye saw there was the flashing Vacancy sign out front. A single light burned in the office, and she parked in front of it and knocked on the door. That's when she noticed the sign in the window.

Back in 15 minutes.

Since she had no idea if that fifteen minutes had started ten minutes ago or one, she climbed back into her SUV to wait. About ten minutes later, she saw a middle-aged guy walking up the sidewalk to the office. She waited until he started to unlock the door before climbing out of her SUV and following him inside.

"Daily, weekly?" he asked as he stepped behind the counter.

"Neither," she said, and gave him her card. "I'd like to ask you some questions, if you don't mind. Ray said it would be okay."

"Oh yeah, you're that PI. He told me you came by here today looking for Carla. I'm Walter. Did you have any luck?"

"I'm afraid not," she said, not wanting to reveal Carla's murder until the police did. "That's why I'm here now. I know it's a long shot, but if there's anything you can tell me about her—if you saw her with anyone, over-heard her talking—anything at all that might help me track her down, I'd appreciate it."

"I thought about it for a while after Ray told me—not much else to do up here sometimes—but I couldn't come up with anything. I wish I could. Carla is nice and never any trouble, but she keeps to herself and that makes it hard to know much about her."

"So you never saw her with anyone?"

He shook his head. "The only people she's ever talked to here that I'm aware of was me, Ray, and Casey, the weekend night manager. And like I said, she wasn't much for lengthy conversations. Just the usual 'how ya doing' and kept going. A couple times when she's been here she dropped off payment late at night, but she hasn't been by this time at all."

"Did you see her leave for work at night?"

"Sometimes, but not often. Being at the opposite end of the motel and night, you don't really pay much attention to one person walking away. I sometimes saw her when I was making rounds, or if I was out handling a complaint."

"Do you remember the last time you saw her?"

"Not specifically. It was last week sometime. Two guys got into a fight in room 9 around two a.m. and she stuck her head out, probably to see what was going on. I waved and told her it was all over and she nodded and closed the door. That's the last time I recall seeing her."

"Thanks. If you see or hear anything, please give me a call. Doesn't matter what time."

"Sure. I wish I could help. I know Ray's worried something happened to her and he doesn't get worked up over things, so I figure it's serious."

"It is. Hey, I didn't think to ask Ray, but do you know where I might find the weekend night manager—I'm not asking for his home address but maybe he has another job? Somewhere that I could find him tomorrow instead of waiting until the weekend?"

"He works for a furniture delivery company during the day. First Rate Delivery, I think is the name of it. They delivered my sofa. Not sure how easy it would be to find him though, as he's one of the drivers."

"Maybe not, but it doesn't hurt to try. What's his last name?"

"Dugas."

"Thanks for your help. You have a nice night."

"You too."

She turned and started for the door.

"Wait," he said.

She turned back around and he shuffled, looking a little nervous. "Look," he said. "Normally, I wouldn't tell anyone this but you're not just anyone, and I don't think he'll mind."

"Don't think who will mind?" Shaye asked, completely confused.

"Casey. He lives in one of the rooms here. His apartment got sold to one of those condo developers a couple months back so Ray told him he could stay here until he finds something else. Discounted rate, of course."

"That's nice for Ray to do."

Walter nodded. "He's a nice guy. He doesn't take any crap, but he's the first to lend a hand if you're doing all the right things and just need a boost, you know?"

"I know some people like that."

"Well, anyway, Casey stays in room 108. I saw him come in a little while ago. Not sure if he's still there."

"I'll check, and thanks for the information."

"Good luck, and let us know if you find Carla."

"I will."

Shaye exited the office and walked up the stairs and down the walkway until she located room 26. She knocked on the door and waited. Several seconds later, she heard footsteps and the door swung open.

"What's wrong, Walter?" he asked.

The man staring out at her was in his twenties, with brown hair and green eyes. He blinked several times and then frowned. "Sorry. I thought you were someone else. Can I help you?"

"I hope so. My name is Shaye Archer. I'm a private investigator, and I've been commissioned to find Carla Downing."

"Carla? The uh...lady who rents here?"

"Yes."

"She's missing?"

"I'm afraid so. Can you tell me the last time you saw her?"

"Oh wow, let me think. The weekend job throws off my sleep and the days are starting to run together." He blinked again and scrunched his brow. "It was last week. The day I had a late delivery of that damned red couch. Tuesday. It was Tuesday. Wouldn't fit through the door and I had to take the whole thing off the hinges. By the time I turned my truck in it was really late, maybe ten or so. Carla was getting into a car when I got here."

"A taxi?"

"I don't think so. It could have been one of those Uber cars, I guess."

"You didn't recognize the car?"

"Not that I know of, but you can find a white Corolla on just about any street."

Shaye nodded. Jackson had chosen a white Corolla for his surveillance car for exactly that reason.

"And you never saw her again after that?" Shaye asked.

"No, but she wasn't much of a talker, and I usually pick up dinner on the way home and settle down for a night of television. You said she's missing? Do you think something happened to her?"

"I don't know. I'm trying to find out."

"That sucks. I didn't know her well but she seemed nice. Always said hello, which is more than most people do even when I'm carrying furniture in their houses."

"Did you ever see Carla with anyone?"

He shook his head. "No. But like I said, I didn't see her that often. Even when I'm working weekends, it's hard to see that end of the motel from the office."

"No one ever called for her or came by and asked for her?"

"Not while I was working."

Shaye nodded and handed Casey one of her cards. "If you think of anything, please give me a call."

"Sure. Hey, you think she's all right?"

"I hope so."

Definitely not on this earth, but hopefully somewhere, life was better for Carla Downing.

15

SHAYE HEADED BACK TO HER SUV, SOMEWHAT disappointed. It didn't appear that the motel employees could tell her much about Carla. She seemed to have adopted a very private and quiet lifestyle—which Shaye could appreciate if she was truly trying to make a break from Rattler. And neither of the managers looked to be a good fit for the killer. Walter was too old and too heavyset to fit Madison's description, and while Casey's description fit, he would have been working the office at the time Carla was killed.

She guided her SUV down the road to where she'd found Shonda and Louise, mulling over the reported change in Carla's behavior. Shonda had said that Carla stayed at the motel when she was done with Rattler but always went back. Ray had confirmed that but this time, she'd paid for a month instead of just a couple days or a week as before. Why would she part with that much cash up front unless she really intended to change something? Granted, Ray said he would have refunded her the unused funds, but she'd still put a dent in her wallet to shell out a month's rent.

Why was this time different from the last?

Something else she'd noticed was a lack of drugs or booze in Carla's room. Maybe she had run out, but nothing in the trash cans indicated that she'd been using or drinking either. More things that were inconsistent with people's description of the woman's lifestyle. It appeared that Carla really was making some changes. Had those changes somehow put her in the killer's sights? Or was she simply a convenient, random choice?

Shaye turned onto the street she'd spotted Shonda and Louise on before and saw them standing at the corner. The street was lined with cars, probably in one of the many bars in the area, so she pulled around and found a space a block away. When Shonda saw her approaching, she pushed herself away from the lamppost she'd been leaning on and watched as she crossed the street.

"You find out anything?" Shonda asked.

"Yes," Shaye said, "but it's not good news."

Louise sucked in a breath. "Oh my God, she'd dead. I knew it. That asshole Rattler killed her."

"She's dead," Shaye said, "but I don't know who did it."

"Did you talk to Rattler?" Shonda asked.

"I did, but I have to be honest, I don't like him for this."

"Because that other girl is missing," Shonda said. "Yeah, if it was just Carla, I'd put my money on Rattler any day of the week, but I don't see him out killing random girls."

"Maybe it was two different guys," Louise said. "Rattler killed Carla and somebody else got the other girl. Wait—is she dead too?"

"At the moment, she's just missing," Shaye said, "but I went through her apartment and it doesn't look good. She hasn't been there in a while but the money and drugs she hid are still there."

"I think we all know what that means," Shonda said. "Ain't no hooker leaving money or drugs behind. Even if she stopped using, them drugs would fetch some money on the street."

Louise nodded.

"Was she killed like your client say?" Shonda asked.

"I'm afraid so," Shaye said. "A fisherman found her near Lake Pontchartrain. The good news is, since they have a body, and it's clearly murder, there's an official investigation now."

"Whatever," Shonda said. "You think they going to take this seriously? One dead hooker and one missing ain't even going get five minutes of police time."

Shaye understood Shonda's frustration, and in a city with a lot of crime to investigate, she also knew some crime took priority over others.

"I think this time is different," Shaye said. "The city is worried about public perception more than ever."

Shonda laughed. "The short version being serial killers ain't good for business."

"They just worried about losing the tourists with their big wallets," Louise said.

Shonda sighed. "We ain't no better. Who do you think we taking money from? Ain't all of 'em local."

"Look," Shaye said, "I know you don't have much reason to like cops and even less reason to trust them, but I know the investigating officer. His name is Detective Maxwell and I told him about you two. He's not interested in busting you for anything, but don't be surprised if he comes around to talk to you. I can't make you speak to him, but I wish you would."

"If you already told him everything," Louise said, "why do we need to tell it again?"

"Because it's secondhand information," Shonda said. "She might have gotten something wrong or forgotten something we said."

"That's absolutely correct," Shaye said, "and to be honest, after everything that happened with me, I'm not exactly on the police department's list of favorites. I wouldn't blame Detective Maxwell if he tried to avoid putting my name in his reports."

Shonda snorted. "Typical. Blame the victim. Like anything that happened was your fault. Hell, girl, you got the worst of it. Fuck the cops. They don't know. They didn't live it. I saw all the news stories. I figure compared to the things you gone through, hooking is a trip to Disney."

"I wouldn't say that," Shaye said. "What you do is very hard. And very dangerous. Now more than ever. Are you sure you can't think of anyone you've seen Carla with lately that raised any red flags? Any repeat customer?"

"I wish we had," Shonda said. "Me and Louise done spent every minute we standing here trying to come up with something, but we got a whole lotta nothing."

"I talked with the manager of the motel where Carla was staying," Shaye said. "He said she paid a month in advance. And when I searched her room, I didn't find any drugs or alcohol. The manager said she told him she was making some big changes. Any idea what they were? Or why? I wondered if maybe there was someone new she was seeing."

Shonda looked at Louise and then shook her head. "Carla never was huge on drugs. She tried the hard stuff a couple times, since Rattler had it and all, but she didn't like the way it made her feel. Said she was all paranoid and queasy. She smoked a little weed, but she sure enough liked her drink and boy could she blow through a pack of cigarettes. She'd buy smoke before she bought food."

Louise nodded. "She didn't smoke while she was working, though. The smell turns some customers off. But if you hung out with her at a bar or something, man, she'd put them away."

"There wasn't any sign of cigarettes in her room, either," Shaye said, "and it didn't smell of smoke."

"That's definitely different then," Louise said. "But I don't know if it was 'cause of a new man. If she had someone on the hook, she sure didn't tell us about him."

"Nope," Shonda agreed. "Hell, maybe she was making changes. I figure she could quit Rattler easier than she could quit smoking. Figures that about the time she decides to do better for herself, something bad happens."

"Do you know anyone who drives a white Corolla?" Shaye asked. "One of the night managers at the motel saw Carla getting into one last week."

They both shook their heads.

"I mean, I see a lot of white cars," Shonda said, "and probably a lot of them is Toyotas, but I don't know anyone in particular that has one."

"And she never even hinted to you about her plans?" Shaye asked. "Not even making it sound like wishful thinking?"

"No." Shonda frowned. "I know you think Rattler probably didn't do it, but maybe you're wrong. Maybe he found out she was gone for real this time and he killed her. Maybe Mitzi is a coincidence."

"If Carla had been killed differently," Shaye said, "I might think so, but given the way it all went down, I doubt it."

"How did it happen?" Shonda asked. "Can you say?"

"My client wouldn't mind, if that's what you're

asking," Shaye said. "I haven't given you details because I didn't want to put that picture in your minds."

Shonda looked over at Louise, who bit her lower lip. "I want to know," Shonda said. "If Louise don't, she can take a smoke break down the block."

"No, it's okay," Louise said. "I don't want to know, but I think I need to."

Shaye nodded and repeated Madison's story. Both their eyes grew wider as she talked, and when she finished, Shonda blew out a breath.

"That's the craziest shit I've heard in a long time," Shonda said. "I see why you don't think it was Rattler. He'd have shot her and dumped her, but all that arrangement...that's just weird."

"Why would Carla even go someplace like that?" Louise asked. "You don't ever go to someone's house, and you don't bring them to yours. It's always a neutral location. She knew that."

"If I knew the answer to that," Shaye said, "I might be able to figure out who did it."

"So how come this man's face ain't flashed up all over the news?" Shonda asked. "Your client described Carla down to her shoes. Why can't they do up one of them drawings and put that asshole on blast?"

"It's complicated," Shaye said. "My client has a disorder where she can't remember people's faces. So while she remembered everything Carla was wearing and even her hair color and style, she wouldn't be able to tell you anything about her face. The same for the killer. She can describe his clothes, but he had on long sleeves and gloves. Aside from his height, build, his hair color, and the fact that she feels like he was white, she can't offer anything else."

"Can't remember faces?" Louise asked. "What kind of crazy shit is that?"

"Unfortunately, it's real," Shaye said. "And a lot of her life is fairly miserable because of it. She's sick over this, but she's done everything she could do, including hiring me when the police didn't have enough evidence to open a case."

"That's seriously fucked up," Shonda said.

"Oh my God," Louise said. "If she can't recognize him, then he could be standing right next to her and she wouldn't know to run or scream or anything."

Shonda narrowed her eyes at Shaye. "Does he know she saw?"

"I'm afraid so," Shaye said.

"That woman in some serious shit," Shonda said. "And this guy crazy. You looking out for her, right?"

"I'm doing everything I can," Shaye said.

Shonda nodded. "Me and Louise keeping our ears to the ground. We hear anything, we calling you first thing. And we being extra careful. Gonna be super-extra careful now."

"That's good," Shaye said. "And if for any reason it's an emergency and you can't reach me, call the police and ask for Detective Maxwell. I promise you, he'll help."

"If you vouching for him, then I guess we okay with

it," Shonda said, "but if it's all the same, I'll just keep praying we ain't got no emergency."

"Me too," Shaye said. "I'm going to head home. Stay safe."

"You too," Shonda said. "And thanks for telling us about Carla."

Shaye nodded and headed up the sidewalk toward her SUV. As she walked she became increasingly aware of how the street had thinned out while she'd talked to Shonda and Louise. Over half of the cars that previously lined the street were gone, and the people who were hanging around outside the bars had drifted off home, leaving the area dark and quiet. She picked up her pace, the unwelcome quiet unnerving her.

Stop being foolish. You're not the target.

But she was helping Madison. What if one of the people she'd spoken to was the killer? The maintenance guy? The parking attendant? The Realtor? Any of them had opportunity. At this point she'd only be guessing at motive, but she'd bet it was psychologically motivated, which made the killer much harder to identify. Profit motive was infinitely easier to pin down.

As she approached her vehicle, she frowned. It looked odd. Then she realized one side was sitting lower than the other, and it wasn't the street. The back tire was flat. Of all the times and places to have a flat tire, this had to be one of the worst. She looked back at the empty street and ran through her options. She had roadside assistance, but how long would they take to get to her?

The quickest way to get out of there was to change it herself.

She opened the back of her SUV and pulled out the jack and the spare. She positioned the jack under the car and began to lift it. The seconds ticked by into minutes as she struggled to loosen the lug nuts and remove the flat tire from the vehicle. When she finally managed to get it off, she pushed it to the side and let it rest against the curb, not wanting to think about the fun time she was going to have lifting it into the back of the vehicle. The spare was smaller and lighter. She made short work of getting it in place and started to put the lug nuts back on.

Then a cool breeze blew across the back of her neck, and she stiffened.

She had no concrete reason to believe it, but somehow, she knew someone was watching her. And crouched on the ground, her back to the sidewalk, she was completely vulnerable. As she started to rise, the gunshot rang out and the bullet tore through the door of her SUV just inches from her head.

16

SHAYE DROPPED FLAT ONTO THE PAVEMENT AND ROLLED under the vehicle, then scanned the street for movement as she pulled her pistol from her waistband. Her heart pounded so loudly in her chest that it brought tears to her eyes. She heard shouting in the distance as more gunshots pelted the side of her SUV. One hit the concrete next to it and took a bounce underneath, sending her scrambling for the other side.

She dragged herself out from under the vehicle and crouched behind the tire on the other side, dragging in air in short, ragged breaths. The shooter wouldn't be able to see her, but he was smart enough to guess where she was—basically, in sitting duck territory. Panicked, she scanned the street, looking for somewhere to run to, some object large enough to hide behind and put more distance between her and the shooter. But the nearest automobile was thirty yards away, and the lights were out in all the stores across the street.

She leaned down and inched forward, holding her breath, and looked underneath the vehicle, hoping to catch sign of movement, but the street appeared empty. Then she saw a silhouette appear from behind a Dumpster about halfway up the block and begin moving her way. She positioned her pistol in front of her and took aim at his feet, then paused. What if it wasn't the shooter?

A second later, another shot rang out and the streetlight on the corner exploded, casting her into darkness. *Shit!* Now it was too late to take a shot. She squinted, looking into the inky black, but with the dark clouds overhead, she couldn't see anything. She rose into a crouch and scanned the streets to the left and right again. The air got still, and then she heard it.

Footsteps coming her way.

They were faint. So faint she couldn't hear them when the wind was blowing, but now she was certain. He was coming for her.

Think!

Her cell phone was propped against the curb where she'd placed it for additional light while she was changing the tire, but if she could slip around the back of the vehicle and snag it, at least she could call for help. She knew it was reaching. Odds of a cop getting to her before the shooter did were practically nil, but at least they'd have a record of what happened, especially since she had no intention of going out quietly. He might end up killing her, but no way was she going to make it easy. She had seventeen rounds in her Glock, and she would go down firing every one of them.

She clutched her gun and stayed stock-still, trying to keep her attention on the footsteps. They disappeared every time the wind whipped up, but when the sound carried back to her again, she could tell they were closer, maybe thirty feet away. She closed her eyes for a moment, taking a deep breath and slowly blowing it out. She had only one chance to hit him, because shooting would give away her location and she had no doubt he'd return fire.

The footsteps sounded again, this time so close she steadied herself and prepared to whirl around the side of the vehicle and open fire. Then they stopped. She stopped breathing, trying to get a fix on the shooter, and then she realized why he'd paused. Sirens sounded in the distance. She put her finger on the trigger, ready to fire if he made a last desperate move, but a second later, she heard retreating footsteps.

He was running away.

She slumped against her SUV, still clutching her pistol in ready position, and it wasn't until the police cruiser pulled up behind her, the car's lights blinding her, that she lowered her weapon. Her relief was so overwhelming that she could feel tears pooling in her eyes.

"Ma'am?" The cop driving the car approached her. "Are you all right? Have you been shot?"

"I'm fine," she said as she held one hand up to block the light from the headlights from her face. "I don't think my SUV fared as well, though."

"Do you mind stepping back here and putting down your weapon?" the cop asked.

"Of course not." She moved deliberately, keeping the gun pointed at the pavement. When she reached the cop, she held it toward him, and he took it from her and took a good look at her.

"Ms. Archer?" he said, his eyes widening.

"Yes. I'm sorry, do I know you? It's hard to see in the light."

The cop waved and behind him, the bright lights went out to be replaced by a flashlight that lit up the area with a bright, but not blinding, glow. She had seen the cop before but hadn't met him. He was young, probably midtwenties, and looked incredibly stressed.

"I'm Officer Freed. This is Officer Lincoln."

"Looks like your vehicle took some hits," Officer Lincoln said, stepping around from the side of the vehicle. "Might just be body damage, but you should have the shop give the whole thing a once-over."

"Are you sure you're all right?" Officer Freed asked. "I can call an ambulance."

"I'm not injured," she said, "but I'm not convinced I'm all right."

He nodded. "Can you tell us what happened?"

Shaye recounted her walk back to her SUV and the subsequent shots fired, then her narrow escape. Freed looked over at Lincoln, and she saw him swallow.

"That was good thinking," Freed said. "But you didn't get a good look at him?"

"Nothing more than a shadow," she said. "I couldn't even guess at his height."

He frowned. "Can I ask why you're out here this time of night?"

"Working on a case," she said. "I needed to talk to some women who work in this neighborhood, and they only work the night shift."

Even though she was deliberately vague, she knew Freed could make an educated guess as to what kind of "working" women she was down here talking to. She heard a noise behind the cops and looked over to see a small crowd of people gathered on the sidewalk. Shonda and Louise were standing just behind two men, looking around them. Their eyes were wide with fright. She looked directly at them and gave them a tiny nod, hoping to convey that she was all right. But even though she was walking away tonight, all three of them knew how bad this was.

Officer Lincoln looked over at the crowd. "Did anyone see anything?"

They all shook their heads. "We all came from the club up the block," one of the guys said. "Heard the shots and one of these gals ran into the bar and called you guys, but wasn't nobody stepping outside to get a look."

"Well, the show's over," Lincoln said. "It's best if you get back inside. Even better, might be a good idea to head on home for the night."

The crowd mumbled a little among themselves and started walking away. Shonda shot one last look at Shaye, and she mouthed a thank-you before Shonda turned and hurried up the sidewalk to catch up with Louise.

"I see you were changing a flat," Lincoln said. "I'd offer to finish it up for you, but I think one of those shots took out your spare."

"We can call a tow truck," Freed said. "And we'll give you a ride home. No use waiting on the tow. He can get the SUV to whatever shop you use, and you can take them the keys tomorrow. No one will be driving it anyway until they get that tire fixed."

"Thank you. I really appreciate it."

Freed handed her pistol back to her. "I know you have a job to do, and apparently it brought you here tonight, but I don't have to tell you how badly this could have turned out. Lots of people down here are hopped up on drugs. You never know what they might do."

Shaye nodded but she didn't respond. She didn't believe for a minute that the shooter was a random junkie. And someone interested in robbing her or raping her or stealing her car wouldn't have shot her until they were done with the task at hand. She'd been targeted.

Whether by coincidental opportunity or by deliberate stalking was the piece of the puzzle she didn't have an answer for. Either way, the situation had just gone from bad to worse.

She was on the killer's radar. Right along with Madison.

HE WATCHED from an abandoned building a block away as the police cruiser drove by. She was inside. Shaye Archer. Woman of the people. Or nosy bitch, depending on your perspective.

He'd seen her going into Madison's building the day before and had worried for just a minute that the Peeping Tom had hired her to track him down. But he'd dismissed that thought when he found out Madison couldn't identify him at all. Shaye Archer had plenty of money, and Madison lived in a high-end building. For all he knew, she could have been there looking at apartments.

But now he knew his initial thought was correct. And that wasn't good. The whores Carla hung out with couldn't provide her with any information because they didn't know anything, but it hadn't stopped her from showing up in a bad area of town, late at night, to speak to them. Unfortunately, Shaye Archer didn't have the red tape that the cops had to work through or a caseload that kept her spread so thinly that things got overlooked and eventually shelved. Most importantly, she didn't need the money. If she took an interest in something, she had the means, ability, and connections to pursue it until the end.

In so many ways, she was more dangerous than the police.

So he'd watched as she talked to the whores and weighed his options. He'd come here tonight against his better judgment. His body ached for the release he'd feel when he finally took Madison as his own, but that finale required careful planning, especially now that she knew he was watching. But his desire was overwhelming, and it wouldn't be denied. He craved the release that came with death the way a junkie craved the needle. So finally, he'd set out, hoping for an easy score. Something that would tide him over until he could have what he truly desired. It wouldn't be a production like what he'd planned for Carla. More old-school as in the beginning. But he needed it.

Then he'd seen that Archer bitch and rage took over. Who the hell was she to try to prevent him from getting what he needed? Who was she to judge his desires? To decide that a bunch of whores were more important than his pain?

Something had to be done about Shaye Archer.

Nothing could stand in the way of his plans for Madison. Madison was the key to everything. The one he'd been searching for with every previous kill but had never found. She was everything he hoped the others would be, and no one was going to stop him from having her.

When he'd spotted the Archer bitch's SUV on the corner, he'd gotten an idea. Puncture a tire so that she had no way to run from his bullets, except out in the open. Then shoot her while she stood there, waiting for a man to come rescue her from the banalities of life. He'd been surprised when she started changing the tire herself, but it made no difference to his plan. In fact, it meant his plan worked all the better. When faced with death, someone might attempt to drive away on a flat tire, but if the vehicle was on a jack, that became impossible.

So he'd waited until the perfect moment, then he'd opened fire.

When he saw her dive under the SUV, he'd bitten his tongue so hard to hold in the stream of cursing that he'd tasted blood. He'd tried to save the plan, shooting out the light and attempting a silent approach in the dark night. And it would have worked if the cops hadn't shown up. A patrol unit must have been nearby. Just his luck.

And now things were worse than before.

Now Shaye Archer knew that he knew, because he didn't think for a moment that she would attribute his attempt to random street violence, especially when a shop checked out her vehicle and told her the tire had been deliberately slashed. He'd put an already-suspicious person with connections to law enforcement and an unlimited budget on high alert.

He cursed and slammed his hand against the wall, knocking pieces of plaster off the deteriorating building. What if the Archer bitch convinced Madison to leave New Orleans? Without Madison, everything fell apart. She was the only one for him. The perfect mate.

It was obvious what he had to do, and he had to do it quickly.

17

Thursday, December 24, 2015

It was only 5:00 a.m. when Shaye rolled out of bed and headed into the bathroom. Despite only a couple hours' sleep, she was wide awake, even though her exhausted body wished she were still in bed. Unfortunately, her mind had other ideas, and Shaye knew herself well enough to know that her mind always won that battle. It didn't matter that it was still pitch-black outside; if her mind was raring to go, then her body had to get on board. Coffee would help move things forward.

A splash of cold water on her face startled a little bit of energy out of her, and she headed into the kitchen to make coffee, trying to stay quiet so that she didn't wake Jackson, who was sleeping on her couch.

She'd called him as soon as she'd gotten to her apartment. The last thing she wanted was for him to hear about what happened at the police station. He'd rushed right over as she'd expected he would, but she hadn't expected the displeasure he'd expressed with the choice she'd made to go talk to Shonda and Louise with no backup. It was the closest to a fight they'd ever been, and she still wasn't sure how she felt about it.

On the one hand, she was glad that he wasn't dancing around things in order to spare her feelings. She wanted their relationship to be one of equal footing. But on the other hand, her decision the night before was about her job, and he needed to accept that risk came with it the same as she accepted it about his job. Then on the other, other hand maybe she should have asked him to go with her, just to sit in the car, given that she knew the killer was stalking Madison. And if one wanted to throw a fourth hand in there for good measure, no one had considered the killer would come after Shaye, so her worry of being in danger was low.

It was a problem with no immediate solution. For the first time since she and Jackson had taken their relationship beyond friendship, she understood why Corrine didn't date. It was hard. The emotions wrapped up in everything, especially the decisions she made about her own life. If she wanted things to work with Jackson, she was going to have to start considering him in everything she did, not just when she wasn't working.

That didn't mean she stopped doing her job, or taking risks along with the job. But maybe she could alter the way she went about certain things to reduce the chance of her getting caught in the cross fire. It was the same thing Corrine had been harping on ever since Shaye opened her practice, but it had been easier to dismiss her worry as the whole mother thing. It was harder to dismiss Jackson, especially given what he did for a living and knowing how much he respected the choices she'd made concerning her profession.

"You making coffee?" Jackson's voice sounded from the couch and his head appeared over the back of it.

"Yeah. I was trying not to wake you."

"I wasn't sleeping all that great anyway."

"I have a queen bed with a nice cushy mattress in the guest room."

He rose and walked into the kitchen. "It's not the couch. It's actually more comfortable than mine."

He looked directly at her, and she could see the concern and caring in his eyes and all the fight in her slipped away.

"I'm sorry about last night," she said. "I should have asked you to ride along."

He narrowed his eyes at her. "What's the catch?"

"No catch. I've just been thinking about the way it went down. The reality is if he'd been a better shot, I probably would have been killed. Then Madison wouldn't have me looking out for her, my mother would be inconsolable, and you..." She looked down at the floor.

He stepped close to her and put his finger under her chin, raising her head so that she was forced to look at him. "I would have been inconsolable too," he said, and wrapped his arms around her, pulling her close to him.

She relaxed into him, the warmth from his body enveloping her like a blanket. Everything could have been lost. Everything that was so important to her. All because she didn't take the time to consider every possibility. She wouldn't make that mistake again. The struggle she'd had to get to where she was now was worth thinking twice before she made a move. It was worth thinking ten times.

Finally, she leaned back to look at him. "I'm still not quitting," she said.

"I would be disappointed if you were."

She smiled. "How did you get so perfect, Jackson Lamotte?"

"I found my perfect match." He leaned in and kissed her gently on the lips, then released her. "Now, let's have some coffee and talk through everything that happened last night. Everything changed, and you need to rethink how you go about the investigation differently from this point forward. I'd love to help you with that. If you don't mind."

"Mind? I think you've got a couple years' experience on me. I'm happy with any help you want to provide."

They fixed their coffees and sat at the bar, Shaye reaching for her laptop as she slipped onto the stool. "I might want to make some notes," she said.

He nodded. "Okay, so recount last night for me. Everything from the time you got back to your SUV."

She took a sip of coffee and started, taking her time to mentally picture and describe every detail that she could recall. You never knew what would be important. She'd heard that from every investigator she'd ever worked with, and they were right. Sometimes the thing that seemed small or even insignificant was the clue that cracked everything wide open.

"The tires are new, right?" he asked when she finished.

"Basically. I just replaced them two months ago."

"New Orleans roads are bad but not bad enough to take out a brand-new tire, and if you'd picked up a nail, it probably wouldn't have gone as flat as you described in that amount of time. It wasn't pulling to one side when you were driving, was it?"

"No. It was fine. Look, I've pretty much decided that he slashed my tire. My guess is the dealership will call me this morning saying the same thing. I don't believe for a minute that he just happened upon me and took advantage of my bad luck, but I have to believe that he knows I'm working for Madison. Otherwise, why target me?"

"No reason to at all. I'd say your assumption is accurate. He could have been watching when you went to her apartment and put it together. I don't have to tell you that you're at a disadvantage to most PIs given that the majority of the city knows what you look like. It will always be hard not to stick out."

"I know."

"You also have to call Maxwell this morning and fill him in. He needs to know that things are escalating."

"I planned on calling him at nine, unless of course, he gets word of what happened and calls me before that."

"Good. I'll take a cab back to my apartment and leave you my truck."

Shaye sighed. Despite talking about the shooting, she'd completely forgotten about the fact that she would be without a vehicle for a while. "I'll get a rental today," she said.

"You sure? I've got the spare car."

"It's a business expense, and given that he's not afraid to shoot at me, I don't want to get bullet holes in your truck, too."

"It could do with a new paint job, but I hear you."

"Okay, so back to the case. We agree that his shooting at me was deliberate, but what I can't figure is why he was there in the first place. I don't think I was followed, and I usually know."

Jackson shook his head. "I'd bet money you weren't followed. Very few people would be good enough to pull that off during the day with decent traffic for coverage. But late at night, in an area with low automobile traffic, he would have stood out like a sore thumb even to a blind man, much less someone with your perception."

"Okay, so we agree he was already there. Why?"

"No good reason, for sure. We know what corner Carla worked and you said another girl from that area is missing, right?"

"He was looking for his next victim." She'd already made it around to that thought sometime in the middle of one of her tossing-and-turning episodes the night before, but saying it out loud put a whole different sense of urgency on it.

"That's what I'm thinking."

"But why so soon? I mean, there was a bigger time gap between Mitzi and Carla. And he'd made plans for Carla's murder even if she wasn't necessarily chosen ahead of time. So why escalate now? Unless you think he already has multiple locations prepared."

"Window-shopping?"

She shook her head. "That doesn't feel right. He knows Madison saw him, and if he's responsible for Carla and Mitzi, why would he return to the same vicinity? It's risky."

"He doesn't know that the police are investigating. And besides, he knows he didn't leave any evidence. You know these perps think they're smarter than everyone else. He knew he could find what he was looking for in that location because he had before. I don't think it's any more complicated than that."

"I have to do something. Louise could have been next. She fits his type. Tall, blonde, thin. I need to call Shonda. Maybe last night will prompt Louise to change her hair color."

"It could make a difference going forward, but honestly, if he was looking for a victim for last night, I don't think it would have mattered. She could have had black hair or even blue. If he wanted a victim right then, he might have just gone with availability."

"Like shooting at me. I just happened to be there."

"Golden opportunity."

"Maybe, but I don't know. I think the blonde thing is important. I think part of the reason he's fixated on Madison and stalking her rather than just killing her at first opportunity is because she fits his profile."

"And you could be right. God only knows what goes on inside the head of the criminally insane."

"Just my luck to get a case with one." She put her hands in the air. "So what now? He's after Madison and won't hesitate to take a shot at me. Maybe he's even after me now. How do we find him? I have a dozen places to start but none of them sound more promising than the other."

"The way I narrow things down is by picking the one fact of the case that produces the fewest number of options and start there."

She frowned and considered the facts of the case aligned with his statement. "The change in Carla's behavior is one thing. I wondered if she had a new man, but no one seems to think that's the case. Neither the owner of the motel where she stayed nor his two night managers recalled seeing Carla with anyone, and Shonda and Louise didn't think there was anyone new. The weekend night manager saw her get into a white Corolla, but he didn't see the driver."

Jackson nodded. "If Carla was seeing someone new,

that's an angle that needs exploring, but it sounds like you've tapped it out. The thing that really stands out to me is the apartment where he killed Carla. How did he get in? If what the maintenance guy told you is true—that he controls contractor access—then there can't have been that many people who could gain entry."

"And we know for certain that he didn't break in. You're right. I have a list of all the Realtors who showed the apartment. I was going to contact all of them and see if they saw anything unusual when they were there."

"Or a weird client that they showed the space to."

Her mind went back to her interview with Trenton Cooper. "Or maybe the solution is right there at the beginning of it all. I need to do some more digging into Trenton Cooper."

"The Realtor who holds the listing?"

"Yeah. I didn't like him. That doesn't make him a serial killer, of course."

"Thank God. If everyone I didn't like was a serial killer, I'd have a lot more murder cases on my desk."

She shook her head. "Now that you're done being funny, where are you going to buy my breakfast?"

"Me? I offer all this free help and I have to pay?"

"You rode in to rescue me, right? Well, you can wrap up the gig by saving me from starvation."

"I see how this is going to be. Well, if I'm buying, then I'm choosing. How about that place on the corner with the incredible blueberry pancakes."

She groaned. "I was going to wear jeans."

"If I don't get to wear elastic-waist pants, you shouldn't either. It's that whole equality thing."

"My man, the feminist." She leaned in and gave him a quick kiss before jumping off the stool and heading for the bedroom to change. She had a lot to do, and it all needed to happen five minutes ago.

Her life and Madison's depended on it.

MADISON AWAKENED before dawn and went straight to her office, trying to distract herself with work. She hadn't slept for more than a thirty-minute stretch and she felt it all over. Her entire body ached and a small headache lingered, threatening to turn into something far worse. Every time exhaustion had taken over and put her into slumber, the dreams came. And he was in every one of them. The faceless figure wearing black. Sometimes he was behind her, and no matter how fast she ran, he gained on her until he grabbed her shoulder. Other times, he had a knife to her throat and he was laughing. The horrible laugh of a disturbed person.

Both had sent her bolting upright, dripping with sweat, and a couple of times, screaming for help. She was glad none of the other apartments on her floor were occupied. She could only imagine the scare she would have given a neighbor, shrieking as though she were being killed. And she supposed, in a way, she was.

After a pot of coffee and a good hour of work, she

lifted her hands above her head and stretched them, trying to ease her knotted back. During one of her jolts awake, she'd strained something and her body wasn't letting her forget it. She glanced at the master bedroom, thinking about the big whirlpool tub or the shower with all those adjustable jets, but the thought of being in either of them, naked and vulnerable, freaked her out too much to try it. Instead, she dug out the heating pad she used for cramps and stuck it in her office chair, hoping the heat would give her a bit of relief.

It was barely 8:00 a.m. when her phone rang. She looked at the display and frowned. It was security.

"Hello," she answered.

"Ms. Avery," Wanda said. "There's a package here for you. I would bring it up, but I don't have anyone to cover for me."

"Your job is more important than delivering my mail. I'll be down to get it in a couple minutes. Does it say who it's from?"

She wasn't expecting anything, but there was always the off chance that her parents or her sister had sent her something for Christmas.

"No return address. It's wrapped in Christmas paper, though."

"Thanks."

Madison hurried into her bedroom and threw on clothes that were suitable for public, or at minimum, the lobby, and headed downstairs. She was more than a little curious who had sent the package. Her immediate family members were the only relatives she had contact with, and that was sketchy at best. She called them on their birthdays and Christmas. They sometimes remembered to call her on her birthday, but that was about it.

Otherwise, her knowledge of their lives was limited to their posts on Facebook. She kept telling herself she should unfriend them all and save herself the misery of seeing her parents' fabulous life with their one perfect daughter, but she never had been able to bring herself to do it. Maybe she did need to talk to someone when this was over. About more than just the killer.

Wanda smiled at her as she entered the lobby and pointed to the small box on the end of the counter.

"How are you feeling?" Wanda asked. "You look a little better today."

"I'm a bit better. Thanks for asking."

"I hope you didn't catch that flu that's going around. My grandson caught it at school, then passed it along to the entire household. I told them that if anyone's still running a fever tomorrow, I'll Skype them for Christmas and we'll do the whole present thing later. When you get old, you get practical, especially when it comes to being sick. Don't heal like you used to."

"I'm not running a fever, so I promise I'm not passing anything along. I think it's probably just a combination of lack of sleep and not eating right."

"It's easy to eat bad in this town, and you don't go out a lot. Management told me the building's gym won't be ready until February. Maybe you need to take some walks...get some fresh air."

Madison wasn't about to tell Wanda that taking a walk might give her a heart attack. So far, the police hadn't made the murder public and for that, she was happy. If the killer knew the police were after him, then he might just take a shot at her from far away. He didn't know she couldn't identify him. If he did, that might make things better or worse. She wasn't sure.

"If I don't see you again beforehand," Madison said, "have a Merry Christmas."

"You too, honey."

She took the package and headed upstairs, scanning the box for any indications as to where it came from. Wanda said it had been delivered by courier, but it didn't bear the stamp of any of the companies she recognized. A single Christmas tag with her name and address was in the middle of a box wrapped in red and green Christmas paper.

Perhaps it was a gift from her client, purchased from one of the local shops. Some of them delivered all over town, especially the ones selling baked goods. As much as her waistline didn't need the extra calories, she desperately hoped for something incredibly fattening and full of sugar. And if it wasn't, she was now seriously considering gifting herself something that fit that bill.

She let herself back in her apartment and headed into the kitchen, placing the box on the counter. Her Keurig was calling to her, so she started up a cup of vanilla latte and then turned her attention to the gift. She lifted the paper from the end and carefully peeled it back from the backside. Yes, she was one of those people who didn't just rip into a wrapped gift. For her, part of the pleasure was derived from the anticipation she felt while opening it up. In fact, lots of times, the opening was the most pleasant part, depending on who sent the gift. She had donated a whole box of ugly sweaters to Goodwill one year, and not a single one had ever been worn. Her late aunt Catherine had always had horrible taste.

Once the paper was removed, she flipped the box around, looking for any identifying markings, but it was just a plain cardboard box like what you could buy at any office supply store. She grabbed her scissors out of the drawer and slit the tab on the top, then pulled back the tabs. The inside was full of shredded paper, and she pulled it off to find a picture frame, facedown, underneath. She sighed. It was probably a picture of her parents and her sister. They were vain enough to think she would want a picture of them in her home. She lifted the frame out of the box and turned it around.

Then she screamed and let it crash to the floor.

18

SHAYE SAT ON A STOOL AT HER KITCHEN ISLAND, prepping her list of Realtors to call. The list started with the most recent showings and worked backward, listing every Realtor who had shown the apartment in the last month. She figured once 9:00 a.m. came around, it would be a reasonable time to start the phone calls. Normally, she preferred to question people in person because facial expressions often conveyed more than words, but the urgency of the matter and the fairly long list of people who were likely going to be hard to catch given the holiday pushed her to go with calling first and following up in person with anyone she felt needed a second look. But first up was Detective Maxwell, who needed to know that his case had taken a turn for the worse.

Shaye's phone rang just before 9:00 a.m., and when she saw Madison's name in the display, she stiffened.

"Can you come over now?" Madison asked as soon as she answered. "Something's happened."

Shaye could tell by Madison's voice that she was not in a good place. "Are you all right?"

"No. I mean, I'm at my apartment so I guess I'm safe, but I'm definitely not all right."

"Okay. Stay put. I'll be there in ten minutes."

She clutched the steering wheel of Jackson's truck as she drove, wondering what had happened that had sent Madison into a downward spiral so early in the day. She seriously doubted Madison had left her apartment, and the killer couldn't get by security without a viable reason and approval from an occupant, which at the moment was limited to only a handful of people. So what had happened? Did she need to call Detective Maxwell? Madison hadn't indicated whether she'd contacted the detective before she'd disconnected but Shaye had been able to feel her panic over the phone.

Without knowing what happened, Shaye didn't want to bother the detective. Madison had said she was in her apartment and safe, so did that mean she was just inside her own head too long and freaking out? Maybe she was having nightmares. Shaye knew all about night terrors and the way they could debilitate you.

Okay, so she'd see what was wrong first, then call Detective Maxwell if it was something he needed to be involved in. Either way, she'd already decided to call Eleonore. Madison needed to talk to someone, and even though Shaye had plenty of experience being a victim and knew what Eleonore would say to Madison, she lacked the credentials, maturity, and general calm that Eleonore could provide. While the life Madison had carved out for herself was admirable, Shaye knew that the girl could benefit from ongoing counseling, just as she had. And no one was better at dealing with strange situations than Eleonore.

The same woman who'd been working security the previous day looked up at Shaye and smiled as she crossed the lobby.

"Here for Madison?" she asked.

Shaye nodded and the woman buzzed Madison and told her Shaye was downstairs.

"Go on up," she said as she hung up the phone.

"Thanks," Shaye said and headed for the elevators.

This time, Madison wasn't standing at her door. Shaye had to knock twice, and it took several seconds after the second knock before she heard the dead bolt sliding back. Madison stared out at her, her face ashen, her eyes red and swollen. She stood back to let Shaye inside and her hand shook as she drew the dead bolt back in place. She pointed to the kitchen, still not uttering a word, and Shaye wondered if she should call for a paramedic. Madison appeared to be in shock.

Shaye followed her into the kitchen and saw the box with wrapping paper on the counter. Madison walked around the counter and pointed to the floor, and Shaye stepped around and saw a picture frame facedown on the tile. Madison stood off to the side, refusing to even look at it. Confused about what was happening, Shaye knelt down and picked up the frame. When she turned it over, she gasped.

No wonder Madison was terrified.

The picture was Madison, walking on the sidewalk near her home, the picture taken as if she were walking toward the photographer. Behind her was a hooded figure, his hand up in the air and a knife clenched in his hand. His face was blurred.

Shaye set the picture facedown on the counter and went to Madison, placing her hand on her arms to steady her as she swayed. She guided Madison onto the stool next to her and grabbed a bottled water from the refrigerator and placed it in front of her.

"Take a drink of the water," Shaye instructed. "Slow and easy or you'll choke."

Madison reached for the bottle but never looked at it. She stared directly ahead, not seeming to focus on anything, her face slack. She lifted the bottle as if a puppeteer were pulling strings, then placed it back on the counter. Shaye leaned down and put her finger on Madison's chin, gently turning her face toward her.

"I need you to talk to me, or I'm calling the paramedics," Shaye said.

Her words seemed to have broken the spell, and Madison blinked then slowly shook her head. "There's nothing they can do," she said quietly. "I'm not sick."

"They can sedate you if you need it," Shaye said.

Madison's eyes widened in panic. "No! If I'm out of it I can't run."

"Okay then. Can you tell me what happened?"

Madison nodded and recounted how she acquired the frame and how there was no return address.

"Did you call Detective Maxwell?" Shaye asked.

"No. I called you, then it's like I went numb. I couldn't think of what to do so I just stood here until you knocked."

"You're in shock. It's perfectly understandable. I'm going to call him now. I doubt there's any forensic evidence on the frame or box, but he needs to have it processed."

"Please. I want it out of my house."

Shaye pulled out her phone and called Detective Maxwell and gave him a brief explanation of the situation. He said he'd be right over. Then she looked at Madison to assess the woman's mental status. The color was still gone from her face but her eyes were focused now, the glazed look gone.

"I want to go downstairs and talk to the security guard," Shaye said. "Can you stay here and drink your water for just a few minutes? I promise I'll be right back and I won't leave the building."

Madison nodded and Shaye hurried down to the lobby. The security guard looked up as she approached and frowned when he got a good look at Shaye's expression.

"Is something wrong?" the security guard asked.

"Wanda, right?" Shaye asked, and the woman nodded.

"Yes. There's something wrong," Shaye said. "That package that was delivered earlier contained a very cruel joke that scared Madison. I was hoping you could tell me something about the delivery."

"Oh my God. That's horrible. Why would someone want to scare that nice young lady?"

"Someone is stalking her," Shaye said, not wanting to get into the details until the police made the investigation public. "We don't know who he is, but I think he sent that package."

Wanda's hand flew over her mouth and she paled a bit. "I sent her upstairs with a package from a stalker. That poor girl. I never would have done that if I'd known."

"Of course not," Shaye said. "The way you can help Madison is to give me information."

"You're working for her," Wanda said, her momentary confusion shifting to understanding. "Good. That's really good."

"Yes, I am. And I'd really like to help her now. How was the package delivered?"

"A courier dropped it off."

"What did the courier look like?"

Wanda frowned. "It was a young girl. I remember thinking she didn't even look old enough to hold a job, but then the older you get, the younger everyone else looks. Or with kids out of school, I figure someone could have brought their kid to work with them."

"How was she dressed?"

"Not very well. Her clothes were rumpled. She wore one of those hooded sweatshirts and it was pulled down over her forehead. Her hair stuck out of it a bit and it looked like it needed a good brushing."

Shaye nodded. Based on Wanda's description, she'd bet money that the killer paid a street kid to deliver the package. She was probably underage, and if she was living on the streets, the police would have a hard time finding her. They tended to scatter and protect their own when cops were around. But Shaye had an inside track. She might be able to find the girl who'd delivered the package.

"Would you have her on security footage?" Shaye asked.

"Yes, but I don't think it would do you much good. She had that hood low and walked in looking down. The only camera in the lobby covers the entry door to the elevators."

"Okay. Then can you give me a really detailed description?" Shaye asked.

"I can do you one better. If you give me a bit, I can draw her."

"Really?"

"Back years ago, I fancied myself an artist. Did portraits in Jackson Square before I decided a steady paycheck suited me better. I've got good recall. I can get her down well enough that you'd recognize her if you saw her."

"That would be fantastic. I'm going to go back up and see to Madison, but I wanted to let you know that a Detective Maxwell is on his way and it's okay to let him up."

Wanda nodded, her expression grave. "I do hope he can help. A stalker. That poor girl must be scared out of her wits. You tell her not to worry about this end of things. No one is getting up that elevator without clearance."

"I'll let her know, and thank you."

On the way back to the elevator, Shaye pulled out her phone and called Eleonore. She gave her friend and therapist a rundown on the situation and Eleonore promised to be there within thirty minutes. Satisfied that she'd done all she could do for the moment, Shaye headed back upstairs to make sure Madison was okay.

As okay as she could get with her life spiraling out of control.

Given what had happened to Madison, Shaye wasn't about to tell her about the killer shooting at her last night. Madison was already aware of the danger and taking every precaution. Telling her about the shooting might send her over the edge of sanity and into breakdown territory. They couldn't afford that. Shaye needed her as aware as possible.

But she would have a conversation with Detective Maxwell as soon as they were out of Madison's earshot. Her cell phone rang and the number for the car dealership came up on the screen. She answered the call.

"Ms. Archer? This is Stan, your service adviser. Is this a good time to talk?"

"Yes."

"Are you all right? I wasn't sure if you were in the vehicle when the, uh, accident occurred."

"I'm fine. Thank you for asking."

"That's good. Well, the mechanic checked out your tire this morning. I don't know who you've pissed off but that tire was slashed and it wasn't no accident. I don't suppose I have to tell you that the bullet holes in the side of the vehicle weren't either. Bunch of punks roaming the streets these days. They're out of control."

Shaye blew out a breath. She'd expected as much, but it was always worse to hear it. "I thought that might be the case with the tire because it went flat so quickly."

"Yes, ma'am. It can't be fixed the way it was cut, but since the tires are so new, you can replace just the one without it affecting the ride any."

"That's fine. Thanks for letting me know."

"You're welcome. Now, that was the easy part. As for the other, it's going to be a bit more complicated." He gave her a detailed description of the work required to repair the vehicle to its previous condition.

"That all sounds fine," she said. "Please go ahead with the repair the way you suggested."

"Do you need for me to arrange a rental for you?"

"Thank you, but I'll handle it myself later today."

"All right, Ms. Archer, then we'll get you fixed up and I'll call you when we're closer to finishing. We're probably looking at four weeks or better. I'll update you once a week."

"I appreciate it."

"There's one other thing."

She could hear the hesitation in his voice. "Yes?"

"Company policy says I have to report the shots to the police. And I won't be able to start work on your vehicle until I get the okay from the cops. I'm sorry about the inconvenience."

"That's okay. The police already know, but please file whatever paperwork you need to."

"That's good," he said, and she could tell he was relieved by her response.

Shaye hung up the phone and hurried back upstairs. Madison was still sitting on the stool where Shaye had left her. Half of the bottled water was gone, which was a good sign, but the young woman was still pale and her hand still shook as she lifted the bottle. Shaye wished there was something she could say or do to make her feel better, but she knew only one thing would do that.

Catching the killer.

JACKSON WALKED into the police station and straight for Grayson's desk. He motioned to the back door and the senior detective followed him out into the parking lot. Jackson moved away from the door and waited until a couple of traffic cops made their way into the building before looking at Grayson.

"We need on the Carla Downing case," Jackson said.

Grayson stared. "You said to let Maxwell have it. That we didn't need the heat."

"Yeah, well, that was before the loon that killed Carla took shots at Shaye."

Grayson's eyes widened. "You're serious?"

Jackson nodded and gave Grayson a rundown of what had happened the night before.

"Jesus, Mary, and Joseph," Grayson said when he was done. "I know I don't have to tell you how serious this is."

"I know. We have a highly motivated individual who thinks he can avoid capture by eliminating anyone involved."

"You sure you want to date her? She seems to attract psychos." Grayson put his hand up. "I know, I know, so do we. But jeez, she has the worst luck of any PI I've ever known."

"Maybe because she takes the cases no one else wants."

"There is that," Grayson agreed, and blew out a breath. "The case has been assigned. Without Maxwell giving the okay, we can't poke our nose in, and the brass will never approve three detectives on one dead hooker."

Grayson held up a hand before Jackson could say anything. "That's not the way I feel, but you know that's what they'd say."

"But this has all the makings of a serial killer, and now he's targeted an average taxpayer. If the press found out that the department didn't put enough resources into this because the original victim was a hooker, there will be hell to pay if something happens to Madison Avery."

Grayson frowned and stirred his coffee. "Maybe. I could try it anyway, but I'm not even going there unless Maxwell says it's okay. Horning in on someone else's case is not the way to get along here."

"I agree, but I think Maxwell is in over his head on this one, especially since he's essentially working it alone. Those beat cops he was assigned don't have the experience to handle this and there's a lot of ground to cover."

"Okay, I'll talk to Maxwell, but until we get the go-ahead, get back on that missing persons we're working."

"You know good and well she's not missing. That woman took off with her old boyfriend. The husband is the only one who refuses to believe it, and if he wasn't friends with the brass, we wouldn't even be wasting our time."

"True enough, but until we produce her alive and well and giving him the bird or divorce papers, we have to approach it like any other case."

19

When Shaye returned to Madison's apartment, she was pleased to see that some of the color had returned to the young woman's face. And although her hands still shook when she lifted the bottle of water to take a drink, it wasn't as bad as before.

"Have you eaten anything today?" Shaye asked.

Madison shook her head. "I don't think I can."

"You need to keep your strength up. I understand not wanting to, trust me, but I'm going to make you some toast. Even a couple of slices of toasted bread are better than nothing."

"Okay."

Although she didn't argue, it was clear that Madison didn't think much of the concept of eating. Shaye knew exactly why, but she also knew what her body felt like when she went too long without food while under a lot of stress. Madison wasn't thinking about what might happen next, but Shaye was, and keeping Madison healthy and ready to flee or protect herself was her first priority.

She pulled two slices of bread from the package on the counter and popped them into the toaster. Then she grabbed butter and jelly from the refrigerator and put them both on the counter in front of Madison. Probably, she'd pick up the pieces and eat them dry, just to appease Shaye, but at least she had options.

"What did Wanda say?" Madison asked.

"She described the girl who dropped off the package."

"Does she know what company it was?"

"I don't think the girl worked for a company. I think he gave a street kid some money to do it."

Madison's eyes widened. "Really?"

Shaye nodded. "He couldn't afford to use a company because it could be traced back to him, but picking a kid off the street is a good way to avoid detection. The police will have a hard enough time finding the girl, and even if they manage to, they'll have an even harder time getting her to talk."

"But if she saw him, then isn't she in danger?"

Shaye had been hoping that Madison was too stressed to put that problem together, but Shaye hadn't stopped thinking about it ever since Wanda had described the girl. The news was full of Christmas stories right now but sooner or later, someone would do a report on Carla Downing. And if the killer succeeded, the news would carry a story on Madison. The killer knew the girl was a liability. Shaye needed to find her and as soon as she left Madison's apartment, that's what she was going to attempt to do.

But first, she had to get the situation stable here and have a chat with Detective Maxwell to bring him up to speed on her end of things. She was plating the toast when the doorbell rang.

"I'll get it," Shaye said as she placed the plate in front of Madison. "You try to work on that. I can fill the detective in and then he can ask you questions, okay?"

Madison's relief that Shaye was taking charge was apparent. She nodded and picked up a slice of the toast as Shaye headed for the door. Detective Maxwell looked worried when Shaye opened the door, and she expected things were going to go downhill from there. She led him into the kitchen, where he gave Madison a once-over and asked her how she was doing. She nodded her reply and Shaye launched into an explanation of what happened and pointed to the picture frame.

"We both touched it," Shaye said. "I'm sorry about my doing that. I wasn't aware of what it was when I picked it up."

Maxwell pulled plastic gloves from his back pocket and pulled them on. "That's all right. Given how he cleaned the crime scene, I doubt there's any forensic evidence to be had, but I'll have it tested."

Shaye had placed the frame facedown on the cabinet behind her and Maxwell lifted it up and turned it over, his back to Madison. He took one look at the picture and shot a glance over at Shaye. Oh yeah, that initial worry she'd seen when she'd opened the door had just shot up into the stratosphere.

"Is that the box it came in?" he asked, and pointed to the container of shredded paper on the island.

Madison nodded and he placed the frame inside the box and put the lid on it. "I'm going to take this with me," he said.

"Please keep it," Madison said.

"Of course," Maxwell said. "Has anything else happened aside from this? Any attempt to contact you?"

Madison shook her head. "I've been staying in my apartment. I won't even go out to eat or have food delivered because I don't want to leave or answer the door. No one can see in during the day and I put the shades down as soon as the sun starts setting. Short of moving, I don't know what else to do."

"You're doing fine," Maxwell said. "This was something none of us could have anticipated, but I'll make sure it doesn't happen again."

"I've already spoken to Wanda," Shaye said. "I told her Madison had a stalker, but didn't provide any further information. She's going to speak to the other guards and let them know to hold all deliveries and call me before contacting Madison."

"Good," Maxwell said. "I honestly don't anticipate he'd try this route again, but I'd rather err on the side of caution. Does Wanda have the girl on security footage?"

Shaye shook her head and explained the situation

with the hoodie and that Wanda was drawing the face for them now.

"Well, if there's nothing else you can tell me," Maxwell said, "I'm going to get back to the station and have this processed. I've requested a ton of video footage from stores along the route to your meeting. It's going to take a while to go through it all, but I'm hoping to find something."

He put his hand on Madison's shoulder. "Hang in there. I know you're frightened and I don't blame you. Patrol units are doing a pass on your building every ten minutes and they've all been alerted to look for anyone who doesn't appear to belong. If you see or hear anything, you call me. It doesn't matter what time."

"Thank you," Madison said, her voice faint.

Shaye knew the young woman was struggling to maintain control. She'd been through this personally too many times. Madison had moved from shock and fear to despair, and she was trying not to start crying. Shaye followed Maxwell into the hallway and partially closed the door.

"Last night, I went to talk to Shonda and Louise again and something happened," Shaye said, and she described the shooting incident to Maxwell.

He listened intently, his expression growing more and more serious until she finished, and he blew out a breath. "Jesus H. Christ. You're lucky you're alive."

Shaye nodded. "If he'd been a better shot, I wouldn't be."

"So I guess it's safe to say he knows you're on the case."

"I think that's a sure bet. And I'm sure he suspects I've got a line on Carla as the victim, given that I was talking to Shonda and Louise."

Maxwell nodded. "We haven't released any information on her murder yet, but I suspect it's going to come out today. Given Carla's profession, it's not likely to be a huge news splash, especially right here before Christmas, but I have no doubt he's going to be watching for it."

"I agree."

"So he knew you were investigating and instead of hiding, he escalated. I gotta say, I haven't had anything like this before."

"Yeah. Me either."

"Is she okay?" Maxwell asked, and inclined his head toward Madison's door.

"Not really, but I'm working on that as well. Eleonore Blanchet is on her way over. If anyone can get her stabilized, it's Eleonore."

"Great. That's great. I know the brass doesn't necessarily share my opinion, but I'm glad you took this on. Madison needs someone with your experience. I can't help her on that end of things."

"Don't worry about it. I've got Madison covered. I just need you to find this guy."

"I'm on it. I'll stop by the security desk and get the guard to make me a copy of the drawing she's doing. I'll pass it to patrol and have them keep a watch for her, but this time of year, it's going to be hard to spot one teen in a crowd."

"We're going to solve this," Shaye said.

"I wish I had your confidence."

"I've got enough for both of us."

HE STOOD in the alley five blocks away, waiting on the girl to return. He'd already spotted two patrol cars from his hiding place behind a Dumpster, but they hadn't seen him and he was going to make damned sure they didn't. It could be a coincidence—the increase in police presence. After all, it was Christmas, and petty theft was usually at its peak during this time of year. But for some reason, he wasn't sure that was the case.

The picture had been a huge risk. Not that he'd left any forensic evidence to be found. He wasn't stupid. He knew it was exposing himself to both Madison and the police, but with no evidence to prove what Madison had seen, the police wouldn't pursue an investigation. They might patrol around her building a couple extra times a day, presuming she had a stalker, but with Madison unable to describe him, there was little else they could do.

And the additional patrols weren't a factor. Madison was already holed up in her building, thinking she was secure, but there were still ways to get to her. She'd find that out soon enough.

He heard the light footsteps coming down the alley and peered out as the girl he'd paid to deliver the gift approached. He stepped out of his hiding place and she stopped walking, giving him the wary look that all the street kids wore.

"Did you deliver it?"

She nodded.

"And the tape?"

She pulled a small video recorder from her pocket and showed him.

He held out a twenty-dollar bill. "Give it to me."

She hesitated, then slowly moved forward to place the recorder in his hand.

And that's when he grabbed her.

Madison couldn't identify him but this girl could, and that made her a liability. One he wasn't going to let loose on the streets of New Orleans. The street kid might avoid the police on a regular basis, but if they located her and questioned her about him, she'd talk. He wasn't one of them. Her loyalty didn't extend to adults with regular employment.

She tried to scream, but he covered her mouth with one hand and reached for his knife with the other. She dropped the recorder and pulled at his hand, trying to pry it from her mouth, but she didn't have the strength to do it. He lifted the knife around her head and smiled, ready for the kill.

Then something wet hit him right in the eyes and he went blind, his eyes burning as though they'd been sprayed with acid. His grip on the girl weakened, and she broke loose and ran. He dropped the knife and rubbed his eyes, trying to get the burning liquid out of them. She'd sprayed him with something. Everything was so blurry he could barely make out shapes, but he knew he had to get out of the alley.

He felt on the ground for the knife and the recorder and shoved them both in his pants before stumbling toward the street behind him. The glare from the sun felt like a spotlight shining right on him as he stepped out of the alley and onto the sidewalk. He lowered his head and pushed forward as fast as he could, shoving people aside when he couldn't find a clear way through. People yelled at him and a couple shoved back, but no one attempted to stop him.

This was bad. This could be the mistake that ruined everything. He needed to get out of New Orleans...take his show on the road.

But first, he had one last piece of unfinished business to handle.

20

SHAYE GUIDED JACKSON'S TRUCK INTO THE PARKING lot of the Bayou Hotel and parked in front of the office. She'd left Madison's apartment shortly after Eleonore arrived and was confident that the young woman would be much better after spending some time with the therapist. When she walked inside the hotel lobby, her friend Saul looked up at her and smiled.

"Merry Christmas," he said, and came around the counter to give her a hug. "I was wondering if we'd see you soon."

"I'm sorry. I meant to get by days ago, but I had to deal with the legal stuff with Corrine, and I took on a new case. Then there's that whole Christmas gift thing, which I suck at under the best of circumstances, but when you're buying for picky people who can afford anything they want and you're a confirmed shopping hater, it adds a whole other level of difficulty."

"New case, huh? Anything I can help with?"

"No, but I thought Hustle might. I also figured I'd give him his gift so he can pick it up today since the shop will be closed tomorrow."

Saul shook his head. "Lord help us all."

"You've been working with him, right?"

"I have, and he's all set as far as the law is concerned. I'm not so sure me and my heart doctor would agree."

Shaye grinned. "He's keeping you young."

"Ha! Yeah, something like that. He's down in the break room painting. I told him to take some time off for the holidays, but he said he was tired of looking at those ugly walls when he went to the vending machines."

He put a Back in 15 Minutes sign on the counter and they headed down the hall for the break room. She could hear the heavy metal music playing when they were halfway down the hall.

"Don't have a lot of occupants right now," Saul said, "so I put them all on the other side away from the smell of paint."

"And the music?"

"There's that too."

They stepped into the break room and Shaye looked over at the former street teen, still marveling at his trans-formation. The once distrustful, unkempt, overly lanky boy was turning into a young man right before her eyes. A steady diet of good food had filled him out, and his work at the motel had ensured it was muscle, not fat. His blond hair was still long and pulled back into a ponytail, but now the hair shone like silk.

Saul knocked on the door and he whirled around, then broke out into a huge grin when he saw Shaye. He tossed the paint roller into the pan and hurried over to hug her, and she felt her eyes get misty. There was a time when he wouldn't have allowed anyone in his personal space, much less to put their hands on him. Hustle had been given a great opportunity to make a new life for himself, but lots of other people had as well and didn't take advantage of it. Hustle had seized the opportunity and was evolving into an entirely different person with a bright future.

"Merry Christmas," he said when he released her. "I was hoping you'd get by here for Christmas."

"Do you really think I'd let the holiday go by without coming to see you?" she asked.

He shrugged. "I know you got all those things going on with Corrine. She's doing awesome stuff so if that kept you from coming to see me, I was okay with it."

"Well, my part is done, at least on the legal front. Now I just need to help her pick out real estate and screen staff and find someone to put together her IT network, and, and, and..." Shaye grinned. "It sorta never ends."

"I can see that. She's kinda intense."

"The understatement of the year."

"Hey," he said. "I've got your present in my room. Let me go grab it."

Before she could reply, he'd dashed out of the break room and sprinted down the hall. Shaye looked over at Saul, who laughed.

"I told you," Saul said. "The boy has unlimited energy. I swear I never had as much as him. When he finishes art school and moves on with his career, I'm going to have to hire two people to replace him."

"Please. You'll just keep this same blue paint until you sell this place. How long has this awful brown been up here? Ten years? Twenty?"

Saul rubbed his chin. "Hmm, I'm not sure. When did dinosaurs roam the earth?"

Shaye grinned as Hustle ran back into the room with a large, flat package. He handed it to Shaye and waved his hands. "Open it," he said.

Shaye could tell he was both excited and nervous as she peeled the paper back and got her first glimpse of what was inside. Her mouth dropped open and she gasped.

It was an ink drawing of Shaye, Corrine, and Eleonore from about chest up. They faded into each other and a background of tiny spirals that formed flowers and hearts. The detail was so incredible it had literally taken her breath away. She'd seen some of Hustle's work and knew he was talented, but this exceeded what she'd thought him capable of.

"Do you like it?" he asked.

"No. I love it," she said. "It's the most incredible thing I've ever seen. Hustle, this is amazing."

He flushed and stared at the ground before looking back up at her. "I didn't want to get something off the shelf, you know. Not like you can't get anything you want anyway. Then I started thinking about everything I've gone through and the things I've seen, and I always came back around to you and then your moms and Ms. Blanchet. Y'all are the most amazing people I've ever met. You do things for other people that no one else can do. So I thought I'd draw the three of you."

Her eyes, which had misted up a bit earlier, now went full tear overload and she hugged him again. "It's the best gift I've ever gotten," she said as she released him.

His face broke out into a smile so big, it must have strained his muscles, and Shaye's chest clenched once more for the street kid who'd helped her save lives and stolen her heart. She sniffed and wiped her eyes as she smiled.

"Well, since we're exchanging gifts, I guess I should give you yours. I'm afraid it requires you to pick it up as it wasn't quite ready earlier, and it was too big to wrap."

She pulled a small box with Christmas decorations on it out of her purse and handed it to him. He gave her a curious look before pulling the top off the box. His eyes widened and his jaw dropped when he saw the car keys inside.

"No way! There's no way!"

"Saul can't chauffeur you around forever," Shaye said, "and to hear him tell it, if he continues to ride with you, he's going to have a heart attack. You need a way to art school and you can't exactly haul canvas around with your skateboard. The car is a Honda CR-V. It will get decent gas mileage and will give you the room you need for your art and supplies. If you take care of it, the vehicle will last you a long time."

He stared at her for several seconds, and Shaye could tell he was at a loss for words. Finally he lunged forward and threw his arms around her and started twirling her around. She laughed until he released her and he stared at the box again, then looked back up at her, fighting back tears.

"I don't know how to thank you," he said. "You've given me so much and this is so huge. I could draw you a picture every day for the rest of my life, and I still couldn't repay you."

"The only payment I need is for you to get your education and become a responsible, successful adult. You're a good investment. One day I might get old and need you to drive me around."

"I'd absolutely do that. I'll do it now if you want."

"I'm good for now, but I do have a favor to ask."

"Are you kidding? Anything."

She pulled the drawing Wanda had done out of her purse. "I'm trying to find this girl, and I think she might be on the streets. Have you seen her before?"

Hustle took the drawing and studied it. "Good detail. She looks like a girl I've seen in the warehouse district, but I can't be certain. I wasn't over there very often."

"Where would you recommend I start looking for her?"

"Is she in trouble?"

"Yeah, I'm afraid so. She might be the only witness who can identify a serial killer."

"Oh man. Try Julia Street. I'm pretty sure I saw her around the galleries, if it's the same girl. You want me to come with you? She might not talk to you."

Shaye shook her head. "I hate to break it to you, but you're looking more suburb these days than street."

Hustle looked a little pained. "I still know the lingo."

"I appreciate it, but this is as close as I want you to this guy I'm looking for."

He nodded, but she could tell he wasn't happy. "Be careful. I know it's your job and if it wasn't, I probably wouldn't even be alive, much less living like I do. But I know how it is, more than most."

"I promise I'm being careful." With any luck, he'd never hear about her being shot at. She still had to share that bit of information with her mother and was seriously considering working it in between glasses of Christmas champagne.

"Listen to the young man," Saul said. "You've already tangled with more than your share of bad guys. You let the police handle one for a change."

"Will do," she said, and gave Saul a hug. "Merry Christmas."

JACKSON HIT the Pause button on his laptop and looked across the desk at Grayson. Maxwell had given them the go-ahead to join his investigation but unfortunately, what he needed were solid leads. So they were officially digging through the haystack for a needle. Maxwell had acquired as much security footage as available from shops surrounding Madison's building and on the route where the killer had threatened her. Now they were going through them, second by painful second, hoping to latch onto something that launched the investigation forward.

"You got anything?" Jackson asked, even though he knew that if Grayson had found anything relevant, he would have already said so.

"Per instructions, I've captured headshots of every guy who might fit our description and who isn't carrying shopping bags. You realize this is the worst possible time of year for this. We're looking for an average white guy with brown hair, wearing a hoodie, and standing around without any discernable purpose. That describes half of New Orleans out shopping with their wives. Hell, it describes me last weekend."

"Yeah," Jackson said, and threw his pen on the desk. "I've sent at least forty images through facial recognition but I've got nothing except some DUIs and a couple of warrants for parking tickets."

"Same here. And honestly, I don't expect to find anything. If this guy is a serial offender, he's going to be extra careful about things. He's not likely to have a record."

Jackson nodded. Grayson was right. The successful ones kept a low profile when it came to law enforcement. It's one of the reasons they got away with it for so long.

"What about that street kid that he got to courier that package for him?" Grayson asked. "I know Maxwell alerted patrol, but we both know the street kids disappear when cops are around. Did Shaye have any luck running down her location?"

"Hustle said it might be a girl he's seen in the warehouse district and told her to check around Julia Street. She's headed over there now."

Grayson sighed. "Then I guess I better start putting together a compilation of these images in case Shaye finds that girl and convinces her to help. She'll be here going through them until the new year, but I can't think of any way to narrow them down more."

Jackson couldn't either. They were already screening for age and weight when pulling the images. But if you added additional screening options for the witness— assuming Shaye found her—it opened you up to eliminating the perp. Brown hair could become blond. Green eyes could become blue. Facial hair could come in a matter of days and be gone in a matter of minutes. Which left the potential witness with a whole lot of images to look through. And eyewitness testimony being what it was, there were no guarantees that anyone she identified was their guy, and that testimony was even sketchier in court. But at least it sometimes gave them a starting point.

Jackson's phone rang and he saw the medical examiner's number in the display.

"Lamotte," he answered.

"Good morning, Detective," the ME said. "I left a message for Detective Maxwell, but since you're on the case now and worked the body, I thought you might like to know my findings."

"Yes. Definitely."

"COD was the slit on her neck. The description of the knife your witness gave fits the wound, so I'm okay with saying that was the murder weapon. She was already dead when she went into the water, but we'd already figured that."

"So everything is what we expected."

"Yes, except for a couple of surprises. The first is that Carla Downing was sexually assaulted. Postmortem."

Jackson blanched but didn't reply.

"Detective?" the ME asked.

"I'm here. Sorry, I've had a couple of cases, but it still gets me."

"I understand. I had my own reaction during the exam."

"It adds a new level of horror to the whole thing, that's for sure."

"Yes, well, the second surprise isn't going to improve that any. Carla Downing was pregnant."

Jackson clenched the phone. "You're sure? Never mind. Of course you're sure."

"About two months along."

Jackson thanked her and hung up. Well, they had one answer. Now they knew why Carla Downing was attempting to change her life.

21

SHAYE CIRCLED THE BLOCK AND MADE HER WAY BACK to Julia Street. She'd been driving the area for the last half hour but hadn't seen anyone who came close to resembling the girl in Wanda's drawing. Finding a kid living on the streets was never easy. They were wary of adults and outright scared of cops. Many ran away because of less-than-stellar situations at home. The last thing they wanted was an authority figure shoving them right back into that nightmare. Shaye had developed a reputation as someone who helped street kids, but that didn't guarantee her an inside track on information.

And the reality was no one was better at hiding than street kids. If the girl didn't want to be found, it would be very hard for Shaye to do so. She pulled the truck into an empty spot at the curb and got out. Maybe she'd have better luck on foot. If she could find any kids who appeared to be living on the street, she might be able to convince them to give her information on the girl in the drawing, especially if she told them the girl was in danger.

She walked down the block, checking the alleys for someone to talk to, but all she saw were adults, hustling around, trying to get home early or pick up one last-minute gift. Her phone signaled an incoming text and she pulled it out of her pocket to look. It was from Jackson.

Heard from the ME. Not good. Sexual assault postmortem.

Shaye clenched the phone. She'd been operating off the theory that the killer had some psychosis based on past trauma, perceived or real, but this wasn't welcome news. It was a small percentage of people who traveled down the road of necrophilia, and they were the most damaged of the lot.

And Carla was two months pregnant.

Shaye felt her chest constrict. No wonder the woman had been making changes for real this time. She was going to have a baby. *Was it Rattler's?* she wondered. *And if so, did he know?* She was inclined to think that the baby was probably Rattler's and he didn't know anything about it at all. Probably because Carla didn't want him to know. That way, any plans she made wouldn't require his involvement, and the last thing Rattler needed to be involved in was raising a child.

I guess we have one answer.

She pressed Send.

Yeah, but not the one we need. Any luck on finding the girl?

She sighed.

No. Still looking but not hopeful. And have to be at my mom's house at five.

10-4.

She could beg off, but for what purpose? She wasn't any more likely to find the girl tonight than she was tomorrow. In fact, with the streets mostly empty due to people being home celebrating with their families, it was even less likely she'd find the girl. Street kids liked crowds they could work for the money they needed to live. Tonight, the French Quarter would start to empty out, and tomorrow it would be a ghost town. All she could do was hope the girl was safe. That she had taken some money, delivered the package, and never seen the killer again. Because he had to know the risk of leaving her walking around. She would be hard to find and it might take a long time, but it wasn't impossible.

At the end of the block, she started to turn around and head the other direction when she saw a delivery truck across the street and Casey Dugas standing behind it, talking to another guy. She took a closer look and realized the other guy was Jason Parks. They appeared to be engaged in some sort of disagreement, which was interesting because the truck was parked in front of an art gallery, so it was doubtful the argument was over a delivery for Parks.

She watched as Jason shook his head, then finally whirled around and stalked off down the street. Casey opened the back of the truck and pulled out his phone, probably checking the delivery. She crossed the street and walked up behind him.

"Lots of last-minute gifts, I see," she said.

He started, then turned around. "Oh, hi. Yeah, lots of people scheduled for today. I'm trying to hurry, but they'll still all be complaining about how long it took."

"I saw you talking to Jason Parks a minute ago. How do you know him?"

"Oh, he stays at the motel sometimes."

"He doesn't have a place?"

Casey shrugged and looked away. "I guess. I don't know really."

"Is something going on with Jason?"

Casey sighed. "Look, I think the place he used to live was condemned. Sometimes the police do sweeps and they run him off. He stays in empty apartments sometimes in that building he works in...and I think maybe he's stayed in some of them when the owners were out of town, which isn't cool, but it's not my business. I'm guessing he stays at the motel when he doesn't have another option."

Shaye nodded. "It looked like he was angry with you."

"Yeah, well, I won't let him have a room for free or give him a big discount. I told him he has to talk to Ray about that, but he thinks I'm blowing smoke up his ass."

"Hopefully, he'll figure it out. Good luck with your deliveries."

"Thanks," he said, and climbed into the truck.

Shaye turned around and headed off in the direction

she'd seen Jason go, but after several blocks of walking, she finally gave up. If he had a vehicle, he could be miles away by now. Even on foot, he could have covered a couple blocks in any direction. Unless he was off from work, the most likely scenario was that he was on his way back to the apartment building.

The information she'd gotten from Casey concerning Jason's residence matched up with what she'd learned from the background search, and Casey had confirmed Trenton Cooper's suspicion that Jason was living in the empty apartments. The fact that he might also be staying in occupied ones when the residents weren't there was troubling, but that wasn't the most troubling aspect of all of it.

The most troubling thing was that Jason Parks stayed at the same motel as Carla.

Maybe she'd finally made the connection she'd been looking for. Now all she needed was motive. She hopped in Jackson's truck and pulled out her cell phone. She wanted to make a play but needed Detective Maxwell's okay to do it. He answered on the first ring.

"I'm running down a lead," she said, "and I want to know whether I can reveal the murder and Carla's identification."

"I heard a few minutes ago that there will be a mention on the news tomorrow morning, so I don't see any reason why not. The brass wanted to hold it until Christmas. Probably hoping it gets buried and no one decides to poke into it further."

"Figures."

"Who's the target?"

"Jason Parks. Maintenance at the crime scene building."

"I talked to him again yesterday and told him I was just wrapping up some details. The guy seems a little strange, but I didn't get anything out of him that made me want to push. What's his connection to Carla?"

Shaye repeated her conversation with Casey. "It doesn't prove anything, of course. He might never have met her, but given the proximity to the victim and access to the crime scene, combined with his reaction, it seems like something worth pursuing."

"It's as solid as the rest of the leads on this case. Except for the girl who delivered that package. Did you have any luck finding her?"

"No. The streets are packed with last-minute shoppers right now but they'll start to clear and when the people go, those kids will fade into the shadows. I hate to say it, but I'll probably have better luck after Christmas."

"I agree. I just hope that kid is safe somewhere."

"Me too. I'm on my way to talk to Parks now. I'll let you know if I come up with anything."

"I really appreciate your keeping me informed."

"I don't want to cause you any trouble with the brass. And more importantly, I want to get this guy. Madison's life, and possibly mine, depends on it."

"We'll get him. I'm not giving up until we do. I didn't

tell you this, of course, but I interviewed Trenton Cooper yesterday as well."

"And?"

"Jackson said you didn't like him and I can see why. I thought telling him that a woman was murdered in his listing would punch a hole in that arrogant attitude of his but all he did was turn it up a notch. Said if I released the location of the crime, he'd sue the department and so on. Got himself really worked up, and then I asked him for an alibi and that stopped him short."

"I bet."

"He gave me the same story as you—that he was at his plantation fishing. The interesting thing, though, is that his car was ticketed that night in the French Quarter, about three blocks from the corner Carla worked."

Shaye's grip tightened on her phone. "Did you know that before you questioned him?"

"Yeah. I wasn't going in there without all the ammunition I could get."

"So what did he say when you hit him with that one?"

"Said it wasn't his car. That the cop must have made a mistake on the license plate. But he was lying. I'm sure he's smooth enough for real estate sales, but he's not good enough to fool a cop. Not one with any experience, anyway."

"Thanks for letting me know. I was going to question him again, but I think you've got it covered."

"I'm going to tail him tonight. I don't expect much given that it's Christmas Eve, but there's something about him that doesn't add up for me. It's like Parks. I'm not saying he's our guy, but he had opportunity and access. I can't tie him directly to Carla, but I can put him in the vicinity."

"Let me know if I can help. And please be careful. I don't think he'd hesitate to take a shot at you too."

Shaye signed off and guided Jackson's truck away from the curb and toward the apartment building, recalling the background information she'd dug up on Jason Parks. It was scant, at best, and nothing in it indicated he had tendencies toward violent crime, much less serial. But sometimes people with the darkest secrets managed to hide them the best.

Maxwell's interview with the Realtor had been interesting. She hadn't believed him when he'd said he was out of town that night, but it was a gut feeling, not something she could prove. At least Maxwell had managed to put his car nearby. She doubted watching him tonight would yield anything, but she appreciated Maxwell's sense of urgency in catching the killer.

She parked in front of the building and headed for the maintenance room. The door was closed, as before, so she knocked on it and waited. Several seconds later, she heard rustling inside and when the door opened, Jason peered out at her.

"You're that PI lady," he said.

She nodded. "Do you have a minute? I have a couple of follow-up questions."

"Um, I guess. If it doesn't take too long. I've got a

leak up on five and I need to figure out where it's coming from before there's more damage than I can repair."

"This shouldn't take long. I just wanted to let you know that the police found the woman who was attacked in the empty apartment."

"So she's okay? That's good."

"I'm sorry. I should have been more specific. They found her body."

His eyes widened slightly but he didn't say anything. Despite the fact that the room was quite cool, Shaye saw tiny beads of sweat forming on his forehead.

"Anyway," Shaye continued, "the woman's name is Carla Downing. I think you might know her."

"I don't think so." He was trying hard to keep his expression neutral but Shaye knew he was lying.

"Really? Then maybe I was wrong. You stay at the Franklin Motel sometimes, right? One of the regulars said he saw you talking to her."

"He must have been mistaken. I don't know any Carla Downing."

"Tall, blonde, thin. Worked a corner not too terribly far from here?"

He shook his head. "Look, I'm sorry the woman died, but I didn't know her. If that's all, I've got to find that leak."

"Yeah, sure. I didn't mean to hold you up. Merry Christmas."

He pushed by her, not even meeting her gaze, and hurried out of the office and down the hallway. Shaye followed him into the lobby, noting that he kept glancing back to see if she was behind him. When she stepped outside the building, she turned to look and saw him standing next to a large plant, watching her. She lifted her hand to wave and gave him a smile before climbing in the truck. By the time she took her seat and glanced back over, he was gone.

She pulled out her phone and called Detective Maxwell.

"I think you need to bring Jason Parks in for questioning."

22

SHAYE PUT DOWN HER CELL PHONE AND SCRATCHED another person off her list of Realtors. This one had shown the apartment two weeks prior but had been at a conference in New Mexico the night of the murder, a fact she easily verified by the drunken selfies the woman had posted on her Facebook account. Of the seven Realtors she'd managed to get hold of so far, all of them sounded appalled that someone had acquired a key to the unit and committed a crime, and none of them could think of any other way into the apartment except for those already known to Shaye.

She hadn't specified what kind of crime had occurred, even though they might put two and two together once the news broke. A couple had commented on the increasing problem with vandalism in empty units, so she guessed most of them were thinking along those lines. Several hadn't answered and she'd gotten voice mail, indicating they'd be returning to business on the twenty-sixth.

She moved to the next number on her list and punched it in. The message that the phone number was no longer active played. She checked to make sure she'd punched it in correctly and frowned when the numbers matched. What Realtor changed phone numbers with no forwarding message?

She did an Internet search for the Realtor, Ramona Babbage, and a picture of an older woman with long blond hair and a little too much eye makeup flashed up with a link to an old listing. Shaye noted the broker and accessed his site, figuring the woman's current contact information would be available. But when she clicked on Ramona's name in the Realtor list, there wasn't any updated contact information.

Ramona Babbage had been dead for two months.

A knock sounded at her front door, and Shaye checked the cameras she'd recently had installed and saw Jackson standing outside. She hurried to the door to let him in and motioned him to her computer before he could even get in a hello.

"That woman showed the apartment two weeks ago."

Jackson stared at the screen. "I know Realtors are pushy and don't like to give up on a commission, but isn't that taking things a little too far?"

"Ha. It's definitely above and beyond the job description."

"What else do you know about her?"

"Nothing. I had just found this when you knocked."

"Then let's see what else there is to find."

"I thought you'd never ask." Shaye slid into her chair and Jackson pulled another up beside her. She accessed the software she used for background checks, typed in the name, and hit Enter. "Now we wait."

"Good. Gives me time to grab some cookies. You didn't eat them all, did you?"

"If I'd eaten them all, I wouldn't fit through my front door. Corrine's putting out more cookies than Famous Amos."

"I swear I'm going on a diet after the holidays," he shouted from the kitchen. "That includes New Year's, though."

"Really? You're going to do the totally cliché New Year's resolution thing to eat better?"

He popped back in the office and pushed a bottle of water in front of her. "Why not? I'm a regular guy. Might as well do regular guy things."

She laughed. "You're anything but regular, but I'll see your resolution and match it with my own. Of course, we might have to hide Corrine's cookie sheets."

"Preemptive strike. I like that."

Shaye's computer signaled that the search was ready and they both leaned forward to see the results. Name, address, and all the usual things popped up. She had a couple of arrests for minor things—an assault that appeared to be the result of a bar fight and a possession charge for heroin that happened during a bust at a previously known drug bar. Other than that, a handful of parking tickets. Cause of death was an OD.

"Cocaine" Jackson said. "Not exactly mother of the year material."

"Mother of the year?"

Jackson pointed at the screen. "A son. Michael."

Shaye looked at the notation and felt her pulse tick up a notch. "He would be in his midtwenties."

"See if you can find him online."

Shaye did a quick Internet search but couldn't find any references to or images of Michael Babbage. "Figures."

Jackson pulled out his cell phone. "Let me try." He called the police station and asked for a driver's license search. A minute later he disconnected and shook his head. "No license issued to a Michael Babbage. At least not in Louisiana."

"Let me check for an obit. Maybe there's a husband."

But the search didn't provide anything.

"A lot of people don't have one published."

"Still, no record of marriage might mean she was single. Michael might have lived with his father. A lot of boys make that choice when they reach teen years."

"A lot of single mothers do as well. Check the address. Someone had to deal with the house and her belongings."

Shaye did a search on the address and Jackson took a look at the map.

"Older building. Probably a rental, and not the best area of town," he said. "Bars, tattoo parlors, pawnshops."

"There's no phone number associated with the address, but landlines are becoming less common these days."

"Well, we know she had a cell phone, and someone used it to access that apartment. I can't think of any legitimate reason for someone to steal a dead woman's phone and use it to access an empty unit. Can you?"

She shook her head. "Maybe we should check the apartment out."

"Assuming we could even get in. If it's a landlord situation, I'll need a warrant."

"Let me check the tax records." Shaye accessed the property records and pointed to the screen. "It's a corporation, so unless Ms. Babbage is the owner, which I doubt, the rental theory looks good."

"It's highly unlikely any of her things are still there. My guess is the landlord cleared it out as soon as he was aware of her death."

"Wouldn't he have to hold her belongings for her son? At least we could get a line on Michael."

"We should definitely look into it. Day after tomorrow." He pointed at his watch.

"Crap!" She jumped up from her chair. "We have to be at my mother's house in thirty minutes. I've got to shower and put on something besides yoga pants or she'll complain until next Christmas."

"I need to grab my clothes out of the car and hit the shower myself. Meet you back here in twenty."

Shaye hurried into her bedroom and jumped in the

shower, glad that she'd washed her hair that morning and that it hadn't endured any tragedies during the day. She'd run a brush through it and twist it into one of those fancy comb things that Corrine kept buying for her, then she'd throw on her newest pair of jeans and the blue sweater Corrine gave her for her birthday and she'd be set. Well, maybe she needed shoes. The brown boots would be great.

While she got ready, the facts of the case kept running through her mind—the Realtor, Jason Parks, Trenton Cooper, the motel, the white car, Carla's pregnancy. So many moving pieces, but she knew the answer was in there somewhere.

She was close. She could feel it.

He walked into the building and headed directly for the front desk. The security guard—James, according to the nameplate—looked up at him and smiled. "Merry Christmas," James said. "Can I help you?"

He pulled out his gun and fired one round into the guard's chest. The guard's eyes widened and he staggered back two steps before crumpling onto the floor in a heap. He hurried behind the desk and accessed the security footage, deleting the last ten minutes of recording, then pulled the lever for the fire alarm.

As the alarm began to sound, he picked up the phone and made the call he'd been waiting to make all day long.

23

MADISON POURED HERSELF A GLASS OF EGGNOG AND grabbed a container of cookies that Eleonore Blanchet had brought earlier. She claimed Corrine Archer was baking her into the next size up and that Madison would be saving her a really expensive alteration bill. After Shaye left, Eleonore had sat with her in the living room and they'd talked. At first, she'd asked Madison about her condition. Being a doctor, Eleonore was familiar with the disorder, but she wanted to establish the severity that Madison was dealing with. Usually, explaining her condition was difficult but given Eleonore's credentials, it was easy.

Then they talked about Madison's family. That part was more difficult.

Eleonore asked a lot of questions about how Madison had learned to cope and walked through the stages of her life with her parents and then into college. Madison had hesitated at first, but Eleonore had made her feel so comfortable that she'd finally opened up and unloaded on the therapist just how much she resented her parents and the way they'd dismissed her as an embarrassment. Eleonore had stressed that her parents' issues were about their own shortcomings and insecurities. Madison knew that, but hearing someone like Eleonore Blanchet say it gave it more weight.

Once she had a basic understanding of her past, Eleonore began to ask about her current situation. It was a long conversation with a lot of fits and starts and crying mixed in. Eleonore was so calm that Madison managed to make it through her story but when she was done, she was utterly spent. Eleonore reassured her that the police and Shaye were going to find the killer and that she was safe in her apartment. Then she'd taught her some relaxation techniques and ways to help focus her mind when she was in a high-stress situation.

Most importantly, she'd agreed to take Madison on as a client, and starting the first week of January, Madison would spend one hour a week with Eleonore. For the first time since she'd seen the murder, Madison had hope that if the police could find this guy, she might be able to get a firm grasp on a normal life for the first time. She just prayed that Detective Maxwell and Shaye could catch the guy before she ran out of relaxation techniques.

She sank into her recliner and looked at the shades, wishing she had the nerve to turn off the lights and raise them. She missed her view, but sitting in the dark was something she still couldn't imagine. Not while he was still out there. She grabbed the television remote and turned it on to the festivities in New York City. Personally, she'd do most anything to stay out of the cold, but the snow made a pretty blanket over the city with all the Christmas lights reflecting off of it. Maybe one year, she'd take a trip there just to see the Christmas festivities. New York was even easier to get lost in than New Orleans. And she'd heard the food was stellar, so there was that.

She took a bite of a cookie and sighed. No matter how much she tried to convince herself that she was doing fine, the reality was she was often lonely. Not all the time. She was too much of an introvert to not appreciate her freedom and the silence she had to work in. But sometimes that silence was deafening. A reminder that she had no one.

Shaye had invited her to Christmas Eve celebrations at her mother's house tonight, and Eleonore had seconded that invitation. But as tempting as it was to spend the evening with good people she admired and respected, Madison couldn't bring herself to intrude on their family event. And beyond that, she'd have to leave the building, and that meant putting herself and Shaye's family in danger. She would never be able to live with herself if something happened to any of them because of her. Logically, she knew the situation wasn't her fault, but if she drew a killer to their home, then that would be.

Things could be worse, she decided as she pulled her

fuzzy blanket over her legs. She had a beautiful apartment that was paid for and already increasing in value. She had a container of incredible cookies and a decent carton of eggnog. Her bills were paid. She had money in the bank. And she had very competent people looking out for her. She ate several more cookies and had almost polished off her eggnog when she finally dozed off.

The fire alarm sent her bolting out of her chair.

Out of reflex, her hands flew up to cover her ears, the piercing sound so loud against the background of near silence. Her cell phone rang, and it took her a second to realize what the sound was. Then she grabbed it off the end table and seeing that it was security calling, pressed it tightly to her ear so that she could hear.

"Ms. Avery. This is Wanda. There's a fire in the building. You need to take the rear stairwell out."

"Oh my God. Where's the fire?"

"We're not sure. The fire department is on the way. Throw on some shoes, grab a coat, and hurry."

Madison bolted for her bedroom, pulling on her tennis shoes in record time. She yanked her jacket off the hanger and grabbed her purse from the kitchen counter on her way out, shoving her cell phone in it as she went. Fortunately, she was still wearing yoga pants and a T-shirt from earlier. She'd lost the bra hours ago, but didn't figure anyone would care given the hour and the situation. She ran down the hall to the rear stairwell that Wanda had indicated and hurried down the stairs as quickly as she could go without tripping.

What if the whole thing burned down?

She tried to force that thought out of her head. The last thing she needed to do was stress over something that might not even happen. It could be a problem with the alarm system. The system was new. Sometimes they needed to work out the kinks. And besides, all the high-rises were built with fire suppression systems.

As that thought went through her mind, the sprinklers in the stairwell came on, showering her with water. She slowed long enough to pull her hood over her head, then continued her flight down the stairs, wishing for the first time that she lived on a lower level. Her thighs started to burn and she could feel her calves tightening. Tomorrow was not going to be a good day for legs.

Finally, she reached the ground level and pushed the button to unlock the emergency exit door. She practically ran out of the building, then slid to a stop and looked around for other residents. There weren't many, but she'd seen a couple of moving vans over the last week, so she knew some were occupied.

But the street was empty.

Then she remembered—Christmas Eve. They probably weren't home. Most people had friends and family they were celebrating with, many in other cities. And if any were at home and on lower levels, they would have gotten out a lot quicker than she did. Maybe they were around the front of the building. That's probably where she should go. She set out down the sidewalk at a half-walk, half-jog pace and heard a voice call her.

The streetlight in the middle of the block wasn't on, making it hard to see because the illumination from the two street corners didn't quite meet in the middle, but as she moved closer to a parked car, she saw someone standing there motioning to her. Long red hair spilled down the back of the jacket.

"Ms. Avery. It's Wanda."

"Thank goodness," Madison said, and headed toward the security guard. "Did everyone get out?"

"You're the last one. I was looking for you."

"Is everyone around front?"

"Yes. Let's get going."

As Madison stepped past Wanda, the moon crept out from behind a cloud and she got a good look at her. She couldn't remember Wanda's face, of course, but she knew something was wrong. And then it hit her—Wanda had waved at her with her left hand.

Before she could open her mouth to scream, he grabbed her from behind, covering her mouth with his hand. A second later, she felt the prick of the needle in her neck and then everything went black.

———

SHAYE HEADED into her kitchen and grabbed two bottled waters. They'd just finished a long but enjoyable night with Corrine and Eleonore, and now she just wanted to curl up on the couch and talk to Jackson before drifting off to sleep. It had been so cool to see her mother and

Eleonore welcoming Jackson right into the mix—joking with him and handing out "man" holiday chores for him to handle. Shaye had worried about the holiday because she knew it would be hard on Corrine without her father there, especially given why he wasn't there, but it hadn't been sad, as she'd anticipated. There was still tomorrow to get through, but after tonight, Shaye knew it would be fine.

"I figured you were worn out on eggnog and wine," she said as she handed Jackson the water.

"God yes," Jackson said, and slumped onto the couch. "And food. I might not need to eat again for a week."

"You're out of luck on that one. Tonight was just cocktail hour. Tomorrow is the full service."

He groaned. "Why doesn't all this holiday food coincide with times that's it's okay to wear sweatpants?"

Shaye sat down next to him. "Preaching to the choir."

"I see now why you moved out. It wasn't all the mothering. It was the food."

She grinned. "Maybe a little of both. You're lucky your parents are in another state."

"Yes and no. I don't get the constant interference, at least not in person, although my mother does rock a good FaceTime session. But traveling means when we do see each other it's for days or a week and not just hours. That's a whole lot of togetherness packed into a short amount of time."

"That's true. I guess it's just as well that neither Corrine nor I wanted to leave New Orleans. I already have to run her out of here every time she starts talking about drapes or rugs or a bunch of stuff I'd have to dust. Are you still going to see them next week?"

"I don't know. If there's a resolution on this case, I'll still go, but if he's still out there loose, then I can't do it. I've already told them that I might have to reschedule. They're disappointed, but it's not like they don't understand the job."

"How long was your father a cop?"

"Thirty-two years. He was shooting for thirty-five, but his blood pressure got too bad and the doctors worried about his heart. They said he needed to do something less stressful."

"Thirty-two years is a long time."

Jackson nodded. "Twenty-five of them as a detective. Fifteen in homicide. You should have seen his face when I told him I'd made detective. He was practically beaming. Then I said I'd be on one of the teams first up on homicides and the light dimmed."

"He knows firsthand how hard it is."

"Yeah. I still think special victims is worse, though. I mean, look at this situation. Carla is already gone and that's sad, but my biggest worry is keeping Madison from going the same route. It's a whole different ball game when you've got live ones to consider."

"I can see that. It would be much easier to compartmentalize if you didn't have personal interaction with the victim. And then in a situation like this, where they're still being targeted, it's a million times worse."

Jackson put his arm around her. "And you're sure you want to do this?"

"I don't think I have a choice. You know, Shonda said something to me about that. She said it was a calling and that I didn't get to decide whether I did it or not. The decision was already made for me."

"Maybe she's right. I know I can't imagine doing anything else. Even during the worst parts of the job, there's still no place I'd rather be and nothing else I'd rather be doing."

"We're hopeless. And we're going to give my mother a heart attack one of these days. She knows Eleonore spent the afternoon with Madison and I know it's killing her that neither of us will tell her what's going on. But the last thing I need is her worrying about me. If she knew about last night, she might be tempted to pull a Pierce and hire a bodyguard."

"Because that worked out so well for him."

Shaye smiled at the memory of getting the best of the men her grandfather paid to "protect" her. The men were embarrassed and her grandfather was unapologetic. At least her mother had been angry on her behalf, even though Shaye knew Corrine wished Shaye would consider protection.

Jackson squirmed a bit on the couch and pulled a long, thin box out of his pocket. "I know we opened our gifts tonight, but there's one more I have for you."

"But you already got me the sweater and the 1911,

which is totally awesome, regardless of Corrine's expression when I unwrapped it."

"We'll take her to the gun range and let her see the hole it can put in a man. She'll like it a lot better then."

He handed her the box and she pulled the string to untie the bow. Then her cell phone rang. She frowned and glanced at the display. Who in the world would be calling her this late?

"It's Maxwell," she said, and grabbed the phone.

"The fire alarm is going off at Madison's building," Maxwell said. "I can't get her to answer her cell."

"We're on our way," Shaye said, and jumped off the couch.

Without even asking, Jackson grabbed his coat and gun and hurried out with her. She explained as they jumped in his truck. He threw the truck into gear and squealed away from the curb.

"No way this is a coincidence," Jackson said.

She nodded. "He knew he couldn't get in the building, so he got her out."

24

He hauled her body up the steps and into the house, his childhood home. It had been boarded up for some time now, condemned by the city. But when he'd collected his mother's things from her shitty apartment, he'd brought them here because this is where they belonged. It was where *they* belonged.

He stumbled a bit as he walked through the living room and down the hall, always surprised at how heavy the bodies felt, even when they couldn't possibly weigh that much. That whole dead weight thing was very true. Except Madison wasn't dead. Not yet. She was different from the others. No quick death for her, although he expected that she'd be begging for him to kill her before it was over.

But this one was special. For this one, he was going to take his time.

He'd already had to take her before he planned on it,

but the Archer bitch was getting too close. And the cops had been by the motel, covering the same ground she'd already covered. He knew she had to be the one who tipped them off, although he still couldn't figure out how the Archer bitch had figured out Carla was the one he'd killed. She was too smart for her own good. So he had to make his move faster than he'd wanted, and that made him angry.

Once he'd experienced the power of delayed gratification, he'd wanted to take longer to play with Madison. But he'd had to adjust his plans.

He placed her on his mother's bed and pulled off her clothes. Her naked body splayed out gave him an erection, but he pushed those urges aside. Not yet. This time, she would be awake when he took her. The first time, anyway. He removed a faded pink dress from the dresser and pulled it over her head, then worked it down her body. The makeup was next. Red lipstick and blue eyeshadow, both just a little too dark for her pale skin.

When he was done, he stepped back and reviewed his work.

Her face shifted, and he saw her again—the face he'd been seeing over and over again since he'd killed her. His mother.

He smiled and moved to the bed again to chain her arms to metal rods that made up the bed frame. Now that she was secure, he needed to get back to his other life. Step back into his normal routine. It kept him invisible.

There was still plenty of time for fun.

This time, he'd make her see him. He wouldn't stop until she did.

SHAYE JUMPED out of the car and hurried into Madison's building, Jackson right behind. She drew up short when she saw the paramedics hunched over a figure on the ground and shot a horrified glance over at Maxwell.

"It's not Madison," Maxwell said, hurrying over to reassure her. "It's the security guard, James."

"Is he dead?" Jackson asked.

"No. But he's got a gunshot wound and it's a nasty one. They're prepping him for transport, but I have to say, it doesn't look good. He's lost a lot of blood."

"Security footage?" Jackson asked.

Maxwell shook his head. "Gone."

"So he shot the guard, deleted the security footage, and then set off the fire alarm," Shaye said. "Damn it! We should have been ready for this."

"You can't prepare for every possible scenario," Jackson said. "We thought Madison was safe as long as she stayed in her apartment. At least for the short term."

"I think she was," Shaye said, "until he saw me talking to Shonda and Louise. He knew we were closing in, so he made his move. And we still don't know who he is."

"No," Maxwell agreed, "but we have some leads. I followed Cooper to a hotel and was sitting outside but I never saw him leave. I've already sent units to the hotel to follow up on Cooper and to the Franklin Motel. Parks wasn't there earlier when we tried to pick him up, but his belongings were."

"He wouldn't take her to the motel," Shaye said. "He stages things, like he did in the apartment."

"He was working with limited time on this one," Jackson said.

"Maybe. Or maybe he already had a list of places in mind before he ever started," Shaye said. "We need to check the apartment building."

"Assuming it's Parks, do you really think he'd risk taking her there after Carla?" Maxwell asked.

"I don't know," she said, "but it has to be checked. Can you send a unit over there? What about Grayson?"

Jackson shook his head. "He left with his family this evening for a skiing trip."

"I can get some patrol units on it. But what are we going to do?" Maxwell asked.

"We need to find Parks's house. Casey said it was condemned but if Parks's issues are tied up in the past..."

"He might have taken Madison to the house," Jackson said. "I'll get someone on that address. Maxwell, you call for the building search."

Shaye watched as the paramedics moved James onto a gurney and hurried outside. She hoped the shot wasn't fatal. Not only did his life matter, he might be the only other person besides the street kid who could identify the killer.

"I've got the address," Jackson said.

"Good," Maxwell said. "I've got two units on their way to the apartment building. They have instructions to question everyone and open every door. Let's go check out that house."

Maxwell looked at Shaye. "I'm sorry, but I can't allow you to come along."

"That's okay," Shaye said. "I've got my own vehicle, and I'm not much of one to listen to authority. Unless, of course, you're going to arrest me for following you."

Maxwell grinned. "No time for that. Let's go, Lamotte."

Shaye followed them out of the building and jumped into Jackson's truck. As she pulled away from the curb, two units pulled up in front of the apartment building. She didn't think they'd find anything, but then she hadn't thought the killer would come after Madison so soon or in her apartment building. She'd thought he'd bide his time and attempt to take her when she left.

She'd been wrong. Maybe dead wrong.

So this time, she wasn't going to work off assumptions. She was going to cover every single angle she could possibly think of. Even if she never slept again.

25

Friday, December 25, 2015

At 6:00 a.m. on Christmas morning, Shaye dropped into a booth at a small café in the Seventh Ward. She, Jackson, and Maxwell had been through Jason Parks's boyhood home, what there was left of it. But it had been clear when they'd taken the first step inside that no one had been there for a long time. The roof had caved into the living room and the floor was rotted through in most places, making traversing the house a dangerous game. The upside was that it was small and empty, so it hadn't taken them long to determine that Madison wasn't stashed anywhere inside.

Unfortunately, that meant they were back at square one.

Maxwell had been running an employment history on

01

Parks and had come up with three other apartment buildings he'd worked in. They'd spent the rest of the night canvassing those buildings, but nothing had come of it. Most of the residents didn't know Parks and the few who did said they hadn't seen him in years. No one recognized Madison.

Shaye and Jackson had just finished helping to canvass the last building and had ducked into the nearest café for much-needed caffeine. Maxwell had already called to say the other buildings were clear as well and Parks still hadn't returned to the motel. So basically, they still had nothing. The only silver lining was that the security guard, James, had pulled through surgery, and the doctors were somewhat optimistic about his chances. Unfortunately, they had no idea when he'd regain consciousness and even then, if he'd be fit for questioning or remember what had happened, as he'd taken a good blow to the head from the desk when he'd fallen.

Shaye took a sip of coffee, then leaned back in the booth. "What now?"

Jackson shook his head. "I don't know. I guess we keep looking for Parks. Checking the places we know he goes until we turn up something."

She blew out a breath. "The only problem I have with that is the huge assumption we're making that Parks is our guy. I know. I know. All clues point to him—I've been pointing to him—but we don't have anything concrete."

"Okay, then play devil's advocate with me. I'll throw

out the question and you give me an alternate explanation for why he appears to be involved."

"Sure. That might open up another avenue of thought. Go ahead."

"If Parks isn't our guy, why can't we find him?"

"Because he has friends or family that he's celebrating the holidays with."

"The hotel manager told Maxwell he never listed an emergency contact in his paperwork."

"Then maybe he's celebrating the holidays in a casino with a bottle of Jack Daniel's. People who have no one do that all the time."

"Okay. If Parks isn't our guy, why was he nervous when you told him Carla was the victim?"

"Because since she stays at the motel and Parks had access to the apartment where she was killed, he was afraid he'd be blamed for killing her."

"Assuming he didn't kill her, do you think that's the line of thought he would have immediately jumped on?"

"Maybe. I don't know. Hey, what if he knew Carla in a professional capacity and didn't want to admit it?"

Jackson raised an eyebrow. "Good one. So he saw Carla at the motel, figured out her line of work, and paid for services."

"It's possible. He wouldn't want to admit to knowing her if that's the case."

"Okay, so let's assume it's not Parks. Who else is there? Cooper alibied out. He was at a party in that hotel in front of thirty other people last night when Madison was abducted."

"He lied about being in town the night Madison saw the murder. Maxwell has his car on camera in the same neighborhood that Carla worked."

"And he could have been up to any number of things he wouldn't want other people to know about. Murder is not the only thing men lie about."

"What if he had an accomplice?"

Jackson smiled. "You really don't like the guy, do you? You and I both know the chances of that are slim. Madison only saw one killer. Serial killers prefer to work alone. And the necrophilia thing is definitely best left to two. Or one, depending on how you want to look at it."

Shaye grimaced. "I don't want to look at that aspect at all."

"Can't say that I blame you. So we know it's not Cooper, and it may or may not be Parks. We have to start somewhere. Where is that?"

"I wish I could have found the girl who delivered the photo. I'll bet anything she can identify the killer. Without knowing who it is, it's too easy to put resources into digging up information on the wrong person. If we could find her, we'd know for sure who to concentrate our efforts on."

"Yeah, and if we show her pictures and she picks out Parks, then we wasted time looking for her when we could have been looking for him."

"I hate this. I feel like there's so much pressure to

make the right choice and that the wrong one will get Madison killed. And please don't say she could be dead already. I'm operating on the idea that she's alive. I can't take the alternative. Not yet."

"I know. And I'm as optimistic as you, but we have to pick a direction."

She nodded. "We're close to Saul's place. Let's stop by and talk to Hustle. Maybe he has another idea of where to find the girl, especially with it being a holiday. I know he said some of his crew used to celebrate holidays together. Maybe this girl does the same. He might have an idea where to check."

"Okay, and if he doesn't?"

"Then we head to the Franklin Motel and question everyone who'll talk about Parks. And we ask Ray if we can search his room. I know one of Maxwell's teams already went through it, but maybe they missed something. Or maybe they saw something that didn't mean anything to them but might to us."

She looked over at him and could see the worry in his expression.

"I know I'm grasping at straws," she said, "but I can't change clothes and go sit down for a five-course meal at my mother's house. Not when I know what Madison could be going through."

"Of course not. And no one is asking you to. I'm sure Corrine will understand, but the reality is, neither of us has slept in a long time and we might not be as sharp as we need to be."

"It will have to do. I couldn't sleep right now if I tried."

"Okay. Then we'll finish up our coffee, force ourselves to eat a couple bites of something, ask for to-go cups, and go speak to Hustle. You realize how early it is, right? We'll probably have to roust him out of bed."

"I don't think he'll mind."

Thirty minutes later, Shaye entered the lobby of the Bayou Hotel and drew up short when she saw Saul standing behind the counter.

"I figured you'd still be in bed," she said as she and Jackson made their way over.

Saul waved a hand in dismissal. "I'm old. Sleep goes out the window right along with your hair."

"Things to look forward to," Jackson said.

"You still got a while. Me, I'm well on the back side of a good set of hair. So you want to tell me what's wrong? Because I know you two aren't out this early, looking like the cat dragged you in, because you're interested in my thinning hair."

"I wanted to talk to Hustle," Shaye said.

"Still looking for that girl?" Saul asked.

Shaye nodded. "Things have escalated since yesterday."

"Then I best get him out of bed. Meet us in the break room. I started a pot of coffee a minute ago. You both look like you could use a cup."

"We've already had three each."

Saul shook his head. "Then I best hurry."

Shaye and Jackson made their way to the break room, and Shaye poured herself a cup of coffee. "Want another?" she asked.

"No. But give me one anyway."

She poured his cup and put them both on the table before dropping into one of the chairs. "Too tired to stand. Too antsy to sit. But tired is winning."

Jackson nodded and took the chair next to her. "I have a feeling it's going to be a while before we see a pillow again."

"When this is over, I might give up coffee for a while."

"Let's not get hasty."

She heard footsteps and low voices and a couple seconds later, a very sleepy but concerned-looking Hustle entered the room, Saul right behind. Hustle sat next to Shaye, and Saul poured himself a cup of coffee and took the last seat.

"What happened?" Hustle asked. "Saul said things are worse and you didn't find the girl."

Shaye gave him a basic description of the situation leading up to Madison's abduction, leaving off how things progressed and ended with Carla. When she was done, Hustle sat back and blew out a breath.

"Man! That is some crazy shit."

Saul gave him the parental look.

"Sorry," Hustle said, and held up his hands. "But it is. That lady sees faces, then can't remember them? And what are the odds that she's the witness? "

"It's definitely not a normal situation," Shaye agreed. "Which is why it's been so difficult to catch the guy."

"And now he has this lady." Hustle shook his head. "He's a serial killer, right? That means if he hasn't already killed her, he's going to."

Shaye nodded. "And the only two people who can identify him are the security guard at Madison's building, who was shot and is still unconscious, and this girl he paid to deliver the package."

"And if you don't know who he is, you don't know where to look," Hustle said. "So finding this girl might be the lady's only chance."

"It's possible," Shaye said. "We have one other line of investigation to follow—a suspect we haven't been able to locate since yesterday. But yeah, the girl is our best chance of identifying the killer. And the quickest—if we can find her."

"You checked Julia Street?" Hustle asked.

Shaye nodded. "I drove that area for a while yesterday, until the crowds started thinning out. I figured when the people went home, the street kids would disappear as well."

"Yeah," he agreed. "No money to be made without an audience, you know?"

"Exactly, and I figured today would be quiet, but I remembered you telling me that you celebrated Christmas with some of the other street kids. It was a long shot, but I thought I'd see if you had any idea where they might do that sort of thing."

"Assuming she was part of a group," Hustle said, "and assuming they celebrated."

"I know," Shaye said. "It's such a thin lead it's almost nonexistent, but we were already in the area and I figured it wouldn't hurt to ask."

"We had a regular place," Hustle said. "An inside place for when the weather was bad. It was an abandoned warehouse. We'd hauled in some couches people threw out and cleared a space so we could skate in there. If she's in a group that's celebrating, you're not going to see them from the street."

Shaye blew out a breath. "So you're talking a search of every empty building in that area. That could take days."

"I'm sorry I can't help," Hustle said. "If I knew anything...that poor lady."

Shaye put her hand on his arm. "You did everything you could. Please don't feel bad. The New Orleans police and I are doing all we can to find her."

Hustle nodded, but Shaye could tell how troubled he was.

"Please be careful," he said.

"Always."

26

HUSTLE TURNED AROUND AND TRACKED BACK IN THE direction from which he'd just come. It wasn't much of a hike, being that the living room was small, but he didn't figure leaving Saul alone on Christmas morning was the right thing to do, even if he was just walking up and down the halls of the hotel.

Saul looked up from his spot on the couch. "You're going to wear out the carpet with your pacing," he said.

Hustle stopped and looked over at the man who was the closest thing to a father that he'd ever had. Hustle had tried to sit and watch the parade with Saul. To listen to the Christmas music and get into the holiday spirit. After all, he had a whole lot to be thankful for. But he couldn't stop thinking about the lady. Was she still alive? He was hopeful until he remembered that dead might be better than some things.

"I'm worried about that lady," Hustle said finally.

Saul nodded. "Me too."

"I can't just sit here knowing she's out there somewhere, scared to death...not if there's something I can do."

"You told Shaye everything you know. You've already done what you can do."

"I don't think so."

"What else is there?"

"I could find the girl." He held his hand up to stop the barrage he knew was coming. "Before you say anything, some of the street kids know about Shaye, but not all of them. And the ones who have heard of her still might not trust her. Shaye sorta knows how to spot them on the street, but she doesn't know how we hide...how they hide."

Saul frowned. "You really think you can find the girl?"

"I don't know, but I've got a lot better chance than Shaye. Searching those buildings could take the police days, and if they wait for everyone to return to the streets tomorrow..."

He didn't say what he was thinking. He didn't need to. Saul knew the score as well as he did.

Saul rose from the couch. "Then I guess I best put on some tennis shoes."

"You're going with me?"

"Regardless of what the law says, you're still not good enough to drive alone, especially in a car you're not yet familiar with. Besides, if that girl saw the man they're looking for, she's in danger too. I know you want to help, and so do I, but I'm not letting you do it alone. I'll hang back when you need me to, but I'm not going to just sit on this couch and hope for the best."

"Fair enough." If he was being honest, Hustle was a little relieved that Saul was coming with him. Someone waiting nearby was a lot better than someone sitting a couple districts over with a cell phone.

Hustle headed to his room to change. Shaye had been right when she pointed out that he looked more suburbia than street. But he'd kept one set of clothes that he used to wear. The jeans were too short due to a recent growth spurt and they were worn in several places. The hoodie was so threadbare on the elbows that it was almost transparent. But they would help him look the part. If he wanted to find the girl, the kids he talked to had to trust him. And they wouldn't even consider it unless he was one of them. After changing, he grabbed his sketch pad and some pencils and headed out.

Saul was standing in the living room, shoving his pistol in his waistband when Hustle returned. Hustle was as happy to see the pistol as he was that Saul was coming. The retired military man was an excellent shot. If they ran into the killer, Hustle's money was on the hotel owner.

"What's the pad for?" Saul asked.

"In case we find her. Shaye said I was better than the police sketch artist, and I know I'll be quicker."

"Good thinking." Saul reached under the tree and grabbed a package. He tossed it to Hustle. "Open it."

"Now?"

"You might need it."

Hustle pulled the paper off the box and lifted the lid. Inside was a military-grade pocketknife, just like the one Saul carried. Hustle had always admired it, and Saul had remembered.

"It's perfect," Hustle said, still humbled by the way his life had changed. "Thank you."

Saul clasped him on the shoulder. "Let's just try to do this without pulling anything out of our pockets, okay?"

They headed out to Saul's truck and when they got to Julia Street, Hustle directed him a block away and told him to drive slowly for three blocks, then move one block over and head back in the other direction.

The streets were quiet, with only a handful of cars moving on them. Because this area of the city was mostly businesses, there were hardly any cars parked at the curbs. A couple walked a dog and peered into the windows of an art gallery but otherwise, there was no one in sight. Hustle studied the empty buildings as they went, looking for the signs that would indicate people inside.

"Wait," he said finally. "Pull over here."

"Why here?" Saul asked as he parked in the middle of the street in front of an antique furniture store.

"Because that building behind us is empty."

"We've passed several that were empty."

"But they were already being developed or were about

to be. That one has the city trespassing signs but no real estate signs. Not yet."

Saul turned around to look at the building. "The doors and all the windows are boarded up."

"Yeah, but the board over the window on the alley side is crooked. Maybe they hung it crooked or maybe someone took it down afterward."

Saul climbed out of the truck and followed Hustle around the side of the building. Sure enough, one of the pieces of plywood was tilted at an odd angle. Hustle reached up and easily lifted it off the screws it was resting on.

"See," Hustle said. "There's a bracket on each side. When they leave, they put that board across the plywood to hold it in place. But as long as the wind's not bad, it will stay propped up here while they're inside."

"How do you know it's kids?"

"I don't. Could be anyone living on the street. We all know the same tricks."

"You're not going in there alone."

"Don't see any other way to find out who's inside."

Saul shook his head. "No way. It could be junkies or even dealers in there. They wouldn't hesitate to cut your throat. If you're going in, I'm going with you."

"If they see you, they won't talk."

"If it's not kids, they might kill you for invading their space. You've only got two choices here—either I go with you or you don't go."

Hustle knew Saul was right. It was just as likely that

junkies were inside as it was that kids were. And Saul did have his pistol. Junkies usually had a shiv of some sort, but few on the street had a gun. Anyone who'd had one usually sold it at some point.

"Okay," Hustle said. "But stay back some. Make sure when people set eyes on me, they don't see you. At least not at first. And be careful where you walk. These buildings are usually falling apart."

"I spent four years crawling through sand dodging land mines in Iraq. You think a little rotten wood is going to get the best of me?"

Hustle grinned. That's one of the things he liked best about Saul. He was a man's man. Tough and ready to back it up.

"Then let's get going," Hustle said and hoisted himself over the window ledge.

Saul grunted a bit getting into the building, and Hustle knew the older man's knees were probably protesting the jump he had to make to get over the ledge, but as soon as he was inside, he waved at Hustle to continue.

With all the windows boarded up, the building was dark inside until they reached the center, which probably served at one time as a lobby. The ceiling was vaulted there and the plywood covering some of the second-floor windows had fallen off. Or been removed. It might have been done intentionally to give them some light inside. Hustle stopped in the middle of the room to listen. He could hear the faint sound of music coming from the back of the building. At least it was on the first floor. It was easier to navigate a healthy retreat when stairs weren't involved.

Hustle pointed to a closed door at the end of the hallway and Saul nodded. He followed Hustle down the hall, peering into the empty rooms as they passed. When they reached the end, Saul slipped into the doorway of the closest empty room. Hustle knocked on the door first. Surprise was not a popular thing among street people. He heard shuffling inside, and then the door opened a crack and a boy about his age gave him a cautious look.

"What do you want?" the boy asked.

"My name is Hustle. I'm a skater from the Ninth Ward docks."

"Yeah, so?"

"I'm looking for a girl who stays around here."

"Maybe you should find a girl in your own territory."

"It's not like that. This girl saw something. I need to talk to her."

"What did she see?"

"A guy who killed someone. And if he hasn't gotten to her already, he's probably looking."

The boy frowned. "What's her name?"

"I don't know." He pulled a copy of the drawing Shaye had from his pocket and showed the guy. "Do you know her?"

The boy opened the door a little wider and took the drawing from Hustle. "Wait here." He shut the door and

Hustle blew out a breath, every second feeling like an hour. Finally, the door opened and an older girl with short, jet-black hair looked out at him.

"How do you know someone's after her?" the girl asked.

"Because a private investigator told me. Shaye Archer. Have you heard the name?"

"Who hasn't? You're telling me Shaye Archer is looking for this girl because she saw a killer?"

Hustle nodded.

"You're not bullshitting me?"

Hustle reached into his pocket and pulled out Shaye's business card. "I have a whole stack of them. I know her and I trust her. If she says this girl is in trouble, then it's the truth. Why else would I be out here looking for her on Christmas Day?"

The girl looked behind the door at someone and nodded, then she turned back to Hustle. "I'm pretty sure that's Sprint. I saw her yesterday evening, and she was shook up. Said some guy attacked her."

Hustle felt his heart beat stronger. "But she got away?"

"Yeah. She ain't called Sprint for nothing. Once she broke loose, there ain't no way he could have caught her."

"Do you know where I can find her? It's really important that I find her now. That guy that attacked her has already killed a woman and now he's kidnapped another. She's the only person who can identify him. He's not going to stop coming after her."

Her eyes widened. "Oh my God. She needs to hide."

"Can't hide forever. But if she could give Shaye a description...or look at some photos, they can catch the guy. Maybe before he kills the other woman."

He deliberately avoided mentioning the police because that word alone created panic among street kids, but even though he hadn't mentioned it, they would know the score. If someone was out there killing and kidnapping people, then the police were involved.

"I don't know," the girl said finally. "Let me check on something."

The door closed again and Hustle could barely control his excitement. He had no doubt this girl knew where to find Sprint, or at least had a good idea. If he could just convince her that speaking to Shaye was the smartest thing Sprint could do, then maybe he could convince Sprint as well.

He heard hushed talking inside, and then the door opened again. He expected to see the girl again, but this time, Sprint was standing in front of him.

JACKSON PARKED in front of the lobby of the Franklin Motel and they stepped inside. Ray was standing behind the counter, and he gave her an exhausted nod. "I wondered if I'd see you," Ray said.

"I'm sorry it's not under better circumstances," Shaye said. "This is Detective Lamotte."

Ray extended his hand. "If you're here about Parks, there's still no sign of him. And you best believe I've been watching. Been standing here so long, my knees are about shot."

Jackson nodded. "I've been on enough stakeouts to know that your knees aren't the only thing shot. Point out the unit and take a break. We'll stay here and watch for you."

"Thank God. If I'd known all this was coming, I wouldn't have had all that coffee this morning. Or that eggnog last night. It's the unit right on the corner." He pointed to a unit about fifty feet away, then hurried through a door behind him.

They stood and waited, watching the parking lot for any sign of movement, but only a handful of cars were parked outside and no one exited their rooms. Several minutes later, Ray hurried back and gave them a nod.

"I really appreciate the break," Ray said. "I've got a buddy I call in for emergencies, but I hated to bother anyone on Christmas Day."

"I'm surprised Detective Maxwell didn't leave someone here," Shaye said.

"He said he was sending a unit over as soon as they did shift change," Ray said.

Jackson nodded. "The guys doing the building search expired this morning, so to speak. He's waiting for the next patrol shift to come on duty and then he's going to snag as many as the brass will approve him for."

"Looks like the two of you expired this morning as well," Ray said. "You been at it all night?"

"Sleep's not a priority," Shaye said.

Ray nodded. "Detective Maxwell told me about Carla. I sure was sorry to hear it, and it makes me sick to death to think that her killer might be someone who stayed here. Probably met her here."

"We don't know for certain," Shaye said, "but we'd definitely like to find Jason and let him tell us differently. When was the last time you saw him?"

"Last weekend. He came in and said he needed a room and asked what kind of discount I would give him for a week. Christmas is slow so I gave him the room at half price. To be honest, I felt sorry for the kid. I guess he doesn't have any family to speak of."

"He's never mentioned any?" Shaye asked.

"Only a grandmother, but she lives in Florida, I think."

"Has he ever talked to you about anything else?" Shaye asked.

"Not really," Ray said. "He's only stayed here a handful of times that I know of and usually registered at night once I was already gone. He was always quiet. Kept to himself."

"Ray, would you mind letting us see Jason's room?" Shaye asked, figuring they had a better chance of getting inside before the patrol unit showed up. "I know the cops already looked it over, but maybe we'll spot something they missed."

Ray gave her a sympathetic look. "I guess we all feel like there's something we're not doing, right? I don't mind at all. Detective Maxwell had a warrant and Detective Lamotte is here now so it's all on the up-and-up, as far as I know."

Ray pulled a master key out of the drawer and they followed him to the unit. He opened the door and stood back so they could enter. Shaye stepped inside and glanced around. The room was the same layout as Carla's, with a bed, nightstands, dresser, chair, and television in the front room and a door on the back wall leading into the bathroom. A duffel bag sat on the chair and Jackson went over to check it out.

"Just some clothes," Jackson said.

"He's got his uniform shirts and a couple pairs of jeans hanging in the closet," Shaye said. "A pair of shoes."

She went into the bathroom and saw a toothbrush, toothpaste, and a razor sitting on the counter. The drawers to the vanity were empty, and nothing was stashed on the bottom of the sink, in the toilet tank, behind the mirror, or behind the picture on the wall. She stepped back into the bedroom as Jackson moved the dresser back against the wall.

"It's clean," Jackson said. "If he had anything to hide, he took it with him."

"It's not a lot of stuff," Shaye said. "But that makes sense if he really doesn't have a place to live. Keeping things simple makes it easier to move around."

"Which brings up another question," Jackson said.

"How does he get around? There was no car registered in his name. And our killer has to have a way to transport the bodies."

"He had an older model Toyota," Ray said. "A Corolla maybe."

"What color?" Shaye asked.

"White," Ray replied.

Shaye looked over at Jackson and knew he was thinking the same thing. Casey had seen Carla getting into a white Toyota.

"Probably never registered it in his name," Ray said. "I sold an old truck a couple years ago to a guy who didn't change things over. Kept getting parking tickets and had to go downtown with the bill of sale to prove it wasn't me."

"Where would he go?" Shaye asked out loud. "He took Madison somewhere. He stages things...makes a production. If he only wanted to kill her, he could have shot her in the building like he did the guard."

Ray ran a hand through his hair. "I wish I knew something. Anything. The cops checked with everyone staying here early this morning but no one had seen him. I even called a couple of the regulars that come through here a couple times a month—salesmen—but they couldn't recall ever meeting him."

"What about Walter and Casey?" Shaye asked. "Did the cops talk to them as well?"

Ray nodded. "Walter called me early and told me the police had been at his house. He's kinda like me, freaking out a little. He'd checked Jason in once before, but he'd never had a conversation with him beyond renting the room."

"And Casey?" Shaye asked.

"He stays in a room here. I was with the cops when they talked to him. He told them he'd rented Jason a room a couple times for the weekend, but Jason had never talked about anything personal. The guy kept to himself."

"If I was killing people," Jackson said, "I'd keep to myself too."

"Well, there's nothing to see here," Shaye said, unable to keep the disappointment out of her voice.

"What about the building where he works?" Ray asked.

Jackson shook his head, clearly frustrated. "The cops have scoured every inch of it. They rousted the property manager out of bed and got the keys to access everything. If the units were occupied, they asked to search and everyone agreed. The units that weren't occupied, they entered and searched. There's not a single closet or crawl space that hasn't been looked at. He's not there."

"Maybe he's hiding in one of the other buildings he worked in," Shaye said. "I know they searched them, but they couldn't get access to everything with it being Christmas. He could have made copies of keys before he left."

Jackson nodded. "It would be a big risk, though, trying to get Madison inside an occupied building."

"There has to be something we're missing," Shaye said.

"I'm sure, but it doesn't mean it's there for us to find," Jackson said. "Parks was maintenance, but we only know the jobs he held that are on the books. No telling how many side jobs he picked up for cash. He could have keys to half the city for all we know. And if some aren't occupied..."

"What about where he dumped Carla's body?" Shaye asked. "Were there any cabins around?"

"A couple of old fishing cabins, but Maxwell covered everything in a ten-mile radius. I'm sure there's some stuff out there so buried it doesn't show on an aerial shot, but I don't think he'd dump the body so close to a hiding place."

Shaye blew out a breath, frustrated and completely out of ideas. Every minute that passed, she grew more desperate to find Madison. Who knew how many they had left, or if they even had any left at all?

"What now?" she asked.

"I wish I knew."

27

THE GIRL WHO PEERED OUT AT HUSTLE COULDN'T HAVE been more than thirteen. Her hair was tied back in a sloppy ponytail, and the circles under her eyes told him she hadn't slept much lately.

"Is it true?" Sprint asked. "He killed someone?"

"Yeah. And he's going to do it again unless Shaye stops him."

"Is it the lady I delivered that package to?"

"No. He killed someone before that, but he's kidnapped the lady that got the package."

Tears welled up in Sprint's eyes. "I didn't know. I swear. I mean, I thought what he asked me to do was weird, but he gave me twenty dollars and said he'd give me another twenty when I brought him back the tape recorder."

Hustle frowned. "What tape recorder?"

"He wanted me to record my conversation with the

security guard when I dropped off the package. I thought he didn't trust me to do it or something, but then he grabbed me and pulled out a knife when I tried to give him the recorder."

"How did you get away?"

"I Maced him and then I ran." She shook her head, her expression a mix of fear and disbelief. "He said he wanted the present to be a surprise. That's why he didn't do it himself. And now he's going to kill that woman. And I helped him."

Her voice took on a higher pitch, and her words became rushed. Hustle could tell she was starting to panic.

"Calm down," he said. "No one is blaming you, but we need you to help save the woman."

"How?"

"No one knows what he looks like but you. If you can describe him, I can draw him."

"And you think that will help?" she asked, her voice hopeful.

"I'm certain it will. A friend of mine drove me here. He's an adult but he's cool. I used to be on the streets, but I live with him now. My sketch pad and pencils are in his truck. I can do the drawing here, but after that I wish you'd come with us. You're not safe on the streets. Not until they catch this guy."

"I don't know..."

"I promise you'll be safe. My friend owns a hotel. He

won't find you there. You can have your own room. They've got dead bolts and everything."

She bit her lip. "Can Raven come with me?"

"Sure. But I need you to come now."

Sprint looked back and motioned, and a second later she and the black-haired girl Hustle had talked to earlier stepped into the hall and closed the door behind them.

"Saul?" Hustle said. "You can come out now."

Saul stepped out into the hallway. The girls stiffened a bit but Hustle hurried to explain. "He came in with me because we didn't know who we'd find inside."

The girls nodded but watched Saul with a wary eye as they walked through the building. In the lobby, Hustle stopped and looked around. "There's enough light in here for me to draw. I'd like to do that first so I can send it to Shaye. Then we'll get out of here, okay?"

"Okay," Sprint said.

"I'll go get your stuff," Saul said. "You stay with them."

Hustle nodded. Given Saul's bad knees, it would have been faster for him to get the pad and pencils himself, but he knew the girls would have been scared to be there alone with him.

"You said your name is Hustle?" Raven asked.

"Yeah."

"You knew Jinx, right?"

Hustle smiled. "Still do. I saw her day before yesterday."

"Really? How's she doing?"

"She's doing great. Her aunt is really nice."

Raven gave him a small smile. "That's good. I liked Jinx. She helped me out of some trouble once when no one else would. I heard she'd gone to live with family, but you never know how that's going to be."

"That's true enough," he said. "But Jinx got lucky. So did I. Saul is a great guy."

"I'm glad," Raven said. "I wish everyone could get a good deal like you two."

"Don't give up. Shaye's mother is working on a plan to help kids like us. I don't know a lot, but the stuff I've heard is really great."

"That would be cool," Raven said, but her tone was wistful rather than hopeful.

Hustle didn't blame her. It wasn't that long ago that he was exactly where Sprint and Raven were—disillusioned by life and in a killer's crosshairs. Sometimes he woke up in a cold sweat, his dreams taking him back to his time on the streets. Those days, it felt as if he'd only been gone for five minutes. All the panic and fear were right back where they used to be. It took hours before they faded away.

Saul walked back into the lobby, carrying the pad and pencils, and handed them to Hustle. He motioned to a huge spiral stairwell and he, Sprint, and Raven sat. Saul stood a bit apart from them where he could see the hallway where they'd entered the building.

"Okay," Hustle said. "Describe him to me."

Sprint nodded and closed her eyes, then she began to talk.

Hustle sketched as she spoke, pausing periodically to clarify something. He stopped occasionally and asked her to look at something, then tweaked it as she made suggestions. Finally, he lifted the pad and she nodded.

"That's him," Sprint said. "It's scary how close your drawing is. You're really, really good."

"Let me see," Raven said, and Hustle showed her the drawing.

"Have you ever seen him?" Hustle asked.

Raven shook her head. "No. But if I do I'll know to run."

"She makes a good point," Saul said. "When we get back to the hotel, we'll make up a bunch of copies and bring them back here. The other kids can hand them out. They all need to know to avoid him and call the cops if they spot him."

Raven and Sprint both nodded.

"That would be good," Raven said.

Hustle pulled out his phone and took a picture of the drawing. "Let me send this to Shaye. Then we can head to the hotel."

Shaye answered on the first ring.

"I found the girl," Hustle said.

"You what?" Shaye asked, her voice filled with confusion and disbelief.

"The girl that saw him. I found her. Saul brought me, so no yelling. I drew him. I'm going to send you a text."

"What about the girl? Is she all right?"

"Yeah, she's all right, but he tried to kill her." Hustle quickly recounted Sprint's story about the recorder and the attack.

"I'm glad she got away," Shaye said. "But she's not safe until he's caught."

"I know. I convinced her to stay at the hotel. Her and a friend. Saul's going to give them their own room."

"Great. That's great. Tell Saul I said thank you, and I can't even tell you how much I appreciate you finding her, even though I wish you were still in your sweats and watching television."

"Yeah, well, maybe I'll do that tomorrow. I'm sending the drawing now."

He accessed the picture and sent a text to Shaye. When it showed Delivered, he shoved the phone back in his pocket.

"Let's get out of here."

SHAYE LOWERED her phone and looked at Jackson, barely able to contain her excitement. "Hustle found the girl. He's going to text me a drawing."

"Of the killer?" Ray asked.

"Yeah," Shaye said. "The killer used her to deliver a package to Madison. I looked for her yesterday but never turned up anything."

"How'd he find her when you couldn't?" Ray asked.

Shaye nodded. "He used to live on the streets, and he's a hell of an artist, so if this girl described him well, I have no doubt we'll have a good picture."

"Good enough to recognize Parks, anyway," Jackson said. "What about the girl?"

"Saul's bringing her and a friend to the hotel and stashing them in a room."

"Good," Jackson said. "She's not safe on the streets."

Shaye's phone signaled the incoming text and she accessed it, expecting to see Jason Parks's face, then she gasped.

She pressed the picture to expand the size and turned the phone.

"We were wrong. It's not Jason. It's Casey Dugas."

28

SHAYE CLUTCHED HER CELL PHONE WITH ONE HAND and grabbed Ray's arm with the other. "Casey's room!"

Ray nodded. "This way."

Jackson called Detective Maxwell as they hurried down the sidewalk and filled him in.

"He's going to issue a BOLO and do a background check on Dugas. I'm sure he wasn't keeping Madison in his room, but there might be another place he has a connection to that comes up in a search."

Ray opened the door and Jackson rushed in, gun drawn. Shaye followed behind but the room was empty. "He's gone," she said. "Probably left right after the police questioned him."

Jackson nodded. "Too close to home. Let's search the place. Maybe we can figure out where he's gone."

"You don't have a warrant," Shaye said.

"It's my motel," Ray said. "I thought I heard screams coming from in here."

Shaye nodded and headed into the bathroom. She drew up short and sucked in a breath. "I found Jason Parks!"

She rushed over to the body in the bathtub and checked for a pulse, but the slit on the neck and the amount of blood were dead giveaways that Jason wasn't going to be providing any information.

Jackson came up beside her. "Were they in it together?"

"I don't think so," Shaye said, pieces starting to fall into place. "I think Casey set Jason up to take the fall. It was Casey who told me he saw Carla getting in a white Toyota, but I think that was a lie. Jason was the perfect fall guy. He had access to the apartment, and Casey pinned him as knowing Carla. If Jason had disappeared, we would have kept on believing he was our guy."

Jackson nodded. "The bathtub's lined with plastic. He probably got Parks in his unit and drugged him, planning on killing him and dumping the body later."

"Then the police came and he had to leave before the noose tightened," Shaye said. "But why would Jason come in here? I saw them arguing on the street yesterday. Casey said it was because he wouldn't give Jason a discount on the room." She slapped her forehead. "I should have caught that when Ray said he gave Jason the room at half off."

"Maybe Jason saw something that didn't look right

and asked Casey about it," Shaye said. "I don't think Jason was quick on the uptake. Casey could have passed off some BS on the street, intending to follow up later."

"Oh my God." Ray's voice sounded behind them.

They turned around to see the blood drain from the motel owner's face. Shaye rushed over. "You need to sit down," she said.

"Not in here," Ray said. "No way. I wasn't going to look. But then..."

She guided him outside and sat him on a bench on the sidewalk. "Take long, slow breaths. The cool air will help."

She went back inside as Jackson walked out of the bathroom on his phone, directing the coroner to the motel. He shoved his phone back in his pocket.

"We have to toss this place before CSI gets here," he said. "Parks hasn't been dead that long. There's two needle marks on the back of his neck. Dugas probably intended to keep him drugged and kill him somewhere else, but the cops showing up this morning made him change plans."

Shaye's stomach rolled. "He's gone to kill Madison."

She rushed inside and yanked open the closet, starting with the boxes on the top shelf and then searching the clothes to see if anything was hidden in the pockets, but came up empty. Jackson searched the dresser.

"I have needles," he said. "And a vial of something. Probably what he used to knock them out."

Shaye pulled the nightstand drawer open. "No wallet. No keys. Nothing to indicate he was actually living here. This room looks like any other short-term hotel guest is staying in it."

"Maybe he doesn't have anything."

"Or maybe it's somewhere else. Walter said Casey's previous apartment building was sold to a developer and that's why he was living here, but maybe that's a lie. We need his previous address."

"They're running all that at the station now. If anything pops, they'll call me."

Frustrated, Shaye pulled the drawer completely out of the nightstand and peered inside, then she flipped the drawer over and found an envelope taped to the bottom.

"I've got something," she said, and opened the envelope.

A photo and a folded piece of paper were contained inside. She lifted the photo and saw a very young Casey with a woman, maybe his mother, but then why hide it? She frowned. Something about the woman looked vaguely familiar.

"Look at this," she said. "Does that woman look familiar to you?"

Jackson stared at the photo. "Maybe. I don't know. It's an old photo."

"Can I see?" Ray had walked back inside. "Maybe she's stayed here."

"Of course," Jackson said and handed him the photo.

Ray took one look at it and the color that had

returned to his face drained right back out. He sank onto the bed.

Jackson glanced at Shaye, then looked back at Ray. "Do you know who this is?"

"I thought I did. Years ago, she was my girlfriend, until she chose drugs and the party life."

Shaye handed the folded paper to Ray. "I think you better look at this."

Ray stared at the paper, bewildered. "I don't understand."

"I think Casey Dugas is your son," Shaye said.

"No," he said, even though the paper he held said differently. "Her name isn't Dugas. It's Babbage. Ramona Babbage."

MADISON AWAKENED CONFUSED, her head pounding, her vision blurred. Where was she? What happened? She remembered the fire alarm going off and rushing downstairs, then nothing. Her arms were stretched above her head and felt heavy. She tried to lower them and push herself upright, but something cold and hard dug into her wrists.

Panicked, she blinked several times and narrowed her eyes at her right hand, trying to see why she couldn't move. When her vision focused a little, she saw the handcuffs and let out a strangled cry. She yanked her arms down, twisting them one direction, then another, as she pulled, desperately trying to free herself, but the cold metal held tight.

She stopped pulling for a minute, her hands throbbing from the effort. Slowly, her memory started to return. Wanda was there on the street, except it wasn't her. It must have been him, the killer. He couldn't get in the building, so he'd lured her out. And she'd walked right up to him.

You thought it was Wanda. It sounded like Wanda.

She shook her head and started tugging again. What difference did it make? He fooled her and there was nothing she could do about it. Nothing anyone could do about it because no one knew who he was. She was totally alone. This was it. She was going to die, and they probably wouldn't ever find the body.

She started to laugh, completely breaking down.

There was a silver lining. Her parents would forever be the couple whose daughter disappeared. Taken by a serial killer because she couldn't even recognize the enemy. At least her final moments on earth would embarrass them for as long as they lived.

You're losing it.

Like that was a surprise. All the relaxation techniques in the world couldn't make this one okay. Even Eleonore Blanchet didn't have a meditation to ward away death by serial killer.

A draft blew up her legs and she looked down and frowned. What was she wearing? It was pink and old and barely covered her private parts. Oh my God. Had he raped her? She didn't feel that anyone had touched her there and surely she would know. It wasn't as though she saw a lot of that kind of activity. She would know if he'd violated her.

He hadn't raped Carla either, though. He'd simply killed her.

So why was she still alive? He'd had time to bring her here...wherever here was, and chain her up. Why not just kill her and get it over with? Somewhere, in the back of her mind, she knew the answer. He was toying with her. It was fun for him. Maybe he even got off on it.

And instead of frightening her even more, that thought pissed her off.

She looked up at the bed, studying the handcuffs and the iron rods they were attached to. The headboard was made of metal that had been painted white. Every place that the rods were attached to the main headboard frame, she could see rust stains. The rods must be weakened, but by how much? The top of the rods had more rust showing than the bottom. Maybe if she concentrated all of her strength on one hand, she could break one of the rods.

Since her right arm was stronger, she started with that one. She lifted her arm up until the cuff was right at the top where the rod connected to the headboard. Then with every ounce of strength she could manage, she threw her body over, yanking her arm at the same time. She heard a popping sound and the rod shifted slightly to the side. Flakes of rust landed on her face and she shook her head to get them away from her eyes.

Pain shot through her shoulder, and she closed her eyes and counted to ten. Then she positioned the handcuff again and yanked once more. This time, the rod popped loose. It rocked back in place, but all she needed to do was tug it enough to the side to slip the cuff off of it. She lifted her hand up again, ready to pull, but froze as a door creaked open.

Her pulse spiked so hard it made her dizzy as footsteps started her way. What should she do? Even if she could get her hand free before he made it to the room, one free hand wasn't going to give her any advantage. The footsteps stopped outside the room and she shifted her arms and head to the same position they were in when she was unconscious.

She heard the door open, and the footsteps came into the room, stopping near the bed. The overwhelming desire to scream racked her entire body, and it took every bit of strength for her to keep her body loose. There wasn't a whisper of sound except for the rhythmic repeat of his breathing.

"You always looked so pretty in that dress," he said. "Other men thought so too, which is why it was your favorite. If only you'd cared enough about my father to stay out of that dress. Maybe then, he wouldn't have left you."

He shuffled some more, and she felt him bump the

bed with his legs. Her body wanted to stiffen so badly, and she fought against the straining muscles.

"I found him, you know," he continued. "My father. And he told me all about the woman he used to love who betrayed him with other men and drugs. You lied to me. You told me he didn't love you, but he did. You made him leave. You never saw him. Just like you never saw me. But you'll see me now. I'll be the last face you ever see. The one burned into your memory for all eternity."

Madison felt a chill wash across her body and she struggled to keep from shivering. Did he think he was talking to his mother? What the hell was wrong with him? She knew he was crazy—he killed people—but this was so much worse than anything she could have imagined. No way he was going to cut her throat and let her go quickly. He was going to torture her.

She could hear his breathing coming closer, and then his finger touched her cheek. She bit her tongue, forcing back the scream that threatened to rip through her. He ran his finger down her cheek, then she felt his lips on hers.

"Soon, my love," he whispered. "When you awake from your nap."

His footsteps retreated, and she heard the door open and close. She sucked in a huge breath, fighting back the overwhelming desire to gag. The only reason he hadn't started with her now was because he thought she was still unconscious. The second he knew she was awake, he'd be right back in here.

She glanced around, taking in the room for the first time. There was a single window, but it was boarded up. She might be able to get the right handcuff off the rod with minimal noise, but no way could she break her left hand loose without him hearing. Then she'd have to jump up and break the plywood from a window. She had no idea how long she'd been drugged, but even if she'd been in tip-top shape, she doubted she had the strength to break plywood away from nails. She needed a weapon.

She canvassed the room again, looking for something she could grab that would give her even a tiny chance of fighting back. All she needed was a sliver of opportunity to get by him and to the door. He was stronger than her, but she'd bet anything she could outrun him. Fear alone should push her forward like lightning. And then there was screaming. If she could get out that door, she intended to scream like a banshee and not stop until she was safe.

She heard noise from the other room and realized it was music. It wasn't very loud, but it might give her a bigger window. She pushed her hand up to the top of the rod and slowly pulled until the handcuff was tight, then she pulled harder, slowly bending the rod out until the handcuff slipped through it.

Immediately, she dropped her hand onto the bed before the cuff could clank against the other rods. The muscles in her arms knotted and she felt a burst of pain shoot across her shoulder and down her arm. But none of that mattered now. She pushed herself up in the bed and studied the rod her left hand was cuffed to, brushing the loose rust away to get a better look. She began to panic when she realized it wasn't nearly as corroded as the other rod. She'd barely had the strength in her strongest arm to break the other rod. No way was she going to be able to break this one, especially in one pull.

She inched closer to the handcuff and studied it. Her hands weren't much larger than her wrists and there was a little play. On a television show, she'd seen someone break their thumb to get out of handcuffs, but she had no idea if that was a real thing or not. She tugged a bit on the handcuff and realized that she didn't lack much to slip out of it. The nightstand next to the bed had a drawer, so she turned onto her side and slowly pulled it open.

A small blue tube lay inside and she drew it out. She knew that label. It was a body oil that her grandmother used. It reeked of lilacs and always made her sneeze. But it might allow her to get her hand free from the cuff. She removed the cap and squeezed the oil onto her hand, making sure it was coated all the way around. The flowery smell wafted over to her and her nose itched. Quickly, she rubbed it with her arm. A sneeze would be the end of everything.

When the urge to sneeze had passed, she tugged gently with her left hand, pushing the cuff up with her right. When it stuck midway, she wriggled her hand side to side, sliding it centimeter by centimeter until it passed the widest part. Then she gave it one last tug and her hand broke free. She clutched the cuff with her right hand and stepped out of the bed, slowly lowering the cuff against the rod, making sure it didn't make a sound.

The floor had creaked when he came in the room, so she had to be careful where she stepped. First, she needed to find a weapon. If she'd been able to get the entire rod off the bed, it would have been a great one, but no way could she break the bottom loose without drawing him inside. She looked in the nightstand again, lifting a small box of tissue out of the way.

And that's when she saw it. An old metal fingernail file.

She lifted it out of the drawer and clutched it in her right hand. It slipped in her oily hand and she reached down and wiped both her hands and the file on the bedspread. She couldn't get all the oil off without soap and water, but it was better than before. It wasn't much of a weapon, especially against the knife that she knew he had, but she had a better chance now than she'd had handcuffed to the bed.

And she had the element of surprise.

He expected to come back in here and find her groggy and secured to the bed. He wouldn't be expecting her to be loose and to launch an attack. But that's exactly what she intended to do. She'd move to the side of the door and tuck herself behind the edge of the wall that dipped to form a closet. He couldn't see the bed unless the door was all the way open, so it gave her a second to launch. When he walked through the door, she'd stab him and run. It was Christmas. People would be around. Someone would hear her yell. All she needed to do was get out of the house.

She inched over to the door and tucked herself behind the small jut in the wall. Now she just needed him to come inside but not on alert, so stomping the floor or throwing something was out. As far as he knew, she wouldn't be capable of any of that while restrained. There was only one option.

She took a deep breath and moaned.

She tried to make it sound as though she was groggy and slightly in pain, and that part was easy enough. Between her aching head and her arm and shoulder being on fire, she had plenty to draw from. The music that had been playing in the other room ceased and she heard footsteps coming her way. She clenched the file and drew in a breath, held it, preparing to launch as soon as he stepped into the room.

The door began to open and she saw his shadow creep onto the floor in the bedroom. She held her breath and prayed that he couldn't hear her pounding heart, and when he took that first step into the room, she sprang. She swung her arm as hard as she could, lodging the file in the side of his neck. He screamed and stumbled forward. She gave him a shove that sent him crashing down onto the floor, then she bolted out the door.

29

MADISON RAN DOWN A HALLWAY AND PAUSED ONLY long enough in the living room to find the front door. His cursing echoed through the house, and as she grabbed the door handle, she heard his footsteps pounding behind her.

"You stupid bitch!" he yelled.

She flung the door open but before she could bolt outside, he grabbed her hair and yanked her back. She saw the glint of the knife and screamed, knowing it was too late. That her plan had failed. Every second of her life flashed in front of her like a movie on warp speed. She saw her parents—the few times they smiled, but mostly their frowns. She saw her college roommate sitting next to her watching movies on a rainy Saturday night. She saw her first apartment in New Orleans and the view from her current place.

The gunshot deafened her, and she felt a sharp burn

on the side of her head. She dropped to her knees, the pain so intense, certain that he'd shot her rather than using the knife. She heard shouting in front of her but everything was blurry. She drew in a breath and her chest burned. Her mouth tasted of blood. Was this what death felt like?

A second later, a hand grabbed her arm and she heard Shaye's voice.

"Madison? Are you all right? I need a medic over here! Madison? Can you hear me?"

"Shaye?" She blinked but everything was still out of focus. "Am I dead?"

"No. You're very much alive. Detective Lamotte is an excellent shot, but the bullet grazed your temple and I'm sure it hurts. Do you have any other injuries?"

She was alive!

She blinked again and her vision cleared somewhat. A woman was kneeling next to her, leaned over and studying her. The long dark ponytail gave her away. It was Shaye. Her eyes flooded with tears as relief swept through her. It was real.

She lifted her right arm and could feel the handcuff still dangling from her wrist, then she lost her strength and her arm dropped back onto the hard floor. "My shoulder."

"Jackson," Shaye called, and a couple seconds later, a man leaned over and released the handcuff from her wrist. Another man knelt beside her and moved her hair, studying the side of her head. His badge indicated he was a paramedic.

"It's a surface wound," the paramedic said. "We'll get her in the ambulance and get the bleeding stopped. They'll want to run tests."

"Of course," Shaye said. "Can I ride with you?"

"Sure," the paramedic said.

Madison looked up at the face that she would forget as soon as she blinked again and smiled.

"Thank you."

THE KNOCK on Shaye's door late that evening surprised her. She had spent most of her afternoon at the hospital with Madison, finally leaving when Madison stopped talking and started nodding off. She'd made the obligatory phone call to her mother while she was there, who'd done the complete shock-and-awe routine, exclaiming how happy she was that Madison was safe and that the man who'd taken her was dead. Eleonore had promised to visit Madison that night, and Corrine had insisted on a redo of Christmas the following day.

So she had no idea who could be at her door now. Corrine and Eleonore always called before coming by, and Jackson always called or texted. Hustle and Saul were back at the hotel, hosting a celebration with Sprint and Raven, and she didn't anticipate the police asking her for a statement until tomorrow.

She peeked out the blinds and saw Shonda standing there. She pulled open the door and Shonda threw her arms around Shaye and hugged her so tightly she might have bruised a rib. When Shonda released her, Shaye could see her eyes were misty.

"I shoulda called first," Shonda said. "But I had to thank you in person."

"You heard already? I was going to call you tomorrow. Come inside."

Shonda stepped inside and followed Shaye into the kitchen, where Shaye pointed to a barstool.

"Would you like anything to drink?" Shaye asked.

"No. Thank you. I ain't gonna take up your time. Lord knows, you probably need to sleep. Or maybe drink. I'm not sure how to fix what you been through."

"Me either."

"Louise has an old high school friend that works as a nurse's aide. She was there when they brought that girl you was helping into the hospital. She told Louise about it. Louise called me. And I called every working girl I know and the news is spreading faster than a cold."

Shaye smiled. "I'm really glad it's over."

"Me too. And I'm sure I ain't heard the whole story. Maybe sometime, you can fill me in."

"I don't know that you want to hear the details. A lot of it is gruesome and sad."

"I figured, but I feel like I owe Carla that much. To know what happened to her and why. She was a good person. She didn't deserve what happened to her."

"No. She didn't."

"And I feel all of us owe you as well. No one believed that woman when she said Carla was killed 'cept you. And if you hadn't, he might have got away with it. And don't give me that bullshit about just doing your job. We both know it's more than that."

"You're right. I liked what you said before. That it's a calling."

Shonda nodded. "Anyway, I wanted to see you in person and tell you that because of this, I'm making some changes. I'm quitting the streets."

Shaye stared. "You are?"

"Not tomorrow or anything. I still got bills. But when it opens again in January, I'm putting in my papers for beauty school. It's what I was gonna do years ago before I got sidelined by a man. Ain't gonna happen this time."

Shaye had no doubt that Shonda could accomplish whatever she set her mind to. "You know there are grants for school. I could help you with the paperwork."

"For real?"

"Then maybe you could get off the streets sooner."

"Maybe so."

"What about Louise? Does she know what you're planning?"

"I told her. I don't think she believes it yet, but once I start making changes, I think she will too. This thing with Carla spooked her. She ain't ever gonna look at a john the same again. Neither of us will. And we'll stick to our rules. Carla didn't."

"I still wonder why she went to the apartment with Michael. I figure it's because she knew him."

Shonda nodded. "That and the money. It's a dangerous thing, though—thinking you know somebody."

"Yes. Sometimes it is."

Shonda rose from the stool. "I gotta get. If you was serious about helping me with those papers, I'll call you next week."

"I'd love to help."

"I'm gonna pray every day that God keeps you safe. This city needs you."

IT WAS WELL into the night before Jackson made it to Shaye's place. He'd spent a long day helping Detective Maxwell run down all the facts they could obtain on Michael Babbage, aka Casey Dugas, and searched every square inch of the house he'd lived in with his mother.

"How's Madison doing?" Jackson asked as he slumped onto the couch.

Shaye grabbed a beer from the refrigerator and handed it to him. He'd earned that and more.

"She's doing good," she said as she sat next to him. "Her head hurts some and she'll need to regrow a patch of hair, but I don't think she's overly worried about it. She's torn a few things in her shoulder, but the doctor thinks it will be fine with some rest."

"And mentally?"

"That one's always hard to call. I'd say that right now, she's so relieved, she's happy. But eventually, she'll come down off that high and start working through everything that happened, piece by piece. She'll have some things to deal with, but I think she can handle it. And she's got Eleonore."

"She couldn't find better on that end of things."

"That's for sure." Shaye credited Eleonore with her ability to live a normal life. As far as she was concerned, the therapist was a miracle worker. "Did you turn up anything at the house?"

"Oh yeah. All sorts of things. The worst being a set of photos—four women, Carla included—it was clear they were dead. All blonde. Maxwell already identified one as Mitzi, and he'll keep working on ID for the other two. There were dates on each photo. The killings started after Ramona Babbage died."

"An overdose, right? Want to place any bets on that one being an accident?"

"Ha! Pass. I'm going with Killing Mommy Made Me Psycho for the win."

"Based on the things he said to Madison, I think you're probably right. I mean, I doubt he was ever quite right, but I think killing her would have tipped him over the edge."

Shaye told Jackson what Michael had said to Madison when she was being held captive.

Jackson nodded. "Something else we found—more

paternity tests. Every one of them a man who owned a low-end motel. We checked. Michael, aka Casey, had worked as a night manager at every one of them over the last two years."

"He must have found out somehow that his father owned a motel and gotten jobs so he could get close enough to the owners to get hair to use for the DNA tests."

"And then he found Ray and he was a match. But why didn't he tell him the truth?"

"I think he looked for Ray intending to kill him. Michael told Madison that he knew about her lies. My guess is he went to work at the motel and Ray eventually shared the story he told me—of his tragic youthful romance—with Michael. Maybe as a warning about getting involved with the wrong woman."

"Then Michael realized his mother had lied all this time and he killed her, setting off a whole different chain of events."

"I don't think we'll ever know exactly what was going on in his head. I'm sure Eleonore would have some theories, but honestly, I don't even care. Michaels's gone and that's good enough for me. What else did you guys find?"

"You're going to love this one—a 3D printer and several plastic keys."

Shaye stared. "That's genius. He used his mother's phone to get the key to the apartment, then made a copy of it right there."

"Maxwell's going to take the keys over to the apartment building and test them, but I'm betting one of them works. The others are either duplicates or keys to other vacant units."

"Other crime scenes. Or potential crime scenes."

"It's possible. Maxwell plans to get a list of every 'showing' that Ramona had after her death and see if any of the other keys match. We also found a dolly and a furniture crate, just the right size to transport a body."

"That's how he moved the bodies without being seen. No one thinks twice about a guy moving a crate when he's driving a furniture truck." She shook her head. "It still amazes me sometimes how people who are so warped can also be very clever. It's frightening, really."

"Yeah. These kinds of cases always leave me feeling uneasy. When crimes happen over money or a woman, you can understand the dynamic on a certain level, even if you don't agree with the action taken. But when people are living in their own damaged mind, there's no way to understand that completely. Unless maybe you're just as damaged."

Shaye nodded. "It makes avoiding danger difficult when you can't pinpoint the inciting incident. It means everyone can be a victim. That's a tough reality to live with, even for a cop."

"Did you talk to Ray again?"

"Yeah. That's where I just came from."

"How's he doing?"

"As well as can be expected when you find out the son you never knew you had was a serial killer."

Shaye shook her head. "Ray is a good man. I feel bad for him."

"He's a strong guy. He'll figure out how to handle it, but yeah. I feel bad for him too. You know, one thing I still can't figure out is how Michael killed Carla when he was supposed to be at the hotel working."

"I have a guess on that one," Shaye said. "I think he asked Jason to cover the desk for him. Probably told him he had a family emergency and not to let anyone know or he'd lose his job."

Jackson's eyes widened. "I bet you're right. Two young white guys, brown hair. People probably wouldn't pay enough attention to notice the difference. And that would explain why Michael was angry with Jason. When the heat turned up on the investigation, Jason must have thought something wasn't quite right."

"Yeah. It's a shame he wasn't smart enough to know why. If he'd gone to the police with his concerns, he might still be alive."

"So much carnage and we'll never know for certain why. Sometimes this job sucks."

Shaye leaned over and kissed him on the cheek. "You have to remember all the people you help. Like Madison. Not only did you save her life, but you killed the man who wanted her dead. She'll be able to move forward because she's safe. Even if you don't have an answer for everything, the outcome matters more."

He looked at her and smiled. "How did I get such a smart, beautiful girlfriend?"

"Well, for starters, you have really good taste."

He laughed and put his arms around her and pulled her close. She leaned into him, the heat from his body comforting her. She'd never met a man like Jackson. A man who didn't just talk about high moral standards but lived them. A man who didn't make promises lightly and put himself on the line every day for strangers.

A man she could trust.

He released her and reached for the present she'd started to open last night. "I think you've waited long enough," he said, and handed her the pretty box with its metallic silver bow.

"I thought you'd never remember," she said. "I've been staring at that thing for the last half hour."

He grinned. "Go for it."

She pulled the bow and slipped it off the box, then lifted the lid and gasped. "Oh my God, Jackson. It's beautiful."

The locket was silver and old. She lifted it from the box to get a closer look. It was heart-shaped, and the etching on both sides was so intricate that she couldn't fathom the amount of ability or time it took to render such a work of art. She pressed the tiny button on the top and it opened. Inside were two photos—her on one side, Jackson on the other.

"I was afraid you might think it was corny with the pictures," he said. "But it was so pretty. I saw it and immediately thought of you."

Shaye sniffed and struggled to keep from crying. "It's not corny at all. It's beautiful and perfect."

He took it from her hands and placed it over her head, letting it rest against her chest, then he took her hands in his and looked directly at her.

"I love you, Shaye Archer."

The tears that had been threatening to fall burst out and she began to cry. She flung her arms around him, so many emotions coursing through her that she didn't even trust herself to speak.

Finally, the tears subsided and she whispered, "I love you, too."

More Shaye Archer coming in 2018.
To receive notice when a new book is available, please sign up for my newsletter.
Janadeleon.com

Made in the USA
Middletown, DE
27 February 2018